The Tree Makers

BOOK ONE of the
WARDENS OF THE SHAWS

BUDDY HEYWOOD

ISBN 10: 0692757880
ISBN 13: 9780692757888

DEDICATION

For Mark
The excitement you show while reading my books continually
inspires me to write.

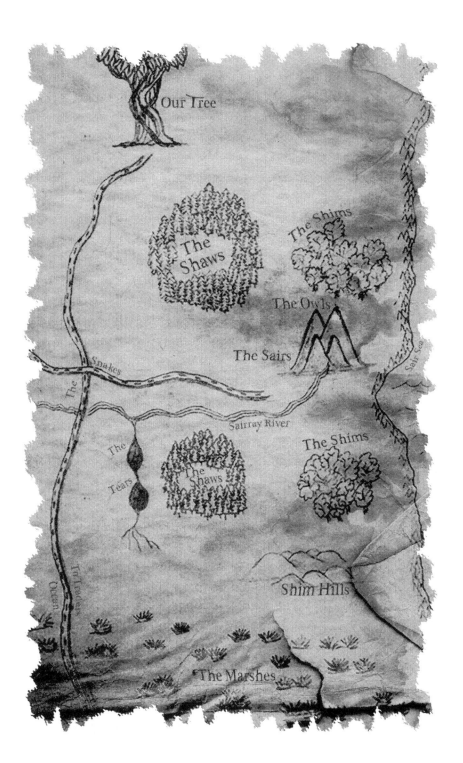

ACKNOWLEDGMENTS

A huge shout out to Dylan for the cover art. What you can do in one night of drawing rivals Van Gogh, ear and all. And the biggest thanks to April, my petite and quiet editor, whose external character contradicts her internal one. I am so glad that tolerance of my neediness can be bought with money and friendship. Also, all errors belong to you.

CONTENTS

CHAPTER 1

The smell from up here told me everything about what was being made for dinner back home. The smell also told me that I would go out hunting tonight in this forest and have my dinner elsewhere. I might even visit my hidden cache of fruit. Once a week I visit the cave where I planted that fruit tree, and once a week I take a single, blue fleshy fruit. This forest, The Shaws, is my home. It's full of large trees, a lot of game, berries, and the like. My stomach grumbled at me to move.

"It's decided then," I muttered. I swung my legs up off the branch and stood. The night sky was favorable this time of season as I could see through the trees and gaze upon our mountain range, The Sairs. Well, I could see two out of the four mountains. The far two, The Owls, always hid behind the comfort of constant fog. I promised myself that one day I'd visit there and find out the truth behind Algrad's story of the perpetual fog. Another stomach grumble reminded me to take care of the present and to seek the truth another day.

With a well-placed hand here and a strategically placed foot there, I shimmied down the tree as if I grew up in one. Which wasn't far from the truth. I am a Tree Maker after all.

Tree Maker is not what we originally called ourselves; it was a title given to us by foreign traders that frequented the two roads that weaved through our forest. It was a long time ago when that moniker was given and the elders chose to let it slide. The knowledge of the real name can carry power and, in contrast to many of their other decisions, the elders actually made the right decision with the naming. Calling us Tree Makers was an oversimplified description of the relationship we had with nature.

For instance, there are trees along The Snakes - separate roads that run north to south and east to west - that could look unnatural to an outsider. The crossing of the Snakes in the center of the forest was sheltered from above due to the overlapping and interconnecting tree branches. We didn't make the trees do that, so much as ask them. But hey, if outsiders thought we made the trees and they awed my people for doing so then I can't complain. It made my job that much easier.

While I'm all for awe, I still grimace whenever people refer to these roads as Snakes. Being called a Tree Maker gave us some power while the name of the roads lacked any sense of power. Alas, while I am the head warden of these lands, no one really asked my opinion on naming things. In fact, rarely do they ask my opinion unless someone needs a sweet, unique treat from afar. Or if they want me to make someone permanently disappear.

"What are you doing now, Brim?" The voice was female, soft and cute. The voice also startled and annoyed me.

My shoulders sagged and I turned around to gaze upon the dark green eyes of Caryanne. Her eyes smiled at me while the rest of her face gave away nothing. As she stepped away from the tree, the rest of her body became less camouflaged. Unlike most of my people who preferred loose clothing to hide weapons and potions, she preferred tighter, overlapping clothing to accent her tiny frame. Her clothes were the same dark brown as her hair, but her uncovered arms showed the natural light brown skin of my people.

As always, her hair was pulled back save a tiny curl that fell onto her forehead. The curl gave her an innocent, youthful look that she used along with the tightness of her clothing to deceive others. She is as physically strong as I am and just as old. Actually, she is a few decades younger - as she likes to remind me. Although when you've walked among these trees for a couple centuries, a couple decades don't really matter.

To the traders, however, we all looked like we were in our early twenties. A perception we played to our advantage. There is a certain joy when some traders think they can bully me because I look so young. It's only a moment before they find themselves on the ground with my foot on their throat. Or in Annie's case, poisoned or bleeding. She didn't have the same subtlety as I did.

"What do you want, Caryanne?" I asked.

She hated when I used her full name instead of her nickname, Annie. I hated that she was the only one able to sneak up on me. If I didn't find her so attractive, well, I would just walk away. I'm pretty sure she knew how I felt since hiding feelings from her wasn't something I'd mastered yet.

"Oh, you know, just sneaking up on you," she coyly replied.

I saw her shimmer a little and a light green aura appeared around her, about a foot away from her body in all directions. It lit up the forest around us, pushing the darkness out. Within the aura, light green stars began to fall as she sauntered towards me.

"No, no, and no. You can't go using your gift to get me to stick around." I shook my head and averted my eyes.

She walked through the brush and broken branches without any sound save the soft tap of her hide shoes on the dirt. Her voice seemed to saunter the way her body did.

"Who says I want you to stick around? I mean, you're only a head taller than me. You always have that beard stubble that doesn't quite grow into something more. All you really have going for you are those blue eyes."

I heard a slight noise in the distance. I tuned out Annie so I could tune in elsewhere. I could already hear better than any other Tree Maker and with my eyes shut I could hear even better.

Each Tree Maker is born with at least one gift and they can develop it into something greater over time. However, some Tree Makers just enjoy the long life and easy living so their gifts do not end up being honed.

My gift, one of my main ones, involved extraordinary hearing and I never squandered my time honing it. Although my hearing is constantly being honed, mainly because I have a rare form of the gift where it is always active. Imagine centuries of instinctively sharpening that blade everywhere you went and it's not hard to envision how you can cut through everything when you need to.

When I focused, I could travel in my mind to wherever my hearing took me. At this moment, I traveled across the worn path and into the forest. I cut through the noise of the leaves and branches swaying as the evening wind tickled the tops of the trees. There were noises of waking baby birds from an unseen nest at the edge of the clump of trees to the east. Just past that nest is where I found him.

I knew it was a male by the breathing. Yes, I know it sounds odd, but females and males of every species breathe differently. Like their exterior, the males are rough and lack refinement in their breathing. Females retain an element of class - even the crabby crones that always complain when I show up after they've put away the dinner. This male breathed slowly, but loudly in a wasted effort to hide from us.

"Get down!" I reached behind with both hands, pulled the blades from under my tunic, and crouched.

"Who me?" Annie was still trying for seduction and unaware of the predator.

I growled. "Get down, Caryanne. Now."

She shimmered again and the green glow gave way to the black of night. She turned away and put her back against mine. There was a thunk-thunk-thunk-thunk and I knew she had extended the specialized javelin she kept up one of her sleeves. We had switched weapons a few nights ago so she could improve her skills with my weapon. I'd taken her blades for a refresher. It would appear the gods wanted to put us to the test.

"Where?" She whispered and pressed closer to me.

"East. Find Big Owl and drop half way between ground." Big Owl was a nickname for the tallest of The Sairs. I shut my eyes and tapped one blade twice against the other's hilt. It was our code letting her know that I'm going blind and she needed to heighten her eyesight. I heard the knock of wood as she acknowledged with a rap of her knuckles against the javelin. Then I heard her feet shuffle and the warmth against my back disappear as she moved to face the same way as me.

"See him?" I whispered.

"Oh yeah. Idiot thief," she replied.

Thieves had always been common in this part of The Snakes. Annie and I constantly joked about how the thieves probably thought the name of the road was meant to encourage their presence. It wasn't, but that hadn't stopped their activity.

"Why do they all smell the same?" I asked as I relaxed from my crouch and open my eyes. Annie and I had spent many days and nights hunting down thieves as it was our duty to protect The Snakes and the borders of our home. Although their activity was increasing more than ever.

"Why do they all insist on wearing their spoils?" She asked in kind. "This one is actually wearing a gold whale earring of one of the northern traders. As if I wouldn't recognize their emblem from here."

I glanced where the thief was and I could make out the glint of the earring thanks to the moon's light blue light. At ninety yards through thick brush and trees, my vision went a bit hazy. Annie, however, could see over five hundred yards through anything except a mountain when her gift was in full swing.

When I asked how her gift worked, she explained it to me as a simple process of changing colors. She knew that certain things had certain colors, like tree trunks being brown, and she would make them gray. Instantly, she could see all the world without any browns. Thus, leaving the other colors to stand out. However, using this gift made her nearly deaf and extremely vulnerable. It's on the list of things to help her with, don't worry.

Annie let out a defeated sigh. "I suppose it's my turn, isn't it?"

I pointed out, "I got last time."

"Fine. Can I at least use my aura on him?" She'd never used her aura to actually seduce anyone because I knew she didn't care for anyone but me. She made her intentions known a while back and, unlike mine, they were quite obvious. I mean when a female falls on me by accident and remains there with her face a few inches from mine, even I get the hint.

Although, I can't quite stand the idea of being with her as my partner for life, at least not in that way. There are too many complications. Then again, it could be nice. I'll wait a decade or so then I'll get around to making a move. Maybe. I'd sooner count the stars in the sky than try to organize and express my feelings.

I sighed in frustration. "Sure. I'm hungry so let's get it over with and I'll share my dinner with you."

"You just like how they make me burp," she responded with a flirty smile.

In all honesty, it's that smile that keeps me from being completely removed from the rest of my people. Trust me, sometimes I just want to live at the edges of the forest or far north where only a handful of my people have been. Always at the brim, they like to tell others about me. Oh yeah, that's why they call me Brim if you didn't know.

I nodded in agreement. "You do belch like an old man full of mead."

"Hmph." She grunted and turned away from me. The light green aura extended a few feet in every direction around her and began swirling. Shoulders back, she headed straight for the thief.

"The poor bastard…" I remarked.

"See you on the back side."

"On it." I made my way to circle around the thief. I shimmered and went invisible. Oh, did I forget to mention I can do that?

CHAPTER 2

"You ain't gonna fool me, mosser," grumbled the thief. "That veil is easy to ignore."

Annie smiled at him from ten yards away. Her aura was filled with tiny daggers of light swirling faster than normal. Usually the aura distracted the looker into seeing someone really beautiful or seeing something so distracting they were nearly mesmerized. I'm guessing his slam at her heritage - calling her a mosser - had set her off something fierce.

I knew the swirling of her aura meant a racing heartbeat. I pushed calm energy to her, but she brushed it off. I wasn't worried about her; she was a formidable fighter even without the javelins. Also, I hunkered down in the shade of a thick, thorny bush about five yards behind the thief and he gave no indication to my existence. After doing this for more than a tree's lifetime, I would hope a scruffy, mortal outsider couldn't get the jump on me.

"Fair enough. I won't fool you," Annie said in a cool tone with an even face.

I knew what was coming. She was in one of those moods and technically we did have the right to end the life of anyone breaking the law.

She shimmered and the aura stopped swirling and solidified into a dark green bubble. The aura was Annie's natural gift and a rare one to boot. The air within the aura protected her or me if she didn't want to slow me down. The aura didn't damage the life around her. Branches, brush, and flowers physically bent away from it before the aura arrived. Nature always knows enemy from friend. Although, anything not of the land was going to get a treatment they never expected.

The thief gulped audibly and took a step back. His ratty, black hair and equally ratty black clothes did not blend in with the night sky thanks to Annie's aura. As he walked backward, he pulled a knife from his belt and held it out. The gesture didn't even faze her.

"Oh boy," I whispered. It was rare for me, but I didn't want to deal with explaining to the elders why we couldn't just catch the thief and gather intel. It was part of my duty, after all.

As I moved toward the thief, I verified the information we all knew about them. The thieves in this area had key things in common. The first was that most of them were part of the Yeryan race. The Yerya were a foot shorter than our people with dark skin, thin hands, and long, nimble fingers. Naturally, those physical features helped greatly with thievery and deception. Although, there were rumors of some that actually utilized their traits to excel in respectable crafts.

The thieves were also easily identified by their earrings. However, the earrings weren't something that was attached as much as it was grown. Rumor has it that the leader of the thieves found a way to manipulate some animal or plant to grow from a cut in their ear. The other rumor was the leader could hear everything because each thief's ear was an extension of the leader. The first rumor I believed while the second was one I simply refused to believe. Although we still cut off the ear with the earring of all the captured thieves just in case. For those we didn't kill outright anyways.

I slipped around the bush and carefully tiptoed over fallen twigs and leaves until I was arm's length from the thief. If I was careful, I could turn this night into something funny and maybe stop Annie from making a bloody mess.

With a little exertion and focus, I extended my invisibility outward until the thief's legs disappeared. The instant I did that the thief looked down and screamed. The invisibility made mortals go numb and typically fall over. Sure enough, the instant after the scream, the thief toppled onto his back. The knife in his hand flew up in the air and fell, dagger down, straight into his right thigh.

The sound of beautiful, musical laughter filled the forest as Annie's aura popped and sent bright white light in all directions.

"I hate it when you do that," she said between gasps. "I wanted some blood."

I let go my invisibility, flipped the blade in my hand to grab the sharp side and knocked the thief unconscious with the hilt.

"And I wanted to hear your laugh," I replied with a careless shrug.

She glared at me, but it was clear she couldn't hold it for long. Her eyes crinkled and a smile brightened her face. The bright light of her aura was still making the trees and bushes glow which cast her in an even more beautiful light. She looked like an angel...which must have been written on my face.

She raised a playful eyebrow and asked, "Like what you see, Cassius?"

With a flick of the hand, vines from nearby bush swept Annie off her feet and she fell onto her back just like the thief. All Tree Makers could manipulate nature in some basic way with barely a thought. So basic was the manipulation that Annie used the same vines to cushion her fall. She only laughed even harder.

Fine. If she was going to be that way then I was, too. Staring her down, I said, "You have to return the thief to the elders. And don't forget how you treated them last time."

Her laughter died and the daggers of light began to rematerialize.

"Nope. You can't take this one out on me. It was your doing, Caryanne." I put emphasis on her name and her aura dissipated again.

"I should have never let you in," she stated. She waved her hand and the vines raised her upright.

"Please, you know you're glad you did." I smiled at her and

pushed a happy thought her way.

We share a bond that neither of us can explain and none of the elders will explain. Well, they did tell us we are not related, just to make sure we didn't run to opposite ends of the planet after the kiss we shared. It was that kiss, under that rare purple moon all those years ago, when we discovered our shared gift. We could push thoughts to one another from nearly any distance. Also, when we combined our will together, we could push thoughts to others. They couldn't respond in any way (which was perfect by me), but we always knew they received it.

So when I pushed her the happy thought of the kiss, her aura began to swirl the tiny emerald stars and all was good again.

"Fine. Go on," Annie said with a wave. "Enjoy your burpy, blue fruit."

"I will. First, let's tell the other patrols to be on alert and give a heads up to the elders." My stomach growled again. "If there is one thief then we should warn them that more will likely be out tonight."

I stepped over to her and put my right hand on her left shoulder and she instinctively mirrored my gesture. Looking into those dark green eyes made her aura shift from swirling stars to tiny falling ones. Yeah, she loved me. Yeah, I loved her. But she didn't really need to hear it. Okay, she probably did need to hear how I felt, but I haven't directly told her and I won't for some time.

"You know you could just tell them. We both don't have to do it." Her voice was soft, her eyes exploring mine.

"I know. And I also know how much it irks them that I involve you because they want me to develop my skills and not help improve yours." I paused and gave her a playful smirk. "I do like to see you happy...and upset them a bit."

She blushed deeply. The deadly fighter was gone and the tiny girl that kissed me all those moons ago stood before me. Her blush deepened as I held my gaze.

"Thinking about how beautiful and ageless I am?" She jested yet I noticed a bit of hope in her eyes.

I shook my head. "Actually, I was thinking about how I hope I don't age as noticeably as you have been."

The off-white stars stopped falling downward and turned into tiny daggers that landed on my skin. Since I was within her aura they caused tiny, annoying pricks all over my exposed skin. Before she could make them pierce skin, I leaned in and kissed her forehead. Her aura instantly melted into soft rain that tickled my skin.

When I pulled away, Annie furrowed her brow at me in frustration at the exposure of her weakness with me.

I smiled. "I'm hungry. I want to get this over with."

"Fine," she replied with a sigh then closed her eyes.

It was only when we were emotionally intense could the telepathy work. Some people thought I could hear every single thought of everyone around me. I let them think that, but it simply isn't true. I'd go crazy if that was the case. They would likely never see me as I'd climb the tallest Sair and be left alone for life just to have my own thoughts. In reality, it took intense emotion which could also be stirred by my connection with Annie. The bond we have allows us to reach great distances. The rest of the time, our fear, worry, or hatred that stemmed from natural circumstances would allow us to use the ability without the other present.

I had a couple more decades of practice compared to Annie so I always took the lead. When I closed my eyes, I always imagined what the forest looked like as if I sat on the clouds. From there I would envision The Snakes and The Sairs, then my fellow wardens would begin appearing as bright blue forms.

I didn't have to focus on each one separately anymore; I could just take my memory of a recent event and push that thought to them. Tonight, I wasn't as grumpy - damn Annie and her seductive ways - and I sent them the memory of the thief falling on his butt with his legs missing.

Different forms of laughter came from each of them. It's hard to describe as it's slightly different for each person, but listening to their thoughts is like an echo of an echo. When I first began practicing telepathy, thoughts could be heard like an echo coming from The Sairs. Thankfully, it was much clearer now. Annie always described it for her as the sound of raindrops on a puddle. With time, she'd be able to hear it better. Since I was leading this one, she heard it the way I did.

Annie commented, "Your way is so much better."

"I've been telling you this for years." I took a long breath and continued. "Now be quiet so we can reach the elders. They always want to try and talk back. It's quite annoying."

I pulled my thoughts away from the patrols and shifted focus. The elders were in our village in The Serenities. The tallest of the trees in The Shaws, The Serenities had thick trunks the size of small hills. Our people hollowed out some of them, but mainly we used the limbs - which were as thick as normal trees - to string our vines, brush, and cut logs to form the houses and gathering places. The elders insisted on occupying the highest point in The Serenities - without being susceptible to the wind of course - and they enjoyed that vantage point. Thankfully, when connecting telepathically, their physical placement didn't matter.

In my mind's eye, I didn't imagine the entire forest. Instead home always showed up as its own place. It wasn't that surprising since all of my people felt close to our home. All of our lives centered around the forest because it provided everything and therefore we protected it at all costs. My home showed up as vivid as if I was physically there. All I had to do was "walk" to the elders' council and they all showed up in blue just like the wardens.

They didn't know I was there because none of them possessed any sense of telepathy. They were the elders only because they had lived the longest without leaving the comforts of where they grew up. Living a long time doesn't grant wisdom, but the elders don't understand that. To be honest, I could be an elder because I know more and have seen more and have fought more and have more gifts than they do. However, being an elder is boring. They sit. A lot. They talk. A lot. No, thanks.

The elders were also somewhat arrogant which was well-known even amongst the foreigners. Granted, most of our older people's arrogance got them in trouble, but that didn't make it okay by me.

Maybe that's why I was more flippant than normal.

I wandered around them. Well, technically, Annie and I did. Three of the eight were there. Two of them were men and one of them a woman. Similar to different sounds made by the genders, females and males telepathically radiate a different color. Females have a softer, sky blue whereas the men are darker blue.

Do they even have a hint of an idea you are there? Annie's voice was clear in my mind as if she spoke the words out loud.

I laughed to myself. *Nope. No idea. And I could snoop on their thoughts if I wanted.*

I didn't mean to let that part slip, but it was too late to take it back.

You what? Annie's voice was full of surprise. *But you said you couldn't do that with anyone except me.*

No, no, what we have is different. I severed my connection with home and opened my eyes to look into hers. I pondered how much I wanted to tell her and she picked up on my hesitance.

"Cassius, I'm not going to tell anyone. You know I'd die for you."

My heart suddenly lurched for a couple reasons. The first was simply because I couldn't imagine my life - especially as long as it can be - without her. The second reason it bothered me was that burden of responsibility. By taking Annie out from the comfort of The Serenities, I put her life in danger with every setting sun.

"Don't say that again," I stated in such a way she knew to remain quiet. "I've been practicing. That's not true; I've been listening more and thinking less."

"I could have told you that last part."

"Yeah yeah." I shook off her jab. "No, I've been meditating more. Not being so angry at the stupid people and the thieves and figuring out the mystery of our bond and Algrad's story. Just been enjoying the breeze."

"And..." She was hanging on every word. I know she was wanting to learn how, but she also was just a snoopy person. Her ability to sneak around and belligerently face any foe made her an ideal protector and a good ally.

"And they are blinded by their arrogance. To them, being an elder lets them believe they are worth more which feeds their pride. Their pride—"

She continued, "Is an emotion that leaves them vulnerable."

I nodded. "Exactly. And once that door is open then I can hear or see."

She looked away for a moment as a thought clearly struck her. When she looked back at me, there was conviction in her eyes. "So, could you dig for something specific?"

"Sure, but why would I...wait. No, Annie, I won't dig for us."

She stomped her foot like a child, furrowing her eyebrows. Green stars in her aura turned into tiny bursting bubbles. "I want to know."

I leaned closer to her even though no one could hear us. "I know where to find out. And we will."

She opened her mouth to interrupt me, but I shook my head. Then I let out a quick breath that caused the bubbles in her aura to stop bursting.

"Annie. Remember, I can mute your power if you push too far. Almost like that's part of our bond."

"I'm sorry."

I shrugged and closed my eyes, knowing she would follow me into the vision. "Pay attention."

Immediately we were walking amongst the elders who were clearly in a heated discussion. One of the men raised their arms in frustration and a tiny red bubble floated from their head.

I reached out to Annie's mind. *Walk up to that and tell me you see.*

In the vision, Annie was a white ghost amongst the elders. She walked up to the bubble, peered into it for a moment. Then she circled it until it hit her.

It's hazy, but Grendar is thinking about the expansion into the neighboring forest, but he's hiding something. It's hazier as I look deeper into it. I see...something, but I can't make it out.

I walked over and peered into it. I saw it, but I still wanted to train her. The better she was at this then the better we were as a team.

Forget the face. What garb is worn?

Excitement pulsed from her. *Ohh! It's a trader. From the northern seas, it looks like.*

Yes. Good job catching that, I replied then reached out and popped the bubble with my finger. The red dissipated.

Her shock was not veiled at all. *You can do that, too?*

Mmhmm. Now let's tell them we are here. I'll bring you in because I don't want them to know you can be here at the same time. I paused to find the wording. *Oh, be annoyed that I interrupted you.*

Not a problem. Lying mossers, she mumbled then disappeared from the vision.

Once she was gone, I simply visualized the elders as their actual physical representation instead of the blue entities and they immediately turned to me. I sent the image of a thief and catching the thief - not the humiliating invisibility part - and an image of Annie. Not the nice image of Annie, but the angry aura that was ready to kill. I could sense all of them turn their focus to Annie instead of the thief which was my cue to bring her in.

She showed up right at that moment. Her white form subdued their blue auras like a midday sun wiping away all shadows. If the elders knew that we saw them cower that much, they definitely would be upset. After all, she'd always been there, just without their knowledge. They recoiled, but I sent the message that she was going to return the thief. Their thoughts were reluctant, but they agreed to handle it.

Without hesitation or our traditional goodbye, I pulled away from the vision. My eyes opened and I looked at Annie. "I love how they don't love you."

She laughed. "Me, too!"

"Take care of the thief. And don't hurt him. He's knocked out and you can use the vines to wrap him–"

Already turning around and weaving her right hand in a figure eight to motivate the vines to bind the thief. "You're such a nag. I

15

know the routine."

"Just doing my job. I am the head warden, you know."

"We all know, boss," she replied with heavy sarcasm.

"Oh, and Annie. Don't hesitate to kill if he resists or you suspect another is following you." I didn't hide my authority. While she was capable, she was still my apprentice and my responsibility. "I'm upset with the elders for not doing anything about the increase in thief activity. If they don't get information out of this one then we are going to do the interrogation ourselves."

Her eyes widened in excitement as if I just told her I loved her. Yes, it's messed up she equates violence with love, but that's just who she is. "Can I tell the elders that?"

I turned away from her and said over my shoulder, "I would never tell you what you can and cannot say to them."

CHAPTER 3

The Snakes wound through most of our forest, but there were other smaller roads and trails that branched off them. They didn't have names and they were rarely used because word got around about the increase in robbery along the road. Coincidentally, the thieves stayed away from these dirt tributaries because they knew the presence of wardens had increased. We do not like people disrupting the harmony in our lands.

I felt a tiny burst of frustration from Annie. I stopped walking and closed my eyes. She telepathically sent me images of the thief trying to run away, hands bound behind him, then running into a tree and knocking himself out. Her trip was going to definitely be slower since she'd have to drag him along. I sent back a message that was roughly equivalent to: "better you than me." Then I resumed my pace south along one of The Snakes' side roads.

Even though it had already been a long night, the light blue moon still held high as the nights are longer in the winter. The long nights suit me just fine as it's the most peaceful and quiet time of day. Most creatures are asleep or lethargic from a long day of pollination, crawling, walking or flying. Even the winds couldn't make it through the cover of the leaves on these trees. The only noises came from the nocturnal animals. They are so different from their brothers and sisters that love the sun. They show their true brilliance as they play with the shadows and the assumptions of those around them. It's from them I learned to be so quiet and hide so well.

For example, there is a brown and red spotted, five-legged creature called a fink. It uses the night shadows to hide two of its three rear legs and crawl in such a way that it appears injured. Without fail, a larger predator will come along (or fly by) and attempt to snag the easy, injured prey. It never works though since finks run in packs. There are always at least a dozen waiting to pounce out of the shadows and on the predator the moment it goes for the kill. Given they have a paralyzing bite, they do very well for themselves. I may not have their bite, but I've learned to use the shadows as effectively as finks.

I thought about using the shadow-hopping ability to sneak up on one of the border patrols since there should be one somewhat near the cave. They do work for me so I like to keep them tested. But my appetite got the best of me so I pushed on.

To speed up the journey to the fruit cave, I shifted my focus away from the moonlight and to the shadows. Immediately, everything else became clear. I could easily run through the forest without catching my garb on a single branch or bush. I could easily leap over the fallen trees and branches without so much as glancing down. Even after a couple centuries of being a Tree Maker, it still is really cool to use these abilities.

Some thought deep in my mind surfaced and flashed a memory. Very hazy, very gray, and nothing perceptible except a feeling like using these abilities was filling a void. Almost like going home again after being away for a long time. I tried to dig at the memory, but gained no ground. I shook it away and continued running, excited at what was ahead.

The Tears were two separate lakes, one after another, stretched oblong thanks to an extra tributary from The Sairray River that cut across The Shaws, through The Marshes and eventually dumping into Trader's Ocean. The first of the two lakes was larger and carried a steady, slow current into the next lake via a small channel. Both lakes had a dock where people could exit and take one of the smaller paths into the woods. Both lakes were protected by trees growing along the shore that reached out and touched one another above the lake's center. It created a safe haven - a canopy of peaceful calm for both the lakes. Thus, both lakes had become a frequent visit for many of my people.

A thicket of thorny bushes brought me to a stop. Just beyond the bushes stood the trees that grew as close together as some bushes did. I knew the branches and trees would support my jumps and swings since I couldn't walk on water. And I didn't feel like getting wet just to eat. If I did then I would have to start a fire to dry myself off. Starting a fire in the middle of winter night with one thief already caught and bound wasn't a good idea. No matter how dangerous I knew I could be, I didn't want to be foolish by underestimating the fact there could be more thieves on the prowl.

If only I was like the Tree Maker of old, Elb. It was told Elb could walk on water for a minute or two and swim underneath for at least an hour before needing air. Only the gods knew what he could do at the bottom of a lake for an hour. Probably getting away from the elders.

Since the thorny bushes grew around the perimeter, I was better off running along the shoreline. With a running start, I leapt over the bushes, caught a branch and swung from one to the next until the shore was in sight. As easily as I swung onto branches, I released my grip from the branch and landed on the shore. Rather gracefully, I might say. Normally, my landings were quiet so no one heard it. Under the canopy of branches and leaves, however, my feet made a noise that echoed halfway across the lake before fading.

I cringed at the noise - it was a little embarrassing - but I noticed something on the water. The moon was barely shining through the thick canopy. The slight ripple on the water came from wind that snuck through the trees. The other ripple came from a makeshift raft someone was paddling to the opposite end of the oblong lake. The person had a lantern in one hand that emitted a firefly glow around the raft and across the lake. From this distance, I couldn't make out the age or race, but guessing from the slender form the person was a female.

The lake wasn't too deep around the edges and the floater figured that out. With her free arm, she pushed a long pole into the water against the lake floor then lifted the pole out of the water to repeat the process. She was making good time, almost too good of time, as if she was escaping.

I thought about letting it be, but my right calf burned and I heeded the warning. I let out a frustrating sigh. "Great. I'm never going to eat."

This lake didn't have wet shores due to the trees keeping the wind to a minimum. The hard dirt allowed me to quickly gain on the rafter. With a quick thought, I sent an image of the rafter and the lake to Annie. There was an acknowledgement of wonder and I could feel a nag of a question, but I shrugged it off. My only answer came in the form of an emotion: cranky hunger. I felt humor from her then I refocused on the night and the foreigner on the water.

There were only a few driftwood logs along the shoreline that I easily skirted. I was making up a lot of ground to the point that I was running the risk of being seen. I shimmered and went invisible. My tracks in the dirt wouldn't be invisible, but no one was tracking me so I didn't have to worry. As I rounded the lake, I could make out more of her features. The glow from the lantern showed dirt and blood on one side of her face. At one point, she turned to my side of the lake, the visibility of her black eye and bruised face easily discernable. Another fact that confirmed she was running from someone.

She was nearing the dock and I certainly didn't want to startle her. I may have forgot to mention that wardens weren't the most liked by outsiders. In fact, we have a reputation for being narrow-minded and executing a sentence before hearing the evidence. Even though I don't run things that way, those before me did so for a long time. While reputations are difficult to change, I tried to mend such a reputation by never letting that kind of Tree Maker to become warden during my reign.

A sliver of bright moonlight crept through the canopy and I noticed movement on the other side towards the dock. I stopped moving and steadied my breath to ensure it wasn't just the light playing tricks or it wasn't a lurking predator. Only a few breaths passed and I saw movement again. Two people were moving in unison and I immediately closed my eyes and focused my hearing.

The sounds from around me rushed forth and I pushed them aside to focus on the two beings. As if my ears were on the wind, the sounds carried me across the lake and to the crunching leaves and bending branches of the two attempting to sneak around. I heard whispers in Yeryan then the distinct noise of metal sliding out of a hard leather.

"Thieves," I hissed under my breath.

I opened my eyes, shimmered away the invisibility and started running to the dock. I'd have to run even faster so the female on the raft didn't see me. My hearing gift was still in tune yet throttled so I could use my vision to find the quietest and fastest way to the other side of the dock. In the span of only a few minutes I had to keep an ear on the intruders, keep an eye on the female and get to a vantage point to stop whatever was about to go down.

I'm able to be swift when I need to be and I needed to be. I made it to the other side and shimmied up a tree a few yards at the edge of the clearing that surrounded the dock. As luck would have it, the men stopped at the same tree moments after I did. I watched them intently, one hand on the grip of my blade, but they didn't notice me. Their focus was only on the rafter.

I adjusted my hearing back to normal and focused my attention on the men. I noticed their single, discolored earrings. I could have stopped them before they even made themselves known to her. However, instincts were holding me back. It didn't make sense why they didn't just stand at the dock since they had the upper hand. Clearly, they were waiting for something else, so I was going to wait, too.

Using the pole as an anchor instead of a paddle, the black-eyed female held it in place and set the lantern on the dock. The glow of the lantern showed me more bruises and blood on her face than I saw from across the lake. I also recognized her race: she was Dewarian.

21

The Dewarians came from another continent in the southern part of the world. Typically, they were good people who primarily kept to themselves except those who came to trade with us. They sailed in one or two large ships solely to haul back chopped trees and branches. Apparently, their land was burned long ago and it hadn't recovered. They made a life underground, but needed material for building. Unfortunately, none of our seeds grew in their land; so long ago my people and theirs agreed to trade metal ore for our trees. They had plenty of caves that provided them endless ores that we smelted for our weapons and for some of our buildings.

Oh, I forgot to mention we gave all the trusted traders a necklace to be worn to prove the loyalty. Typically, this trust was only established by decades of trading and usually within the same family line. Also, the necklace was enchanted with a magic that kept predators from nearing them as they traveled to Varokkar, the gathering point of all trade in our land. Loosely translated, Varokkar meant Our Tree which I always felt was a little smug. Yet the name had been used by traders for centuries and tradition is tough to break. Our Tree had been hollowed to serve as a large archway and the gateway into the home of my people. I didn't see any necklace on her, but I'm guessing she had other things on her mind.

Usually, I leave myself out of the business of others unless they were damaging my forest or when a death was about to happen. So when the men moved from underneath the tree and into the clearing around the dock, I chose to act.

I jumped up and forward, grabbed a branch then used the momentum to somersault forward and land between the thieves and the female now standing on the dock. In an instant I had a knife in my left hand and pulled the short sword from underneath my cloak. The sword hummed with a green glow like Annie's aura. Actually, it was exactly like Annie's aura because she imbued her protection into it. By putting part of herself into the sword it meant that she knew when I used it.

Immediately she was in my thoughts. *Help?*

Not yet, I replied.

Typical Annie, she ignored me. *On my way.*

I thought about telling her to stay, but this many thieves in one night within such a short distance of one another was suspicious. I sent her an image of the dock and the men then returned to the moment.

I took one step toward the thieves and they stopped walking forward immediately. The woman on the dock also stopped moving. The only noises were heavy breaths of fear and the humming of the blades.

CHAPTER 4

"You should know that I'm kind of cranky. It's been a long night and I'm really hungry." I meant to say it with a little humor, but holding glowing weapons and being a warden doesn't lighten anyone's mood.

One of the thieves was a few inches taller than the other. They both, however, were still a head shorter than I was. One of the thieves had a crude goatee and seemed to be carrying himself with a little more confidence than his friend. However, the one without facial hair decided he had a little more courage than his friend.

"Ain't none of your business, moss'r," he grumbled. He spoke slowly, but distinctly.

"That's twice in one night," I mumbled then I threw my knife before the second thief could get his left foot off the ground. The knife went through his foot like it was wet moss. How poetic.

The thief cried out and the shivs that he'd loosened from his sleeve fell to the ground. He reached down to pull the knife out.

"Not wise, scrub," I whispered an enchantment and vines from the closest bush snaked across the clearing and wrapped around the knife and the thief's feet.

"Stupid moss'r!"

"Really? You think more insults are going to help this?" I nodded at the vines and they twisted the blade and the thief screamed in more agony. As he looked to the sky, I was able to verify he was a Yerya by the light-colored neck. While their skin is almost as dark as a shadow, the skin under their chins was almost as light as the sun by contrast. I speculated that the thieves developed a downward tilt of the head to best hide the fish belly neck.

A timid voice behind me whispered, "Thank you."

I turned around and faced the female.

The damage to her face was extensive. There were several cuts that could only be from repeated blows of a fist. The swollen cheek was that deep purple of recovery and the other cheek was swelling from a recent punch. Muddy and bloody hair covered her face, indicating she'd taken a knock to the head. Her hands were trembling in fear as she looked over my shoulder at the thieves. The only part of her that remained clean were the sea green eyes that showed more fear than her petite body did.

Anger in me stirred as I imagined what they did to her. In response to that anger, the sword's green light began to float off the blade and fly towards the unrestrained thief. I heard a gurgling sound and I knew the aura had enveloped the thief's face and within a few seconds his unconscious body slumped to the ground with an audible thud. The green aura returned to my sword as vibrant as when it left.

I took a long deep breath and exhaled equally as long. The sword's aura calmed down to a subtle glow, blending into the light blue moonlight. I sheathed my weapons and walked around the female to sit on the dock several feet away. If I wanted information then I couldn't startle her any more than the knife throwing already did. And I wanted to keep my eyes on the thugs.

The woman looked at me and looked at the thieves. "Am I safe?"

"You're never sa–," the conscious thief started saying through the pain of the knife in his foot. I cut him off with a wave of my hand as the vines started pulling him back into the forest. Before he disappeared out of our sight, he was completely enveloped in vines.

"Yes, you are safe," I replied softly. "My name is Brim. I'm the head warden of this land."

She clearly knew enough about my people and wardens because

there was an immediate sigh of relief and her shoulders slackened.

"Cantiga," she said. "Thanks for the help."

I nodded and watched her out of the corner of my eye. She fidgeted with her garments, straightening her shirt the best as possible and tried to fold under the torn parts. Using some of the water at her feet, she leaned down and cleaned off her face and hands.

I only spoke up when she tucked her hair behind her ears. "You're one of them."

She tensed and sat up straight immediately. My blades began to glow brighter. Quickly, she covered up her ears to hide the thieves' earring. To my surprise, she didn't run. Instead she looked at me in a challenging defiance.

"No. I'm not."

"I'm aware not all are thieves, but I can feel that thing from here."

The earring gave off a disturbance that my people had learned to detect. It wasn't hard to do since it felt like a kick to the gut like the senseless killing of an animal or the cutting down of one of our great trees. Now hers wasn't as strong as others, but that only meant it was not quite matured.

She hung her head and turned away from me. With deep embarrassment, she said, "It was forced."

I almost laughed because that is something anyone would say to save their life from a warden's wrath. Yet she clearly wasn't the typical thief since she wasn't Yeryan. Something still felt off by the whole situation.

"Why should I believe you?"

"Because of this." She pulled a necklace from underneath her shirt and held it out.

It was one of our necklaces. Those given to people proven faithful and loyal to the land and thus our people. It wasn't unheard of for a Dewarian to have a necklace, but it was unheard of for a thief to have one. Plus, there were measures in place to guarantee if someone stole the necklace that they would be punished.

I stood, sheathed one blade and covered the distance between

Cantiga so rapidly that she gave a startled jump. Bearing down on her with furious eyes, I stretched out my palm.

She looked at my outstretched hand, but her attention quickly shifted to the glowing blade in my other hand. With shaky hands, she lifted the necklace off her neck and placed it in my hand.

The necklace was made of a water-resistant, stretchable leather that came from a water fowl in the northern regions of The Shaws. The jewel in the necklace was a rare kind that originated from petrified trees deep in The Shims - the thickly-packed forest that surrounded The Sairs.

When the necklace was given to the trusted person, a Tree Maker forged a bond into the jewel with their blood and the blood of the wearer. This bond created a unique reaction when the blood of a Tree Maker and the person touched the jewel. The reaction incited a magic that would cause smoke to rise from the jewel and form into the tiny version of Our Tree. The color of the tree - a deep, rich brown - would be surrounded by a fog in the color of the necklace wearer's eyes.

If the necklace was stolen then a vibrant red glowed whenever the jewel touched the skin of the wearer. This glow could be seen from over a dozen yards. Of course, if blood of someone other than the owner touched it then the jewel cracked and spilled a poison that would slowly petrify the wearer. There were only a few so foolish, but their petrified bodies still remained intact across our lands.

I pricked the tip of my finger and let a drop of blood fall on the jewel. I nodded at Cantiga and with her free hand she stuck her finger in a fresh wound on her face. Her eyes never wavered from mine and she didn't cringe once.

This one has fire in her, I thought.

Without taking her eyes off me, she touched her bloody finger to the jewel. Something happened that I did not expect.

Instead of the color of Our Tree, a vortex of gray, sea green, and sky blue smoke swirled upward from the jewel. The colors lit up Cantiga's face and I could see the wonder in her eyes. Four separate columns formed for a moment then shifted into a silhouette of Our

Tree. I'd forged a few of the necklaces myself and intimately know the details of my magic, but this was entirely different. The jewel recognized three entities: our people, Cantiga, and myself as my eyes are that shade of blue. And I definitely had never met this person which means I didn't forge this necklace.

This knowledge frightened me and I don't frighten easily. Living a long life especially within the confines of the same area allows a great wisdom to settle. All living things including those who wandered to our lands were as well known to me as the very leather shoes I have been wearing for over a century. To come across something I didn't know was unnerving.

Annie picked up on my fear and reached out. *I'm close.*

Her timing couldn't have been better. As I was about to ask Cantiga questions about the necklace, I heard the distinct and familiar sound of a mourar's wings.

The mourars are closely tied to our race. Most other races bonded with less intelligent, three or four-legged animals. For our people, we bonded closest to these older birds since they were similar to us in long life and intelligence. Although mourars possessed intelligence and power beyond ours and were thus revered above all. We didn't know their true life spans and some guessed they did not die. Instead they flew to other lands only to return when the next generation of Tree Makers were born. There were a lot of theories pertaining to the ancient beast and I didn't put credence to a single one. All I know is from my interaction with the mourar that landed behind us.

"What is that?" Cantiga jumped to her feet and turned around. The vortex from the necklace disappeared immediately. "Another one?"

I slowly turned around and looked into the dense trees. I could feel the mourar's power pressing on my mind. I reached out to face the power head on. Of course, my power was like a boulder next to the mountain that was his power. I still held my ground and reached out telepathically. *Why are you here?*

The mourar did not answer me. Well, not directly. There was a flash of brightest white that made both of us turn our heads.

Cantiga opened her eyes before I did. Her hands frantically grabbed my arm and her fingernails pierced through my tunic. "What in the five hells is that?!"

My eyes opened slowly. The light was so bright that small stars were still in my vision when my eyes fell on the mourar at the end of the dock. Even though I'd seen him a lot this last year, I am still awed by his presence.

His body is five feet wide and at least eight feet tall. The ancient bird was decorated in light and dark gray feathers, but they had a faint, white glow like the fog that swirls atop The Sairs. A large, sharp black beak stuck out beneath a row of four, black eyes. Four massive wings - each one as long as his body - spread out from the bird's torso. The mourar slowly flapped them with such power that three-foot waves rippled away from the shore. The middle two eyes blinked then the outer two eyes blinked.

Cantiga's grip tightened more and she moved behind me.

"His name is Jaired. And he's our ride," I said with a small, satisfying smile and started down the dock. I love having powerful friends.

CHAPTER 5

"I didn't think your people hid from thieves," commented Cantiga from atop a stable yet high branch. Judgement came out with each word and stayed on her face after she spoke.

I grumbled and growled for a few breaths. She had been carrying about this air of entitlement and it was grinding against my nerves. There was no gratitude for lifting her up into the tree courtesy of my will and the friendly vines. I could have reached out to the closer bush that had thorns - maybe I should have. There was no gratitude for the salve I snagged for her wounds from a warbeye bush moments before the thieves saw me. There was no gratitude for giving her my cloak to keep her warm and camouflaged.

"We live a long time because we are wise with our actions and not hasty, Teega."

She seethed. "It's Cant–,"

"Mmmm...no. I decided I don't like your name. So I'm going to call you Teega. And I saved your life and I continue to do so by having you up here." I don't know why I insist on nicknames, but I do. I gave her a level gaze indicating that I was done talking about it. "Now, be quiet. Help is coming and she'll clean house so we can figure out what you are."

She looked down at her chest where the necklace dangled, the vortex started swirling, albeit faintly, once we landed. I didn't know what to make of it and the mental imprint I sent to Annie resulted in only more confusion.

Jaired wasn't exactly helping out either. He sat perched above us about ten feet, all four eyes tracking all the thieves. He'd carried us here on his back then dropped us off. Then he immediately transformed into a bird the size of a small owl and took to the tree branch. He didn't look as intimidating as before, but I knew his fiercest form was a shimmer away.

I'd witnessed the predatory panther before. His wings would turn to legs and his beak would turn to a long, fierce jaw. His eyes, well, they were the only part that didn't morph into anything else; they would only adjust to be proportionate to his current form. The gray blue feathers would turn to a rough, black fur and a tail - which somehow gave his leaps a short flight - would grow a sharp, fanged tip the size of my head. There are many times I'm glad I didn't meet that side of him first.

I looked up at Jaired and one eye swiveled down at me. *Me too, Brim.*

Every time he spoke with telepathy, his words echoed in my head like a not so distant thunderstorm. He wasn't threatening; it was just that his depth of power was so old and so profound that he would always be heard.

I let out a sigh and calmed myself. He is the only one who made me feel like a child in this world and that's a position that I am not used to. I'm not the oldest, but I am the wisest amongst my people, much to the chagrin of the elders. As much as I hate to admit it, Jaired helps me grow and learn.

I extended my mind to him. *How many?*

Jaired swiveled the one eye away from me then closed them all. *Come with.*

During one of our first interactions, he entered my head, took my mind and we ended up flying over The Shaws for half the day. Now Jaired tells the story differently. Something about me being stubborn, stupid and not trusting him so he took my mind and left my body in a tree like the one I'm crouched in now. Naturally, I prefer my version of the story.

Since that first time, I learned it's best to trust him because having your will pulled from your body is more painful than you might think. We become used to the walls of our mind and being in our skin - not having them is just scary.

Any time Jaired asks if I want to leave with him, I know it's a courtesy because he could just yank me out. It took a while, but I just have to close my eyes and let go of the control that keeps me rooted to my body, to my lands. I still didn't have the entire method figured out so Jaired pulled me along, gently. He was gracious enough to actually invite me even though he did most the work.

Okay. I closed my eyes, imagined I was leaving my body then...I was gone.

I took flight. Well, Jaired took flight, but I got to see every step of the way. My vision went from the single target of two eyes to four separate areas of focus courtesy of his eyes. The eyes captured various distances and one saw the heat outlines of all the creatures in the trees, on the ground and even those swimming in The Tears. I'm a smart guy, but it was too much to process all at once. I felt a headache started to push in on me even though my physical head was somewhere far below.

Focus not on all. Only what you want. Jaired's voice wasn't as loud when I was a visitor in his consciousness.

I can do that. I made sure the reply sounded more confident than I truly was.

Similar to the shimmer when I turn invisible, I shifted my focus to thieves. Specifically, I focused on the abomination that grew in their ears. Immediately all the heat signatures disappeared and dark red outlines of the thieves filled my vision. As Jaired floated mostly stationary on a breeze, he looked down so I could get a bearing on their locations. I saw my body, in the blue of my eyes, and I saw Teega in the swirling colors of the necklace. There were the two thieves that I'd wrangled with by the tree where I left Teega. Also, there were the six that were scattered in a semicircle around the dock.

Jaired flapped his powerful wings and took us higher. The

pulsing red and black outlines became dots and what I saw made me gasp. As much as I can gasp without a body, anyway. There were several small groups of thieves, all in their semi-circle predatory approach, scattered across most of The Shaws. The only area free of the thieves was near Our Tree and The Great Ice Shores to the north.

I was completely shocked by the infestation. *How long has this been going on?*

Jaired paid attention to our world even if sometimes he insisted that it didn't matter to him. I knew he cared. At least he did for Annie and myself.

Weeks. Been in hiding. Moving only under this moon.

Why this moon? I asked. To my knowledge, I didn't know if this moon was different than any other. The elders didn't know either even if they tried to pass off their guesses as truths. Annie said she felt different under this blue moon, but she couldn't really put words to the feeling.

Stronger.

Stronger? I repeated.

There was a feeling of impatience coming from Jaired. His voice was softer in my head than normal. The calm before the storm. *You are wise with your people and those beneath. Be wise with me. You will not be punished.*

I laughed and he let it go. Our relationship had been a slow-developing one as he'd been there since the beginning, but only visited at scattered times across these long years. Here I was thinking I was being kind and humble by not exacting my thoughts on him like I do with others. Turns out I was being child-like.

This time Jaired laughed. Audibly it sounded like rolling thunder, but from within his conscious it sounded like a beautiful sunset - if a sunset made noise, of course.

Annie feels stronger during that time. Yet I do not. I know I'm stronger than her.

Silly, little brother. Think.

I like it when he calls me little brother as I believe it was the one thing I caught during our conversations that he likely didn't mean to let slip. Somehow, we had a familial connection.

He may not like me asking simple questions, but he never scolded me for working through a problem. *Hmmm. I am able to do this more easily. And my telepathy is growing.*

Yes.

I threw out a guess. *That means the thieves are led by one of us?*

Before he could answer, I decided that wasn't right. The ear growths were foreign. They were bastardized and unwelcomed by nature.

No, the leader has turned nature against himself.

Manipulated, Jaired clarified. *Very bad. Very strong.*

Care to get rid of him for me? I'll even lend a hand to make sure you get them all.

Jaired laughed then kicked me out of his consciousness. It was playful. Mostly. Immediately I was back in my body, perched on the tree with Teega holding onto my wrist.

"Are you okay?" Her voice showed great concern and her eyes were sincere.

"I'm fine. Just had to go for a flight."

She opened her mouth to inquire more, but a bright green light burst from the forest in the distance and interrupted her. Teega gripped by wrist tighter. "Who is that?"

"That's the help. Her name is Annie. She's...impatient especially when she has recently killed."

Teega's dark complexion lightened considerably. "Killed whom?"

I laughed lightly. "The thieves, of course."

"You're not going to bring them to your elders?"

Elders. Hmm, she knew more about our people than she led on. Shaking my head, I laid it out for her.

"No. That takes too long. There are many groups of thieves spreading throughout my land. They are up to something and we need to find out. The elders take too long to decide. I think you are a part of it, too. And, no, I don't know why."

"You could let them take me away," she replied with little conviction. The jewel betrayed her words as the light vortex brightened at the heightened emotion. We both looked at it then at each other.

"Yeah, that's not going to happen." I jumped and grabbed the limb above me. "Stay here, I have to get my bow and arrows for you."

I pulled myself onto the branch then looked up at the cache hidden in a giant, abandoned nest. I reached out to the tree and asked for help. The moment I jumped up, the branches shook in such a way that they created a strong breeze to help propel me. Just as I was within arm's length of the cache, the branches stopped moving and my momentum slowed so I landed softly in the nest.

Teega's voice carried up the tree. "Can they get up here? Is that why I need weapons?"

I looked over the ledge. She looked up at me then looked down around the tree.

I shook my head, a smile creeping up the corner of my mouth. "No, it's for Annie. It's possible she might try to attack you."

"Oh. Thanks, I think." She slumped against the trunk and covered herself in the cloak.

I grabbed the bow and quiver then leapt down to Teega. My feet touched the branch without a sound or any movement of the branch. Falling slowly was an art few had mastered, but any warden of mine had specific training on falling. Most of us lived in trees and patrolled from them. Therefore, quick, safe exits from trees were necessary to enforce the laws.

I set the weapons at Teega's feet then I reached out and touched her face. In a low, slow voice, I said, "You'll be fine, Teega. This bow and these arrows are for me, for later when the thieves are gone."

There was a loud crack like a giant tree splitting from a lightning strike followed by another giant burst of green light emanating everywhere.

I looked toward the light and let out an angry grumble. "She's going to attract more." I turned to Teega, "Stay here. I'll be back. Jaired is watching you so you'll be safe."

"He's just a bird. What coul–," Teega started to complain and was interrupted as Jaired landed on a branch just behind me. I felt him shift from bird to animal form.

I turned around and stepped to the side so Jaired could see both of us. Moreover, so Teega would be aware of her protector.

Jaired stretched forward with two legs, sharp claws leading the way, then laid down his large panther-like body on the branch. It bowed a bit under the weight of all the muscle. His tail flickered back and forth, the tip carelessly slicing through leaves and tiny branches without stopping. Four red glowing eyes stared out the midnight black fur and intently at us.

Jaired abruptly whipped his tail and sunk the tip into a neighboring branch the size of both my legs and chopped it cleanly off, as easy as a hand enters water. The tumbling sound of the falling branch was punctuated by the sound of pain as it landed on an encroaching thief. The mourar bared his teeth then purred approvingly at the sound.

Go. Now. I'll protect.

I nodded at Jaired in thanks then looked at Teega as she wrapped the cloak tighter around her body as if it would help her disappear from the prying eyes of the predator on the limb.

CHAPTER 6

I heard Annie's anger long before I felt it or saw it. There were sounds of screams being quickly silenced by the snapping of branches then bones. Flesh muffles the sound of broken bones, but not by much. And when Annie got mad, the bones really snapped.

The blue moon was waning, the sun was slowly rising and Annie's raging aura made the forest greener than I'd ever seen. Like a rainy-day fog descending from the skies, her aura filled the area with green hue. Even the normally deep brown trees glowed like a rampantly spreading spring moss.

I remained still against the base of the tree, the thief Jaired knocked out was still unconscious a few feet from me. Teega's rapid breathing could be heard and I could feel Jaired's presence reaching all around, ensuring nothing could sneak up on us.

More thieves yelled. The sound of them crashing through branches and brush let me know Annie was making her way west. I looked to her direction, but the thick tree trunks and branches blocked any view beyond a few yards. Added with Annie's angry, foggy aura, I would have better luck listening than straining my vision.

I closed my eyes, took a deep breath, and let out my breath as I let go of the imagery in my head. My ears began to pick up the rustling of bugs and other small creatures as they hurried away from

Annie's raging storm.

I walked my mind towards Annie purely by sound. The tree trunks remained still, but the branches shook and shivered a bit in anticipation of the violence coming their way. As I moved deeper, the movement of the undergrowth and animals increased rapidly. The rapid heartbeats of finks, wallas, and veddies echoed in my ears as they scattered away from the epicenter.

Eventually, I pushed past the noise and through Annie's inner aura. Absolute silence fell. She was in the zone. Her breath was steady and her heartbeat slow and measured. Not even a drop of sweat fell from her forehead. She was finally learning to channel the anger into a controlled fury. My pride in her ability swelled as goosebumps rippled across my body.

She acknowledged my presence with a whispered curse at the thieves. I laughed and opened my eyes, immediately pulling myself away from Annie's location.

She is using the moon, too, Jaired announced.

My heart skipped a beat. *I thought the thief leader was the only one using it?*

That's your assumption. Not mine.

I glared. Sure, he was at least twenty feet above me protecting Teega, but it felt good to glare anyways.

"Hurry! We have to tell him!" A thief yelled over his shoulder moments before stumbling through the trees into the clearing where I stood. Shortly after another thief crashed right into his friend who had stopped to catch his breath.

"No, he won't," I stated matter-of-factly.

Both of them turned. The first guy swore under his breath, but the second brushed past him with a sweeping arm. He was more muscular than most of his kind and swaggered as if that mattered.

I thought about pulling the blades out. I thought about shimmering invisible and taking a few long strides and slicing their throats open. I thought about knocking them down, tying them up, and letting Teega take out some aggression on them. I thought about a lot of things, as I leaned against the tree without a care as if the thieves weren't set on ending my life.

Jaired's thoughts interrupted my own. *Hold on, little brother. I want.*

I looked up at the tree, completely turning my back to the approaching thief, and said, "Really? Now you want to kill them?"

I heard the footsteps behind me come to a halt.

"Who are you talkin' to, moss'r?" The muscular man's voice wavered at the end. "Got another one of ya hiding do ya?"

I turned around. "No. He doesn't have to hide."

There was a slight breeze over the top of my head followed by Jaired landing between the thief and me. His massive hind legs and shoulders tightened and he bared his ferociously sharp teeth at the thief. I could barely see the thieves over Jaired's massive body.

The thief didn't even have time to turn his shoulder before Jaired had leapt forward and swiped his massive claws at the thief's neck. Blood sprayed directly up from the neck as his head went sailing into the trees to the right. His body slumped to its knees then fell forward on the ground with a subtle thud.

The other thief wasn't nearly as dumb as his decapitated friend as he ran away. He was near the end of the clearing when he came to a stop, turned around and walked back.

Through the green haze I could see a pack of finks, each of them the size of my foot, scurrying across the ground. There were about two dozen of them, but they were so tightly packed that they moved like one large animal.

They eagerly pursued the thief until he darted left toward the other side of the clearing and leaving clear sight of Jaired. Upon seeing the black beast, the group stopped moving and fell into a single line as if to make themselves smaller.

Jaired turned to me and smiled. The thing is he forgot to wipe his mouth after taking a bite out of the thief. So his smile was full of pink teeth from the thief's blood and a couple pieces of flesh.

The impressions of the finks were pouring into my mind. They were scared. They were hungry. They were in awe of Jaired. I relayed the images to him then added, "They need it more than you. The thieves took their home."

Jaired must have known because he looked to them and let out a low, somewhat non-threatening growl then looked the way of the thief. The finks chirped in unison then ran after the thief. In short order, the finks swarmed the thief and brought him to the ground. It was going to get messy and I already had Jaired's smile burned in my brain. I didn't need another bloody image, too.

Before I had time to yell at Teega, I felt a flash of concern from Annie. Immediately, I began sprinting towards her with Jaired quickly on my heels. He could have easily morphed into flying form and got their quicker, but we were in battle mode. The enemy was on the ground so we were on the ground. I was tempted to climb on his back and ask him to sprint there, but I wanted to approach Annie from two directions. I told Jaired my intention then he took off to the right.

The branches and the bushes were all bending towards me which meant they were bending away from Annie. While it made finding her easier than normal, it was also difficult to navigate because nature was adjusting to her energy. I didn't get knocked down, but I did get a couple bumps and scratches en route.

With each step towards Annie, the intensity of her aura was becoming more fog than mist. Part of the reason for the transformation I knew to be a defense mechanism. The Tree Maker part of her was sensing not only danger, but a possible demise. That possibility shook me to the core. Aside from Jaired, she was the closest thing to what I considered family. I did not want a life without her that's for sure.

"There's another thought I hope doesn't slip out so she can hear," I mumbled as I leapt over a broken-boned thief.

Hurry. Three groups on me. Annie sent an image of the clearing where she stood and the groups surrounding her.

Just as she said that, my mind felt a sudden drain of energy. She must have killed off a couple more and she was running dry. Even the mist was beginning to lift as it retreated back to form a protective bubble around her.

I pulled sword and dagger out - which were losing the potency she imbued in them - and sprinted towards the clearing. It only took me a few long strides to get there, but it was long enough that one of the groups was closing in to attack.

"Not on my watch, boys!" I yelled and jumped as high as I ever had, grabbed a branch, and used it to swing myself forward a great distance and land with my back to Annie. The familiar presence of her back against mine fueled us both. I felt her heartbeat increase at my presence and I felt her strain to maintain the aura.

"We don't need the aura; we need it in the weapons. Drop it," I barked.

The world became clear again as the emerald aura disappeared and the weapons thrummed again with her power.

Annie's voice was weak, but still determined. "Javelin?"

"What happened to the one I gave you?"

Annie hesitated. "I broke it."

I sighed. Thankfully, the javelins could extend and contract so it was easy to carry a spare. I reached under my tunic, grabbed the extra javelin and passed it to her.

I heard the familiar four clicks and knew she extended it both ways to reach a length greater than her body. The javelin possessed my magic now, one that is capable of freezing on the touch. If Annie had been practicing the javelin then all she'd have to do is hit a major joint and the limb would be rendered useless. Hopefully, with her aura being condensed into just two weapons it would still have the lethality of poison. Instead of freezing the arm with my magic, it would poison the limb and render it permanently useless. If she had an aura protecting her, however, her aura for my weapon would just paralyze the person. An effect I was okay with given that her protection mattered more to me than the damage caused.

"A lot of broken bones echoing," I commented as we waited for the thieves to get closer. I had four coming from my left and she had four from her left.

"The waves are improving. Jaired helped me focus them in the ground." She giggled. "Always breaks the legs."

"You are seriously messed up."

"Mmhmm."

I just shook my head. I suppose having a murderous person on my side was better than the alternative.

"You're tired." Another statement of the obvious, but one that had to be said to keep her in reality.

To my surprise, she didn't argue that point. She simply muttered, "Very."

"Let's get this over with then. I met a girl. You need to meet her."

Annie's sudden anger was so violent that the earth started trembling at our feet.

In retrospect, I probably could have worded that better.

CHAPTER 7

"Oh, grow up. It's not like that," I stated calmly. I really didn't want to deal with her jealousy.

Turning her back to the thieves, she leveled me with her green eyes. They blazed with emotion - half fury, half pain - as beads of sweat trickled down her cheeks. Her aura filled half with tiny white blades (focused on me, of course) and tiny white rain drops. The aura was still semi-translucent and I could see the thieves walking toward us.

I took a breath, leaned my head to the right and threw a friendly wave at the thieves. "Annie, you're an idiot. Now is not the time."

The white rain drops all turned to daggers. The pain from her eyes immediately vanished and turned all fury. A gust of wind burst between us and sent her hair in a flurry. She passed me then faced the encroaching thieves. "Turns out I'm not that tired after all."

She lifted the javelin, reared her arm back and threw it. I expected the weapon to travel faster than sight would catch, but it did not. The javelin only travelled a few feet then hung in the air. Time started slowing for everything except Annie and I. The leaves dancing on the wind a moment earlier now hung in the air as if frozen.

Then she extended her arms outward - usually an indicator she was going to release the waves - and I could feel something different in the earth. I could feel her tapping into nature the way the elders do when they gather in a circle to heal someone or to help grow a tree to a specific shape. Except this magic was much deeper. The protective side of me wanted to stop her as I didn't know what the magic would do to her.

Without so much as a sound, Jaired leapt behind me then jumped up to land on my shoulder in his tiniest bird form. Despite only being the size of my head, his talons pierced through my leather cloak and dug into my skin. I got the warning.

Wait. Been teaching. Need to see results.

I nodded. *Okay. But I don't like it.*

He pierced his talons a little deeper, reminding me of just how much he cared about what I liked and didn't like. Sometimes he's a jerk.

Annie's eyes closed and I could feel her starting to lose focus in Jaired's presence. She always had trouble focusing even when I was teaching her. Too many emotions, too many doubts, and far too much strength. Whether Jaired wanted me to or not, I was going to help her.

I closed my eyes and focused on Annie. Except instead of looking into her conscious and helping focus her mind, I saw a vivid emerald energy gathering around her extended arms. I added my own strength to it and her focus steadied. While seeing the world through my gift was amazing, I wanted to see what reality made of our influence.

When I opened my eyes, I noticed the javelin still hung in the air, perfectly straight, except the tip was glowing blue. With each slow beat of my heart, the blue glowed brighter and brighter. Each pulse slowly drained a bit of my energy like a tiny bead of sap from the crack in the bark of a tree. The draining energy fed Annie's power and fueled her focus. Our minds were becoming closer than ever before.

She turned to face me. A calmness exuded from her every pore. Her determination was unwavering and her excitement and approval bounced in her eyes.

"Now!" I commanded. Jaired's talons gripped deeper, but I

ignored them.

Annie slapped her hands together and a loud thunder roll echoed from them, spreading throughout the forest. The javelin vibrated violently then snapped into four equal segments, exactly at the points of extension. They flew in the direction of the thieves, streaking with a deep ocean blue trail, and found their target. The thieves were in complete shock and didn't have time to react. Each part of the javelin found their pairing of thieves and skewered them in the heart. One by one, each thief died with a hole in their chest and shock on their face.

Before they could fall to the ground, the javelin pieces returned to Annie's outstretched hand. They reassembled (which I didn't know they could do) and the energy lent to Annie returned to me.

Annie handed over the javelin and gave a slight bow to Jaired. He acknowledged her with a flap of his wings then lifted off my shoulder, shimmered, then landed on the forest floor in beast form.

Follow, he commanded.

For a moment, I thought we were going to run alongside him. However, he slightly crouched down for us to climb atop. Since the beginning, he'd been strict in his beliefs especially those pertaining to being a creature of immense power and intelligence. Yet sometimes he let us ride on his back like he was a beast of burden. Annie and I never complained when he did and we didn't now. We exchanged smiles and jumped on his back.

———

Something was off. I could feel it, but neither Jaired or Annie recognized it immediately.

I stood, flipped backwards off Jaired and landed with my weapons out in front of me. My instincts protected me as I shimmered into invisibility without thought. I looked around and saw nothing so I closed my eyes and listened. I heard nothing and I should be hearing something.

It took a moment for Annie to respond to my absence. While I was physically invisible, my energy was not. Annie could feel my presence as easily as I could see her, yet she looked startled nonetheless. Her emerald aura extended out enough to cover Jaired - not that he needed it - and she looked around nervously. That's when the arrow flew out of the clump of trees to the right of them and struck Annie in the arm.

That was not supposed to happen since anything that came from nature would wilt upon entering the aura. Hence why nature literally bent itself out of the way when Annie's aura was present. Anything not of nature that entered the aura would dissolve into dust. An arrow definitely wasn't made by nature so it should have dissolved immediately. This arrow, however, made it through her aura and glanced off Annie's arm.

Jaired stopped the instant Annie was hit. He bucked her off his back, jumped in the air to transform into a bird and flew off into the trees. I heard Teega shriek then Jaired flew down with the Dewarian holding desperately onto one of his legs. While Jaired had no physical way to display anger in flight form, I could feel it coming off him like heat off the sun. I thought about sending him peaceful thoughts of some kind, maybe even a bit of humor, but you don't give a flower to a hurricane and expect the winds to stop.

Jaired more or less set her on the ground then he transformed into the black beast. She tried getting up, but Jaired immediately put one of his large, thick and sharp-clawed paws on her chest. He growled at her then looked at me. *Explain.*

Before I could relay, Teega interrupted me. "Okay, I'll explain. Just take your paw off me, please."

All three of us looked at Teega. None of us knew of any other race possessing telepathic powers. I thought Jaired would be impressed or even intrigued by this revelation, but it only angered him. He pushed his paw down more to the point that Teega grunted in pain.

"It's this," she said with a gasp and pulled out the necklace. The vortex of smoke was still swirling. "It vibrates when you, well, talk if that's what you're doing."

Jaired growled again. *Yes, I talk.*

We didn't see the necklace vibrate, but the light of the vortex did quiver as if it was being vibrated.

"See what I mean?" Teega held the necklace up higher.

Jaired seemed satisfied and slowly lifted his paw off her.

I walked to Annie to check the wound on her arm. It was already healing up; the blood having been wiped away by her aura. The gash from the arrow was already closing.

"You okay?" My voice cracked. I'd never seen her spill blood. Ever. My heart didn't know how to respond and my mind was racing with all the possible outcomes.

She just nodded, but never made eye contact. She only had eyes for Teega. "Why did you shoot me?"

"I didn't know who you were. And he saved my life," Teega replied. Her reply didn't land well with Annie whose aura only deepened in color.

"He'll have to save it again," Annie stepped toward Teega so her aura would envelop the stranger. Except it didn't knock her out or even daze her. It didn't do anything. Annie stepped back and her aura retreated with her. More shock resonated through the rest of us.

"Look at the necklace," I commented.

The vortex that swirled above the gem now contained the exact emerald color of Annie's power. We all looked to Jaired for answers, but he offered none. His tail was straight, his eyes fixated on Teega, and he was blocking me out from his thoughts.

Annie faced me. "How'd she get the necklace? I can feel that thing in her ear."

I filled her in on what I knew. She looked to Jaired who nodded in affirmation of my story. Annie's demeanor immediately changed as all her anger towards the stranger disappeared and her sweet side came out. Her face relaxed, her shoulders slackened and she knelt in front of Teega.

"May I?" Annie gestured towards the necklace.

Teega was clearly unafraid of anything except Jaired, because her eyes stayed on him. She grabbed the gem at the end of the necklace and set it in Annie's outstretched palm.

The instant the gem touched Annie's skin, a vortex of smoke expanded like a tornado with the four of us in the eye of the storm. Then the necklace lifted off Teega's head and flew to the center. The world outside disappeared as the smoke thickened as if to shield us from something. No dirt or fallen leaf stirred. We couldn't see the sky because the vortex had covered that, too.

Jaired transformed and tried to fly out, but he bounced off the sides and top of the vortex. He transformed back into a beast and swiped at the vortex with his claws, but nothing happened. He roared in frustration then settled back into a predatory stance, eyes scanning and muscles tensed.

Annie extended her aura, but it could not penetrate beyond the swirling smoke. I think she would have roared in frustration like Jaired if she could.

I was entranced. I should have been frightened at the unknown or angry at being contained like a fly caught in the mouth of a frog. Yet I was as calm as the air in the eye of this storm. More importantly, there was something about the floating, vibrating gem that pulled me to my feet and toward it.

The moment I was within reach, the gem began vibrating so rapidly that it hummed. I took another step forward and the humming gave way to singing. I closed my eyes to focus my gift and heard the faintest sound of distinctive voices, singing in a foreign language. Another step and the singing became a little clearer. The gem also pulsed a blue hue that increased in intensity the closer I moved toward it. By the time my eyes were just an inch away, the blue smoke exactly matched the color of my eyes. Instantly, something unlocked within the gem. There was a flash of the brightest blue, the world around me disappeared and I was looking at a different one.

There were trees everywhere. They were strong and thick like those in my land, but they were younger. They hadn't reached heights and lengths like those in The Shaws or The Shims. I wondered what the world would look like from the clouds and instantly my view changed.

From the clouds, I could see a river cutting across the lands as the Sairray River cuts across ours. However, unlike The Sairray River, this river dropped away in the middle of the continent and never reappeared.

Then I noticed dozens of beautiful, silver birds clustered over a patch of trees. They were far enough away that I could only make out basic shapes, but they looked like mourars. A black light streaked across the sky, obscuring my vision for a moment, and struck the middle of the forest. The silver birds were engulfed in black and fire.

Then my world went black.

CHAPTER 8

Have you ever wondered what it would feel like to have a giant boulder on your chest while you're trying to breathe? Honestly, I have not. I've travelled many places and asked many questions about what nature does and what people do, but I've never asked myself the boulder question.

Turns out the answer is simple: It hurts. A lot.

And I have Jaired to thank for the answer. His claws pierced the skin on my chest, but it was the weight of his muscular leg and shoulders that I really felt. Then more weight was added as his words boomed in my head. *Brim. Wake. Up.*

I wanted to wake up, but I was stuck in the dark without a light to lead me out. And in this darkness, all my thoughts dwelled upon the vision into the gem. That place was so familiar, but it wasn't home. I know, even as I say that it doesn't make sense. Yet in my very bones I could feel a bond to the place.

The weirdest part of all is that it felt like my own memory. Although I don't know how it could be a memory. I mean I'm old, but certainly not that old. And that place was young, out of this time. The trees were still finding ground for roots and sky for branches. And the mourars, they were filling the skies yet in this world I'd only see one and Jaired never mentioned another.

The harder I focused on these thoughts and followed the logic, more cobwebs cleared in my mind and images began surfacing.

Jaired yelling in my head finally jarred me awake. *Wake. NOW.*

"Okay, okay. I'm up." I opened my eyes to a worried audience. Annie and Teega were kneeling at my side while Jaired remained in panther form and on guard. His concern was obvious, but a being like him wouldn't kneel to anyone. Not even me.

"You okay, Brim?" Annie asked with a great look of concern. Her green eyes showed that love yet to be confessed and yet to be welcomed.

"I'm okay, Caryanne." I grabbed her hand and gave it a reassuring squeeze then I looked at the mourar. "What was that? Your memory?"

"What was what?" Teega spoke before Jaired could. The swirling vortex was gone and the necklace had returned to her.

I ignored her question and asked again, "Whose was that?"

Jaired's tail whipped back and forth as his eyes scanned the forest. *Ours.*

I tried to process what that meant while holding onto those revealing images, but they were fading back into the dark.

Annie sounded as confused as me. "How could it be ours?"

I addressed Teega. "You have never seen that before? In your homeland?"

She shook her head. "Land burned to a crisp, remember?"

Jaired interrupted the exchange. *Later. Thieves coming.*

We all let out a sigh of resignation. Annie helped me up. Not that I needed the help, but I knew it would make her feel better.

I whispered, "Part of me wants to tell the elders what's going on, but…"

Annie, as always, interrupted me on this topic. "But they are worthless morons."

"And I'm not too keen on meeting them given what they do to people with one of these," Teega added, pointing to her ear.

I walked over to her and examined the ear more closely. The discoloration wasn't as significant as with the true thieves. When combining with their naturally dark skin, the ear growth was a gruesome, sickly black like an arm that didn't get blood flow for far too long. Since Teega is a Dewarian, the ear growth looked out of place and not nearly as gross. However, it did stand out since Dewarians don't have a dark complexion due to living primarily underground. It stood out like a dark, water-soaked log on an otherwise beautiful, sandy beach.

"When we get to safety, we will need to hear how this happened," I whispered as I stared into her sea green eyes.

Her slender face grimaced for a moment, but she eventually nodded. "I know. And you will."

"You think we should go to Our Place?" Annie asked. Her eyes still scanned the forests and her aura pulsed a gentle green around her hands and began expanding. Something was coming.

Teega giggled then covered her mouth like she was clearing her throat. After a few breaths, she gained her composure. "You two are together?"

I dodged the question although I'm certain my face didn't as I felt the blood rush to my cheeks.

"She didn't mean the place where we live together. It's our place away from Our Tree so we call it 'Our Place'. It's her jab at the elders naming the tree in our home Our Tree."

Teega was perplexed. "What else would they call it? It's known all over our world."

"Oh, Varokkar sounds better," I answered.

The Dewarian looked at me with more confusion. "What does that stand for?"

I mumbled, "Our Tree."

Annie's aura pulsed a little more quickly as it was always a foretelling of the imminent frustration. "It's arrogant. We know that it's for our people, but they didn't name it as such. They believe it is their tree. Named for them and not for the rest of us."

"It's one of her many issues," I said with a roll of the eyes. Teega let out a chuckle then took one step away from Annie as her aura pulsed brighter. I looked over at Jaired and gave him the nod. He'd been nagging me with emotions of urgency since I woke up and I was finally ready to relent.

Jaired transformed into a bird again except this one was much larger than the one that stood on the dock. The three of us could lay end-to-end with our arms above our heads and maybe we'd be as long as one wing. His torso was at least three of me thick and the feathers were now a mixture of silver and light blue as to best blend with the sky and the clouds.

"You've got to be kidding me!" Teega exclaimed with wide, excited eyes. "I thought these were just from the tales parents told kids."

I smiled. "You'll never get used it. Although you feed his ego when you do that so try to keep it in. Besides he's just the ride."

Jaired fluttered one wing at me. I knew it was coming so I could keep my feet on the ground, but I couldn't prevent being pushed back a few yards.

I wiped the dust off my tunic. "He doesn't like to think he's some simple animal we ride."

Teega actually bowed at Jaired. "Master, I would never presume to deem you so simple."

Jaired also bowed his head at her and pulled his wings back to look less intimidating. *I like you.*

I waved my hand irritably. "Yeah, yeah. You like anyone that gives you a title. Come on, Annie, let's go."

We all climbed on Jaired's back. I immediately grabbed hold of whatever feathers I could. The one thing they never tell you about riding a bird in the clouds is just how windy the ride is.

CHAPTER 9

"Really?!" I shouted into the wind. Of course, no one responded. Why would they? Teega was standing on Jaired's back, head back and laughing like a little kid as we soared in and out of the clouds. Annie was doing her stretching and fighting workout which involved a lot of acrobatic movements across Jaired's back and his wings. With her aura, the wind had no effect on her.

"Really?!" I shouted at him again. "Anytime we fly, I'm bouncing all over and hanging on for my life. Now, you're barely even moving."

Despite being in bird form, his laugh was a beast's growl. Annie continued her acrobatics and Teega kept smiling at the sky in amazement. Since Jaired was keeping the ship steady for Annie, I let go of the feathers and laid back, clasping my hands behind my head.

Flight truly is awe-inspiring. There are so many things that I've done over these last couple centuries that mortals are blown away by, but none of them compare to flying. The closest feeling of awe came when I was tasked to handle a situation at a port on The Great Ice Shores.

The warden of that region needed help with a couple pirates adventuring onto land. I took care of them in short order, but the real fun was learning about the foo. A foo is a long, slender creature with deep purple scales and a pouch on their backs for their offspring.

The pouch seals underwater and contains oxygen for the offspring since they are born on land. The warden informed me that the baby foo takes a few years to adapt to breathing underwater. A few times I actually stayed in the pouch of a more docile foo. The pouch is translucent which allowed for a near crystal clear view of the world underwater. Being in the pouch made me feel like I was one of the countless swimming about without a care in the world.

As a Tree Maker, the land of my people has always been something I appreciate every day. How nature has woven plants, bushes and trees together in harmony is something especially enjoyable for those in tune like my people. The colors dance closely with each other, but not so close that they blend. The smells are so numerous and so diverse that it would take me another two centuries to catalog a tenth of them.

Up here that all changed. The colors are few, but their purity overwhelms my vision. The world is separated into the simple greens of the land below, the simple silver white of the clouds and the simple blues of the morning sky above the clouds. And the air up here is sweet and pure. There aren't any dancing smells just the simplicity of a world barely touched by the living beneath. Different wind currents swirl about at different elevations and bring with them smells from all continents and islands of this world.

I sat up and looked to Annie. She was sitting legs crossed, eyes closed, and, when I reached out to her mind, I found she was gone. Jaired must have taken her mind into his for another lesson. I don't know what their lessons involved, but clearly she was making progress as evidenced by her spell in the forest.

Teega still sported her excited smile, but had finally sat down a short distance behind Annie. I could only imagine how this experience compared to a person whose race primarily lived underground.

Since the wind was strong and loud, it was impossible to have a vocal conversation with Teega. However, she had been able to hear Jaired's unspoken words so maybe I could try telepathy with her. If all else failed, I know that Jaired would let me speak to her through him.

I reached out to the Dewarian. *Teega, can you hear me?*

I watched her smile disappear and her body jolt. She grabbed Jaired's feathers and squeezed until her knuckles were white. Her eyes were wide as if lightning had struck her.

Jaired immediately pulled both of us into his consciousness. *You're too strong, Brim. Not speaking to me. Not speaking to Annie.*

"Sorry," I mouthed to Teega. She nodded and relaxed her grip, but did not fully let go.

I took a breath and tried to calm my inner voice. I always had to put something extra into my intention when talking with the mourar. Jaired had instilled the habit of making yourself heard if you want to be respected. Annie and I never had to try to connect or speak in a certain way; all of our exchanges just worked effortlessly. I changed my approach with Teega and I imagined I was whispering my thoughts.

Is that better? I looked at her and saw a brief nod.

I could feel her reluctance and I guessed part of it could be the intense eye contact. While Teega had shown defiance before, I knew that only the likes of Annie actually enjoyed confrontation. I laid my hopes on Teega seeing us enjoy the flight to Our Place. Then she might open up more.

I continued. *Just talk how you normally would, but in your head. And no, I can't read your thoughts.*

Liar. That was my thought. Teega's reply was curt, but it carried a hint of humor not heard before.

Given that telepathic communication can be awkward for many people because it is intimate, I was pleased she was showing some humor. When we speak aloud we can hide behind our facial expressions and distract others with our body language. Also, we are able to take time to form our words so they are expressed the way we want - truth or lie. With telepathy, our communication is in its barest form with almost no chance of deception.

Can Jaired hear everything? The feeling of reluctance and embarrassment carried with her words.

I sent reassuring feelings before I replied. *He hears the simple conversations or ones that have no privacy.*

What do you mean?

If we are talking about how fun it is to fly or if we are hungry then he catches it. If he's interested that is. However, if you are sharing something from your heart or something intended for a specific person then he hears nothing.

I could feel confusion coming from her. Since I was still a student of telepathy, I didn't always explain it the right way. *Jaired, will you help explain?*

He responded with a flip of his tail and an increase in speed. As I looked at Teega, I saw her eyes close and her body lull back and forth slightly like a ship moored to a dock. After a few moments, Teega's eyes jerked open and she let out a gasp as if she had held her breath the entire time.

I get it now. She looked at me then closed her eyes. *It's easier for me to close my eyes.*

In the beginning, it is. Over time, you'll get better. Now I want to ask you some questions. Is that okay?

Yes. Did you want the others to know as well?

I debated this point since more minds were typically better as we faced this unknown situation. However, I am the warden and the responsibility falls on my shoulders for all that happens in these lands. And Annie has a penchant for interrupting every time she has a question. A habit I've yet to break her of since, as she claims, "When you're cute like me then you can interrupt all you want." I wasn't denying the cute factor, but I wanted answers not a bedlam.

No. It will be just us.

Ok. However, I want to show you a memory before I answer questions. It is necessary for you to understand me. Her words and impressions were unsettling. They were so assured and deeply rooted in her heart. Where did the hesitant foreigner go and who was this woman?

Very well.

Teega asked, *What is the best way to show you?*

BUDDY HEYWOOD

Imagine I am part of your memory. Paint me in the scene and I'll see it as you do.

That's so cool. Her excitement rippled. *Give me a moment…*

Telepathic connections allow me to feel impressions of emotions. Also, impressions of her thoughts came my way similar to what my eyes notice at the very reaches of my peripheral vision. However, she wasn't a Tree Maker or a Yeryan; she was a Dewarian and I had very little experience with those people. Each race gives off different energy that usually means something different than my own people. While Teega gave off a definitive excitable energy, it may not be genuine excitement. It could be building towards anger or some other emotion. I simply did not know.

I felt her energy spike higher then heard her voice in my head. *Okay, I'm ready.*

Let's go. I calmed my thoughts and entered her mind.

CHAPTER 10

I found myself standing between rows of chiseled gray columns in an underground cavern. Each column had two torches about twenty feet up. One lit up the space between the columns while the other faced out into the massive cavern. The light from those torches dissipated just a few feet beyond the columns. There was only a black abyss just beyond the emitting light which prevented me from determining the size of this place. Since her people lived underground, I guessed the columns were made of stone to support the weight of the earth above it.

"It's metal actually," Teega's reply echoed throughout the cavern.

I turned to the source of the echo. Teega wasn't wearing the torn and bloody garb anymore. In this memory, she dressed in what must be her people's native clothes. She wore dark, black leggings that reflected light in multiple directions and a long sleeve jacket of the same material. Her hair was pulled back out of her eyes and a decorative, gold pickaxe the length of a finger stuck through the hair, holding it in place.

"Are your clothes metallic as well?"

She didn't acknowledge my question. Instead she walked around me, each footstep crackling on the gravel, as if she was looking at a ghost. I understood the shock since our memories are permanent and now she had someone new in it.

I cleared my throat. "Takes some getting used to, huh?"

"It's so...weird. You are in your clothes as you sit on Jaired, but I'm wearing what I was wearing when all this happened. Yet...you're here."

I chuckled. "Yeah, it's pretty amazing."

She stopped circling me and looked at me. I felt another spike of energy from her. "Will you show me one of your memories? It seems only fair."

"Yes, I will," I answered. I felt a pulse of relief from her. "Do your people not share things?"

Her sea green eyes focused on me, trying to make sense of the question. "You mean food or crafted items or...?"

"No, I mean personal thoughts and feelings." That energy spike hit me again.

She looked away to the depths of the cavern. "Oh no, not the way we are doing it now. Or even in person."

"Why?"

"I don't know." Her reply was as automatic as the shrugging shoulders. She walked forward, but she turned around after a few strides.

"Something your people may let go isn't something I will let go of." I stood my ground with a gentle smile. "I mean to say that I will push to get answers."

Teega walked back to me, tiny speckles of orange light dancing off her jacket and pants, as if she climbed out of a bed of campfire coals. As she approached, I noticed how powerfully she carried herself here compared to walking in my land. It made sense to me; this was not only a memory of her homeland, but she was in a foreign land and injured which made tapping into this memory empowering.

I looked her up and down. "The difference is quite drastic."

"I'll tell Annie," she said with that hint of feminine wile.

"No, you won't. What you will tell is your answer to my question."

Stopping a few inches from my face, Teega squared her

shoulders and balled her fists. I knew she couldn't harm me in here, but she was intent on making some point.

"Yes, we share our lives with one another. We share them with our brothers and sisters, mothers and fathers." She paused, averting her gaze, then continued. "And our wives and husbands."

The energy she sent was intense and caused the columns in her memory to shake as if there was an earthquake. The firelight from the torches also started to blur. Clearly, I stirred up an emotion that her people kept deep within. Maybe that's why they didn't share with everyone.

I let out a deep breath and sent as much calm her way as I could. The columns and the firelight returned to normal. "I understand now. Thank you for sharing, Teega. I am trusting you with so much and I have to make sure I can trust you at the same level."

She scoffed. "You haven't trusted me with anything!"

"I saved your life. I brought two friends to protect you. Two that I would do anything, kill anyone for. So yes, I do trust you."

I looked into her eyes and brought forth power in my words. "And I usually kill anyone with one of those in their ears. With no hesitation."

It may have been her memory, but my power made Teega stumble back. The colors on her garb started to dance with fire again which made me wonder if it was tied into her emotions. She flexed her hands then balled them up. She began to say something then decided against it. Turning away from me again, she walked to the center of the cavern.

As I followed her through the memory, more details came alive. The sound of crunching gravel beneath my feet echoed off the distant, unseen walls. I also noticed the air was significantly cooler from my knees down. I looked around for natural light letting a cold wind through or a source of water that could be dropping the temperature, but didn't find either.

Finally, I started to take serious notice of the rows of columns that supported this place. There were distinctive designs on each column. The lower parts of the columns had various languages - some

I knew, but most I didn't. The feet and claws of various beings were chiseled in the stone at the point where languages stopped. Their lower appendages visible in the torchlight while the rest of their bodies hid in the darkness of the upper portion of the column. Like the languages, some of them I recognized, but most of them I did not.

My mind was captured by these drawings to the point where I didn't realize we'd made our way down a sloped entrance some ten minutes later. Time moves as fast as the memory holder wants it to, but it always passes by slower for the person not part of the memory. By the time Teega stopped walking - and I almost walked into her - the columns were even larger than our largest trees.

"May I?" I asked as I reached out, but didn't touch the column.

Teega let out an adorable little laugh. It was so child-like that I can't imagine such a serious person making such a sweet noise. "It's just a memory remember."

I shook my head at my own stupidity. As I reached toward the column to touch the etchings of a language, I felt an energy similar to the kind emanating from Teega except this one was much more powerful.

"Is this the source?" My whisper was softer than ever, as if I was speaking to a god.

"Yes." Teega's reply was equally soft. "That's why I brought you here. I wanted to explain that energy you've been feeling."

I took my hand off the column and turned to her. "I didn't know that you knew I could sense it."

She nodded. "I didn't know at first. In fact, it should only reflect when talking with my people."

"Reflect?" I furrowed my brow. That concept didn't make sense to me since it wasn't light. I consider myself more sensitive than most to the world around me. All I've known about energy is exchanging it. Whenever I reach out to one of my patrollers or even to Annie, my energy is given and accepted, then their energy is sent to me. Even when my people reach out to the trees and begin weaving the trees into what we desire, it's still an agreement of exchanging energy.

Never is it reflected.

"Yes, it reflects like this light off my clothing," she said then held up the jacket sleeve.

I felt like a student listening to Jaired explain how the world really worked. I felt entirely ignorant. It was like standing on top of a mountain looking down at everything one moment then trying to get out of the mud the next. A dozen questions flooded my mind, but I have learned to dig for that one question to answer the rest.

"That reflection on your clothes...is part of that energy being reflected along with the light?"

"Exactly." She seemed to approve of my question. "This is not easy for me to talk about. It's not that it's a secret of our people or a weakness. It's just…"

I finished her thought. "Personal."

She simply nodded and looked up at the column I just touched. "We're not sure who he is as we have never seen that race of people before. Until today."

I followed her gaze up to the column. "I don't see anything I recognize."

"Come over here by me and take a look."

I walked over to her which I could have done with my eyes closed because that energy was now stronger yet more stable. It was like a pulsing light leading me home. I turned around and looked up at the column.

"That's not possible! That looks like Jaired!"

My heart was racing. Why would there be an etching of his race on a column underground, let alone in her land? They lived in the clouds and only occasionally graced us with their presence. Yet here was one. The carving was old, but age only added emphasis to the features. The four eyes bore down on anyone looking up. The wings were expansive and the claws long and sharp. Clearly the artists found a way to stain color into the stone because the bird's color looked similar to the start of a rain cloud. Just like one of Jaired's forms.

"Look at this." Teega walked around the column.

I followed her as my eyes stayed fixed on the column. As the bird-in-flight carving disappeared another carving appeared. A four-legged beast with a deadly tail ready to strike any unseen prey. We continued around the column to discover they had also carved the tiny owl. The last carving was Jaired's usual form of a large bird that we were currently flying on.

"This is unbelievable," I remarked.

"You're telling me." She added, "You see why I brought you here?"

I nodded. "I do see why. What is this place anyways?"

"We visit to clear our minds or talk to the gods or, in my case, to wonder what happened to my land and who marked these columns."

I faced her. "You're saying that none of your people did these carvings?"

A slow almost pitying smile found her face. "We don't live as long as you do, Brim. And no one knows any of their kin that chiseled these."

I shook my head in disbelief. "Sometimes I forget about how the years go by differently. Yet it's so crazy to think that someone doesn't know who did this. Even among our people, we pass down the legends and stories from times before us."

A pulse of energy flowed my way that was different than the previous exchanges. However, I was able to make sense of it since she opened up. It was confusion, maybe shock.

I looked to Teega, my voice sincere. "Yes, my people do die."

The look on her face told me she wanted more information, but I clammed up. She held her gaze and mouthed the word, "Personal."

I nodded in agreement. She showed wisdom I didn't have or maybe it was just part of what her people respect that ours do not. Yet she had brought me this far into her mind and her heart.

"Our deaths are few because we are such a resilient people. But there is another reason that we don't bond easily to other people. Why Annie and I don't have 'Our Place' as you put it."

My heart started racing, a feeling I rarely felt since the world was so easy to control and predict. The secret of my people is not one readily shared, but something within told me to trust her. I looked around for a place to sit and saw none so I leaned against the column. This may be a memory and this wasn't real, but leaning close to one of Jaired's kind gave me calm.

Teega followed in kind and leaned against the column next to me, her shoulder touching mine. I could feel her touch against mine; proof she was mentally and telepathically stronger than she probably realized.

"When we bond, when we marry, it comes at great risk. If one dies then the other has a mortal's life span. Your people's life span."

Teega let out a long breath as she started to understand what that meant.

"We become stronger together. Our powers can grow. We can have children. In fact, that's the only way we can have children. That's why there aren't many of us. It's not that we don't like offspring; it just comes at such a risk to our own lives and the lives of our people. If too many marry and too many get killed then…"

"Your people die out."

"Yeah."

"Yeah," Teega echoed.

We leaned against that column in silence for a good long time. I closed my eyes and tried to stem the scary thoughts of a life without Annie, without my people. I took several deep breaths before I was able to stand on two stable feet. I turned to her, grabbed her shoulders and gripped them tight.

"That fact is a secret of my people. No one knows. Telling that to an outsider carries the punishment of death. Yours and mine."

Her eyes explored mine. Light from the torches reflected then danced around her eyes. She nodded then did something I did not expect. She stood on her tiptoes and kissed me on the forehead. As soon as her lips touched my head, the room quieted and the energy dropped to a low, steady sway as if I was being rocked by a gentle wind in a hammock.

I've learned it's a gift given to all females of all species: a kiss to the forehead can calm any male. Maybe it comes from every mother imprinting serenity on the forehead of her newborn.

I let go of her and she stepped back from me. "I understand, Cassius."

"Wait, I didn't tell you that name."

She shrugged and smiled like a little girl. "Things have been leaking from this connection of ours. I wasn't prying, I promise."

"Well we should continue through your memory before you find out how I feel about Annie." I started to walk to the next column, but she grabbed my arm.

"Please, everyone knows you love her. Didn't need to share this connection to know that."

Females. So arrogant and so correct.

CHAPTER 11

"Come on. I want to show you this one." Teega led the way to the other column.

As we walked away from the first column, I noticed a change in the air. Specifically, I noticed how I couldn't smell anything. In fact, I hadn't been able to smell anything since I entered this memory.

"Why can't I smell anything? Do you not remember smells in your memories?"

Teega stopped immediately and turned to me. "Wait? You get all your senses in your memories?"

"Of course. Why wouldn't I? I was there."

She let out that little girl laugh again. "Tree Makers."

"What?"

Shaking her head, she turned away and continued walking. "Your people assume too much of others that it gets under the skin of too many. It's arrogant."

"And you find arrogance funny?" I felt the heat of anger rising within me. It's possible I get a little defensive, a little prideful when others mock my people.

"No, I just realized that your people aren't arrogant. You're ignorant." Her energy was definitely a happy one. She was toying with me. "And I find it funny that I just now realized it."

I let out a grumble which only resulted in another innocent

snicker from her. She was right. Which made her right twice during this excursion into her memory. Twice is enough for me. It's not that I don't like learning; it's that I don't like when I'm not in control of the lessons.

I could at least redirect the conversation to something not demonstrating my shortcomings. "So how often did you come here?"

Teega's energy changed from the comfortable thrum to erratic pulses. "Once."

As I was about to ask why just the once, she pointed up at the next column. We were still in the half-lit shadows cast by the opposing column torches, but I could make out the shape. Once I did, I ran the rest of the distance for a closer look.

"You're joking. This can't be." I spun on Teega, full of anger and more shock, and laid into her. "This is not a memory! What is going on!?"

To my surprise, she didn't recoil. Her reply was calm and measured. "Brim, you can feel when something is a memory and a dream. You are the king of all lie-detectors."

"How do you know that? I could just be another Tree Maker trying to take advantage of an outsider."

"Because I know you. I know where you came from."

"The hell you do." My fuming wouldn't stop. Fury continued rising. "Why is Annie on this column? What are you playing at, mortal?!"

She only nodded for me to follow her to the next column. Once we were within sight of it, my body froze. The shock hit so hard that Jaired pulled us both out of the memory walk.

Brim.

I opened my eyes. Distantly, I was aware we were still flying. Distantly, I was aware that Annie's eyes and consciousness were trying to reach me. I was not going to let her or Jaired in. My focus was on Teega whose eyes met mine with a severity that could not be ignored.

I'm fine, I replied to Jaired and Annie then shut them out. I do not have to explain myself to anyone. But I'm no fool; I don't have to be rude to a creature that could destroy my consciousness and my physical body before I could even cover my eyes.

I nodded to Teega, closed my eyes, and entered her memory again.

CHAPTER 12

I opened my eyes and looked up at the column that caused such a reaction it scared me. Carved into the column was a depiction of a warrior with a javelin in each hand. Javelins that were clearly marked with four different sections. Javelins I knew because they were my own just as the face on the metal column was my own. The instinct to pull away at this unsettling vision rose up.

I felt someone squeeze my hands and I looked down. Teega was sitting on the gravel opposite me. She had her legs crossed like mine and her hands were holding my own. Her left hand was on top of my right and her right hand underneath my left. A practice of my people. One she might have heard about, but surely didn't know the steps because we kept that from outsiders. The wonder on my face must have told her to put me at ease.

"You flashed it during your outburst. You and Annie sitting like this under trees I've never seen." Teega's voice was so reassuring, as if she'd been putting children at ease for centuries.

"We were at the base of The Sairs. We are the only ones of our people that have been there with any regularity," I replied. A tiny smirk creased the corner of her mouth similar to the one she gave me with my earlier arrogant comment. Before the mother-like aura turned to that of a giggling girl, I stayed her. "As far as I know, we are the only ones."

She nodded in approval then switched gears. "If I told you what I was going to show you, you wouldn't have done this. I feared you would laugh at me."

"Why would I laugh?"

One shoulder shrugged and her gaze broke from mine. "It's always there. The fear of my people."

I squeezed her hands and sent energy of absolute conviction. "Never fear. Just caution."

Her eyes found mine again and she gave me a short nod. "I want to show you the last column. It's of me. Except it's me like I've never seen before."

Energy came in waves from her. Waves like the gods wanted to pull water from the bottoms of the ocean to clean the tops of the skies. Her hands started to sweat with the coldness of winter.

"I got you." With a firm grip, I stood and pulled Teega up with me. I let go of one hand, but kept my right one firmly grabbing hers. We walked toward the column, hand-in-hand, like a friend helping another make steps that fear discourages. Teega didn't let go. In fact, she walked so close to me that her shoulder brushed mine with every other step.

We stopped in front of the column and I stared in fascination. This column looked more weathered than the others. The lines were deeper and not as distinct, almost like a different mason etched this artwork.

"Looks like this one came first," I commented as I released her hand. Her energy waves were slowing now. I ran my hand along the stone and felt an odd comfort from the touch.

"I believe it did." Teega's voice was that of a scared child slowly waking up from a bad dream.

"Hmmm."

Teega asked, "What is it?"

I took a deep breath and shared thoughts that finally came to the surface after seeing all these columns. "This column is the oldest, followed by mine, Annie's then Jaired's."

"My guess, too."

"Yet the languages I do not understand except this specific spot right here." I leaned to the right so Teega could see me.

Her steps were so light that I could barely hear her.

"You walk like one of us when you want to."

"I've been told that before." She mustered a tiny smile then turned to the words on the column. "So what does it mean?"

"See these two," I pointed at two stems coming up from the bottom of the ring of words. "All Tree Makers have this…on their right calf."

In the same delicate voice, she asked, "Another secret of your people?"

I nodded. Then swallowed down the nervous betrayal. "That's two beheadings in one day."

She reached forward and touched my shoulder. "My people haven't needed trees from your people for decades."

I immediately jerked my head at her. She might as well have told me the moon wasn't blue. Or there was only one sun in the sky in the summer. Her people were always so deeply thankful for the help like giving water to a man after a long desert trek. Before I could ask for an explanation, Teega continued.

"We continue to trade out of profound respect for your people and what you've done."

"You know if the elders found out…"

"A secret for a secret." Then she added as an afterthought, "Plus, I've learned that you and Annie are as likely to tell the elders that information as you are to joining them."

A sharp bark of laughter left my mouth and echoed throughout the cavern. "Very true."

I turned my focus back to the column. The nervous betrayal dissipated into a distant nag as I continued. "As we get older, the stems or vines grow around our calf. Usually, within the first year or two a simple form will show indicating the gift the gods gave us."

"What's your gi–," Teega started asking, but I was already pulling up my right pant leg.

Teega crouched down and looked at my birthmark. Her fingers

72

were light and warm as they outlined it. The two vines, in a dark green almost black ink, wound up my leg then split to outline most of my calf muscle. In the middle of the muscle stood a mountain blocking out the light from two concentric suns. A massive shadow cast from the mountain base toward the bottom of my calf.

"Are those the summer suns?" Teega asked as she stood.

"Yup. And a stone protecting all from their heat and glare. The protector. That's me." I let the pant leg fall, but not quick enough.

Teega pointed down at the back of my knee. "What else is growing there? There is another shape."

"It's...nothing." Thankfully the cavern was dark so she couldn't see my face redden. I was sure it was forming two hearts coming together, but I didn't want to acknowledge it yet.

"Hmmm..."

"Look, I'll tell you later. But I should tell someone else first."

Teega looked at me with a quizzical eyebrow. "I see."

"The birthmark is our strength. After that, it's more of a tattoo to tell the story of our life."

"Brim, I don't need to know. Remember, I'm okay with not sharing everything. It's second-nature for my people."

I nodded and turned back to the column. "Do you recognize any of the other languages?"

The tattoo must have distracted her enough because her energy didn't pulse anything noticeable when I asked. In fact, she surprised me when she walked up to the column. And it was even more surprising when she traced her fingers across a set of characters next to the birthmark of my people. The moment she let go there was such a release of energy that it shook both of us from the memory and back to reality.

When I opened my eyes, I immediately back-flipped to where Teega was sitting on Jaired and grabbed her shoulders. "What happened?!"

Teega was shaking and crying. I knew they weren't tears of sadness, but of pure uncontrollable pain. She only managed a few breaths of tears before her eyes rolled back and she passed out.

Jaired immediately stopped flying forward and arched his wings so he could use the wind to hover. Annie, who had been lost in Jaired's mind, went back to her body and jumped ahead to sit on the other side of Teega. Her aura instinctively enveloped Teega and held her upright in a protective cocoon.

"What happened?" Annie's voice stressed great concern. "She was fine one moment and gone the next."

"Too much to explain." I replied curtly. I also didn't want to explain as that could come later.

Birthmark. Jaired's voice boomed in our heads.

Annie and I looked at each other in shock. I nodded at Annie. Slowly, she reached down at Teega's right leg and pulled the pant leg up to her knees.

"That's not possible!" Annie exclaimed.

I shook my head in disbelief. "Apparently, it is."

At least we knew why Teega passed out. The redness of the Tree Maker birthmark glowed brightly on her skin as if it was on fire. Vines of green ink crept up from her ankle, split off to outline her calf then join again just below the knee. The birthmark hadn't fully formed yet. Only two tiny, oblong shapes that were clearly raindrops appeared on the left side of her calf muscle.

I urged Jaired. *Quickly. Our Place.*

CHAPTER 13

Jaired's feet touched down on the branch as gentle as dew dropping from a leaf to the soft earth. Except this branch wasn't as small as a leaf; this branch was as large as Varokkar and stretched out from the trunk at least twenty times that size. Even Jaired in his largest form looked small next to one of these trees. Our Place isn't what I called it when I first made my way here. In fact, I didn't know that I was going to stay when my feet first walked among these trees.

I found this place a year ago while wandering through the Shim Hills after a meeting with Gregare. He's a weird one, but he's been a warden of The Marshes for as long as I've been alive. There was a point that the Elders wanted him as the head warden, but Gregare likes them as much as I do. Since the Elders would be most upset with me as the head warden, he cast the final vote to make sure it happened. That's a standup guy in my skies.

After visiting with Gregare that day, I crossed from the northeast part of The Marshes into the Shim Hills. I noticed an old trail among the ancient trees. The gray bark and dark brown leaves aren't as easy on the eyes like the rest of our land, but there is a beauty in something that's existed for so long. Since I'd never dabbled much in that land - and never heard of any trails - I found myself intrigued in testing my tracking skills. Also, I had to satiate my curiosity and find out where the trail went.

It took a full day of walking and leaping through the trees before the trail ended at a rock face that was almost wider than my peripheral vision. I walked to one end then the other in attempt to find a continuation of the trail, but there wasn't one. What I did notice when I walked back to look up at the giant rock face was that it wasn't a rock face. It was actually a tree, the biggest I'd ever seen. It put my people's symbolic tree to shame. Its width was easily that of a dozen of the tree trunk in The Shaws.

I must have stared at it for well over an hour. The tree is so expansive that it blocked the sun at all times of the day except twice when the steep angle could sneak under the expansive branches.

Despite the overwhelming shock of the size, I was more blown away by the tunnels and steps etched throughout the tree. I couldn't tell how many decades and centuries had passed by, but I knew many had. They weren't recently carved. In fact, they were worn by those destroyers of all things: time and weather.

One aspect that wasn't decaying was the language on the walls. I hadn't seen the language before, but I knew enough to know they weren't scribblings of a mad man. Finally, after a year since I first saw them did I finally see that language in another place: in Teega's memory.

"Do we wake her?" Annie asked.

She finally stopped pacing in the main room within Our Place. Her shadow had been flickering around the room thanks to the four fire pits situated in the four corners. The flames were low so there was no risk of fire. Of course, this tree is so old that I don't think fire could even darken it. Still, I'm a cautious person when it comes to survival and burning anything that is alive on my land.

"Yes, please," I replied.

Annie didn't hesitate and slapped Teega across the face. The slap echoed loudly in the main chamber and quickly faded as it traveled through the different tunnels. Jaired sent an emotion of slight concern, but I just sent him the image of Annie's slap. He replied with a bit of humorous approval.

It took a breath or two, but Teega eventually gasped fresh air into her lungs as she opened her eyes. Immediately, she reached down to her calf. She gingerly traced over the recent mark then rubbed her hand over the reddened skin. When she pulled her hand away, I noticed the red had lessened significantly.

I remained sitting on the chair-like knot protruding from the wall, contemplating what I had seen. She could be a healer, but it seemed unlikely. My people could do many things with basic healing thanks to the symbiotic love between us and the land. True healers that can mend broken bones with a whisper or stop the flow of blood were extremely rare. Those people were only mentioned in bedtime stories.

One such healer in the stories of old, Tinslee, was said to whisper the words to regrow the limbs of Tree Maker or tree. People tried to figure out what words she whispered, but they could not decipher them. Her secrets to healing are wrapped in mystery much like her disappearance.

Teega sat up and looked around the room then at me. "Your place?"

"Our Place." I put stress on the first word. "You're one of us now."

Annie nodded reluctantly. "He's right."

My voice scratched in shock. "Is that...approval in your voice?"

"Yes. It is. She's one of us." Annie glared at me in her typical defiance and I just put my hands up in defeat. "I know what it's like to be an outcast. To be considered less because of who I am."

Teega raised an eyebrow. "How are you an outcast?"

I shook my head. "Let's not get into that now, Caryanne. We need to get this thief situation taken care of."

"This tree looks different than the others," Teega commented. She ran her hands along the floor that had been worn smooth over time.

"We're in The Shims. The oldest part of our land," I told her.

Standing and taking in her surroundings, Teega asked, "Did you make these rooms?"

The main room was half the size of Jaired's wingspan with a ceiling barely high enough for me to stretch my arms. The doorway to the adjoining room was more narrow than most doors that outsiders like Teega had been allowed to see. Even the steps weren't as long as they best fit the smaller feet of my people. Clearly, this place was built solely for Tree Makers.

I shook my head. "Nope, I found it like this. I made a few changes to the entrance steps so they weren't as hidden, but the rest was already done."

"The gem in your necklace is made from crystals in this forest, too," Annie added.

Teega instinctively grabbed the gem with her left hand. She rubbed her thumb and forefinger slowly over it. "Where are the crystals?"

I walked over to the wall and rapped my knuckles against it. "Inside trees like these."

"Are they petrified or something?"

"Honestly, we don't know," I replied.

Teega let out a light laugh. "You're making progress, Brim. The arrogance is fading away."

I smiled then gave her a bow of acknowledgement and respect.

"Are you going to explain about what happened to her?" Annie pointed at Teega. "That shook all of us and I'd like to know."

Me, too. Jaired boomed in our heads.

I infused so much energy in my voice that the walls shook. *No.*

Teega and Annie simultaneously covered their ears as if it would stop the echoing voice in the head. Jaired flew down one of the tunnels and perched himself on Annie's shoulder. Birds don't have much for facial expressions, but I knew he would be telling me off if he could.

"Look, I'm frustrated, tired, and really hungry. I don't want to get into it because it's one helluva story. And I can't make sense of it all." I felt Jaired's energy surging and I put it to rest. "No, Jaired, not even you could make sense of it. Unless you remember posing for a metal carving on a column in an underground cave on another continent."

Annie's mouth dropped open. Jaired flew off of Annie's shoulder and angrily flew around the room as if throwing a temper tantrum would get him answers. Eventually, he settled back on Annie's shoulders.

"I'm going to take that as a 'No.'" I paused then turned to Teega. "That's what I thought."

Teega gingerly stood and slowly walked to my side.

"It's my story to tell. And I will tell it." Her voice was delicate and calmed the energy in the room significantly. "But I'm with Brim. We need to find these scrubs. And I want this damn thing out of my ear."

I turned to Teega and gave her a nod of approval. Then I reached towards her ear. "May I?"

She nodded. "Gently. It's really sensitive to the touch."

As lightly as I could, I moved the black hair out from her face and tucked it behind her ear. She let out a little whimper like an injured animal. I grimaced. I hate causing people I actually like pain.

"Annie, would you mind?"

"I'll try," she replied behind me.

"What's she going to try?" Teega's voice had a hint of concern.

"She can numb people with her aura...if she controls it."

Annie got a little defensive. "Hey! I've been practicing."

You'll be fine, Jaired said to all.

Teega let out a deep, controlled breath. "Thanks, Jaired."

I felt Annie's aura before I saw it. It didn't numb me - another one of those oddities between us. Her aura calmed my heart and focused my thoughts. The aura broke down my mental defenses and made me love everything more, including Annie. Teega must have noticed the change in my face because her eyes locked onto mine.

I whispered, "I'll explain later."

She let out a light laugh. "Oh, you don't have to. I get it."

I simply glared at her and waited for the green aura to envelope her. I didn't know what it would do and I wanted to be ready to protect her. If I touched someone while Annie's aura was around them then they would feel what I felt instead of being numbed or paralyzed.

The green haze passed my vision and slowly moved to cover Teega. Her eyes didn't gloss over like it did with others. From what I could tell, nothing changed at all.

"How do you feel?" Annie asked.

"Hmmm…" Teega searched for words. "Happy. It feels like I'm back on Jaired and riding through the clouds."

"Euphoria. I didn't expect that." I commented.

Annie hit me with another question. "Isn't that what you feel when I do it."

In a definitive, high-on-life voice, Teega answered for me. "Oh no. He feels loooovvveee."

I shook my head. I had hoped for the right moment and clearly that was never going to happen. So I turned around to face Annie. She looked expectant.

"It wouldn't kill you to say it," she said. It's amazing how adorable her voice is when she's not murdering someone.

"Hey, I've said it before." At least, I think I did.

Annie grunted in disapproval. "More than once."

Teega raised an accusatory eyebrow. "Really? Only once?"

I sighed. Again. Then one more time with my eyes closed, hoping when they opened the moment will have passed. Annie's aura started to prick my skin which meant the moment definitely hadn't.

"Jaired, a little help?"

Jaired bailed me out. *Thieves now. Love later.*

"Thanks, Jaired. I love you."

As it has happened so many times before, tiny daggers of energy appeared in Annie's aura and began to poke at my skin. I yelled out in pain as Annie's eyes seared mine.

"I deserved that," I mumbled.

CHAPTER 14

"All right. Narrow that down to her leg," I ordered Annie. "I need to take a closer look."

Annie obliged and her aura shrunk down to envelope Teega's calf. The drunken stupor on Teega's face immediately faded.

"Brim, I'm so sor–," Teega began saying.

I waved off her apology. "You're not the first to say embarrassing things when under her aura."

"Or do embarrassing things," Annie added with a sideways glance to Jaired who was perched on a peg sticking out of the wall.

I looked at Jaired and smiled. The mourar flew off the peg, down the tunnel and out of sight.

Teega raised one light brown eyebrow. "What was that about?"

I kept my eyes on her right calf. "I'm going to not speak about that so I can keep breathing."

"Ha-ha. Really, what was that about?"

Annie cleared her throat. "He's serious. Jaired will kill him. And I can't speak about it."

Teega continued with the interview. "He won't kill you?"

Annie shook her head. "Can't."

"Why?"

"Can't explain." Annie shrugged.

Teega's face washed over with that look she gave me in her

dream. I stepped in for her sake and Annie's.

"It's not our arrogance. It's not a secret either." I paused to gather the correct words. "There are some exchanges between our people or other creatures that cannot be shared unless you were there. The physical act of speaking the words or writing them down cannot happen. It's nature's way of protecting vulnerability."

She let one eyebrow fall and nodded in understanding. "Yet you know and can share, but he'll kill you. So how does that work?"

I let out a sigh of defeat. "You're worse than Annie sometimes."

"Hey!" Annie exclaimed.

"Well, she is. Always asking questions when I don't want you to and not paying attention to anything when I actually need you to."

"That doesn't answer my question," Teega said.

"And now you're back to being Annie again. Stating the obvious." I gave her a wink, but didn't share anything more.

I wanted to tell her the story, but I honestly couldn't. I found out about the memory because Annie accidentally shared it during one of our telepathy trainings. Apparently, Jaired had done something embarrassing when he first encountered Annie's aura. He tried to shapeshift from a bird to his panther form and ended up in between with a panther's head and tail and the rest remained as a bird. And he was covered with black and silver hair.

Even though the memory belonged to those two, the moment Annie let it slip to me, I wasn't bound by that magic. However, Jaired knew that I knew. Subsequently, he flooded my head with painfully-detailed images of torture as a guaranteed threat if I spoke. I was a good boy and never mentioned it again, at least not directly. I'd make some roundabout comments when Jaired was being particularly condescending or impatient since it always shut him up.

"Lift your pant leg and kneel." I ordered Teega. "Thieves are multiplying and we need to find out why as soon as possible."

"Shouldn't we get a couple to interrogate?" Annie asked.

"You mean interview," I corrected.

Annie's shoulders slumped. "Fine. Interview."

She mumbled something about how I'm no fun, but I ignored

her. *Jaired, please get us two thieves. Alive.*

Unharmed?

I clarified, *Able to speak.*

Be back.

I didn't hear him fly off, but I felt his presence fade away from Our Place. "While we're waiting for him, I want to make sense of this tattoo."

Teega stood, lifted her pant leg then knelt. We walked closer to examine the wound closely. The flickering firelight showed a lot, but I wanted to verify my theory under closer scrutiny.

I ran my fingers on her skin, tracing the new lines. Then I stood and stated emphatically, "That's what I thought. She is a healer. Or she's at least part healer."

Annie bent down and looked at Teega's calf. She rubbed at her eyes in disbelief. The red skin had lessened drastically. The wound looked more like the natural birthmark tattoo of my people. "How did you know?"

"I've seen something similar on Gregare." I couldn't pull my eyes off the calf. "He's a partial healer, Annie, not a full blown one."

In my peripheral, I saw Annie stand and look down at me. "What else does he have?"

"Forever the nosey one, Annie." I shook my head and gave no further reply.

It's not that the birthmarks are a secret only shared with family and spouses. They are personal, however, and we don't show them to everyone. If most people paid attention to the person then they wouldn't ever need to see the mark. For example, Gregare showed me his birthmark, but I already knew about the healing portion. I'd cut myself on a thorny bush unique to the Marshes. As talented as I am at navigating the wild, some parts of the land will touch even the most gifted. I noticed that Gregare had the torn clothing from the same bush, but there was a lack of blood. That's when I was able to figure out he was part healer.

"I just like to know things," her innocent voice replied. "To be more like you."

I laughed loudly. "Oh, please. You just need to pay more attention to how people say and do things and not what they say and do."

"Always the teacher," she grumbled.

"Always the pupil," I retorted immediately. "You want to share your tattoo with Teega?"

Annie glared. "You know that I don't."

"Why?" Teega asked without a moment's hesitation.

I locked eyes with Annie and challenged her. I always treated her as an equal even if she was my apprentice. However, sometime she needed a reminder that I was in charge. It was a long moment and a long stare, but eventually Annie broke eye contact and gave a brief nod. Slowly, I'll break that horse and it'll probably kill me.

"Mine only has color," Annie whispered.

Teega whispered in reply, "Okay. Why are we whispering?"

Annie blushed so much that her green aura couldn't hide the discoloration in her face. As much as I wanted her to swallow her pride, there are times when she also needs to let others help her.

I reached out to Teega's mind. *It's personal because it's viewed as underdeveloped. I looked at her eyes then at her chest. Imagine if you were an adult female yet you lacked the physical developments of a woman.*

Recognition hit Teega immediately and she dropped the inquiry. Simultaneously Annie's color slowly faded back to normal.

"Annie, I want you to show her because her tattoo feels different than yours."

Annie turned around and lifted her right pant leg. I'd seen the tattoo countless times before, but I always scrutinized it with a fresh perspective each time.

The tattoo had the same ink vines climbing up from her ankle before splitting off to leave space in the middle of her calf. The ink vines were nearly black against her dark skin, but I knew if I leaned closer then I'd see the black was actually a dark brown.

"Whoa! That's so cool!" Teega couldn't contain her excitement. "It looks like it's fog above your skin and not actually in it."

Annie's aura responded to Teega's happy energy by noticeably darkening. "You're definitely not one of us."

"You know, I never looked at it like that before," I commented. I knelt closer and admired Annie's tattoo. In the empty space between the vines hung a light purple color and turquoise color of ocean water. I poked it with my index finger and the "fog" actually swirled.

"Well, it's never done that before," I stated calmly. I looked up at Annie and she just shrugged. "Teega, do me a favor. Touch her calf."

Tentatively, she reached out with her middle finger and touched Annie's calf. I held my breath for a moment, expecting something to happen, but nothing did. She pulled her finger away and the purple blue fog continued its slow swirl.

"I thought something would happen," I remarked. "Especially given today's events."

Teega nodded. "So did I."

"I actually am happy nothing did," Annie began. "As much as I want mine to show up, I don't want the excruciating pa–."

Suddenly Annie's eyes went wide. She let out a gasp then collapsed.

———

Jaired. Hurry. I urged as I ran my fingers through Annie's hair. My heart was racing, but not nearly as fast as Annie's.

"Where is he?" Teega asked. Her face had gone pale the moment Annie collapsed.

"Coming." I replied curtly. The truth was that I didn't know. I couldn't feel him and he wasn't responding. I took a slow breath then let it out.

"Her breath is so fast." Teega's voice was strained with concern. "I'm so sorry, Brim."

I kept stroking Annie's head. I swallowed the lump in my throat and looked up at Teega. "It is not your fault. I asked you because I had hoped to give her some relief. The lack of markings gives cause to doubt herself, her heritage."

"That's absurd. She's the embodiment of all the Tree Maker stories I heard growing up. Her power, her grace, her beauty."

I added, "And all that rage."

"The balance of all the power is not always found through peace, Brim," Teega chided.

"It can be."

"Yes, it can be. But some of us must burn bright before we learn to glow," Teega replied. She leaned over and kissed Annie on the forehead. She whispered words unintelligible then bestowed another kiss.

Annie's eyes slowly began to open. First the left then the right.

"What did you say?" I asked Teega.

"It's a prayer of my people," she replied.

"Thank you." I reached out and squeezed her hand.

"I fall asleep for a minute and you're already onto the next girl," croaked Annie. She started sitting up, but fell back into my arms. "A little help, please."

I stood, lifting her with me. My eyes bore into hers as her hands held tight in mine. "Don't do that again."

"I won't, warden."

"Caryanne, I mean it. My heart..."

She let go of my hand and placed it on my chest. Her legs wavered for a moment, but I put my free hand on her hip to steady her. The warmth of her touch reached through my tunic and slowed my heart to normal. Slowly, she put weight in her legs and quickly found her balance.

"I'm sorry, Annie." Teega stood with us, but stepped back as if trying to blend into the walls.

Annie stepped forward and hugged her. In all my life, I never saw Annie hug anyone. Not even me and she loved me.

"Thank you for bringing me back. And thank you for this." She lifted her exposed right calf up. The turquoise and purple had finally stopped swirling and had taken sides in the exposed tear-shape inside the vine outline. The turquoise settled on the bottom half and the purple on the top.

We both looked at Annie's tattoo. Something in the back of my mind stirred. It was that echo of an echo feeling similar to when my abilities were taking over my conscious mind. And just like every other time, the moment I reached to understand the echo, it disappeared.

Teega interrupted my mental search for more. "I wonder if it's supposed to be the night sky and the ocean below."

Annie lifted her leg so only she could see her calf. "Could be. Could not. I'm just happy that I have something now."

"Of course you are," I replied with a shake of my head. "I think it's time for you to continue your training. You need the exercise anyway."

I almost kissed the heel of her foot a half second later. I did feel the breeze it created as it went by. "Getting slow, Annie. You really need to practice."

Her eyes went wide and she lifted the same leg to swing it back at me. I dropped to squat, her leg flew over my head and I swept my right leg at her standing leg. She lost her balance and landed on her back, all air expelling from her lungs.

Teega tried to cover her laugh with her hand, but failed miserably. Clearly frustrated, I watch Annie start to sweep her leg at Teega. I wasn't going to allow that. Teega didn't have our training and I wasn't going to let Annie attack her.

So I prepared to somersault over Annie by jumping towards her. Before I tucked my body to spin and land on my feet, I grabbed her ankles. With the strong grip, I pulled Annie with me for the somersault. I flung her away from me when I tucked to land on my feet. I heard her hit against the wall and let out another lung-emptying gasp.

To my surprise, Annie laughed when she caught her breath. "I am getting slow!"

Teega looked at her then at me with a face painted in shock. She muttered while shaking her head, "Tree Makers." She turned away from us and headed toward the adjoining room.

I watched her walk away and felt that she still needed to learn. Not in a scolding parental way, but she was one of us now. And if you're on my team then you're always learning. I waited for her to step over the tree root separating the two rooms then I acted. With her right leg lifted, I reached out to the tree and asked for the root to grow up by a foot.

It did. Annie and I laughed as we watched Teega fall.

"You're a Tree Maker, too. Careful who you mock," I stated with a lifting of one eyebrow.

Teega squinted at me as she slowly stood. "Oh, so you're off the hook. No one makes you fall down?"

"Wouldn't make sense for the most powerful among our people to be knocked down so easily," Annie answered. Then she tried to sweep her feet to knock me down. I flipped backwards away from her without a thought. My ability to feel everything (even if I couldn't see everything) within close proximity was one of those innate gifts from the gods. I didn't need to see what was coming, my body felt it and I moved accordingly.

"See what I mean?" Annie said to Teega, "It's pointless."

Teega just shook her head again, but kept her mouth shut. She wandered out of sight in the other room.

"Go practice with her," I whispered to Annie. "She is hiding something. And she likes you so maybe something will slip."

Annie lifted her hand to move that curl of hair out of her eye and off her forehead. I'd seen her make the gesture for over a decade and it was adorable every time. The curl never behaved, but she had a childlike determination in her eyes whenever she did it.

My voice croaked. "Hey, thank you for coming back to me."

Her eyes began to water, but the water never found the crest to become tears. She nodded and took a step toward the anteroom. She paused for a moment to get on tiptoes and kissed me on the cheek. The warmth from her lips spread to my entire body. All my focus and all my tense muscles relaxed immediately.

I turned and watched her walk away. Each sauntering step slowly lulled me into a stupor. She is truly a beautiful creature, but dammit is she distracting.

She must have read my thoughts because she turned to me, her devilish smile melting me.

"I am a rock. I don't need anyone. I am a rock. I don't need anyone." I said to the empty room. I closed my eyes to reflect on the day's events, but all I saw was Annie's smile and my body relaxed all over again.

I said a small prayer and begged for a giant rock to fall on my head.

CHAPTER 15

"Where. Are. You. From." With each word Annie broke a finger on the taller thief's left hand. And with each break, the thief's scream echoed around the chamber and throughout the tunnels of Our Place.

"Please. He can't tell you," the other thief said after the screaming stopped.

"Yes. You can." My stern voice made the broken-fingered thief jerk his upper body off the floor. The reaction made me smile - on the inside at least. I had to keep my outward appearance menacing.

I had been in the main room since Jaired had first dropped off the thieves. Thankfully, he had interrupted the thoughts that Annie had left me with. And Jaired had obliged my request - mostly - as both thieves were able to talk. Clearly, one of them had tried to struggle and had a thick stream of blood at his shoulder that was soaking through his clothes. After the thieves got a glance at me, Annie pulled them into the anteroom and started interviewing.

The psychology between the thieves and wardens is simple: they are frightened of us in close quarters. More specifically, they are really afraid of me. The reputation of the head warden mostly came from tall tales and speculations, but they spread like wildfire especially amongst the criminals. So I stayed out of the room until the right moment when they were broken - mentally or physically.

The anteroom doesn't have braziers in the corners to light the room. Instead, a hole in the upper corner of the room provides the light. There are a lot more knots on the walls in this room than the main one. Whoever made this place home clearly spent a lot of time communicating with the tree. I'd been here off and on for a decade and only managed to manipulate a few, small growths.

Annie had thrown the tall thief into the spot where the outside light shone. As the wood in this room is significantly darker than in the main room, that light was a stark contrast. Yeryan thieves hated the light and Annie knew that well. The thief would instinctively try to scoot out of the light, but Annie stopped him every time and hurt him for trying. He even tried to pull the black and dirty hood of his tunic over his head, but Annie punished him for that, too. The only time she didn't punish them from hiding was when her aura illuminated the room with an angry, pulsing green.

"You will tell us," I repeated. The light shone on his bruised face as Annie had spared no punches. A cut at his hairline had bloodied the right half of his face and ran down his neck.

The broken-fingered thief glared at me. "We're not afraid to die. We would die to get this way."

I waved my hand dismissively. "I know your mantra and I don't care."

Annie stepped forward, her aura nearly a solid green. I could barely make out her body in the bubble.

"Wait, Annie." The bubble stopped and pulsed a couple times, reflecting her frustration. "I don't want you to kill him. I want you to continue hurting him."

In response to those words, her aura pulsed so quickly that Annie became an awesome blur as she resumed walking toward the thief. The thief tried to move away from Annie, but his legs were numbed by the aura and broken fingers don't get much grip on an already smooth floor.

Teega yelled, "STOP!"

Something in her voice cancelled Annie's aura and broke my resolve of anger at the other thief. Annie and I turned toward her in unison. Our mouths dropped in shock. Teega's entire body was glowing red like embers of a fire.

"There is another way." Her voice came out eerie, so eerie that Annie and I both shivered. "I will take care of this."

"Okayyy," Annie said as she stepped back a few more steps so she was behind me. "I'm going to be over here in the corner. By Brim. And not you."

I didn't say anything. Instead I watched in awe as Teega changed from a dim red glow to a bright orange and red one like a log on fire. The colors reminded me of the lights in the cavern from Teega's memory. It was a deep fire from the depths of an underground world. What I was seeing had to be something unique of her people.

"You will tell me." Teega's voice purred like a hungry predator. She kept her gaze on the uninjured thief as she floated, a couple inches above the tree floor, toward the other thief. The other thief, broken and bleeding, gave up trying to get away. He lay there, trying to muster as much courage as possible, while a walking flame loomed over him.

"No, no, I won't," the other thief said. He was shorter than his mate, broader in the face and the shoulders. His voice cracked at the end, right as Teega's outer flaming aura reached his comrade.

"You will." Teega pronounced. Then she stepped on the foot of the injured man and his leg immediately caught on fire. He didn't scream and he didn't move. His mouth opened, but Teega extended her hand forward and his face engulfed in thick, black smoke.

She turned away and looked at the other thief. Another flick of her hand and the burning thief had two legs on fire. The fire from the first leg climbed up his leg and toward his torso. A light, dull gray smoke rose from the charred, black foot. Teega flicked her hand and the smoke around his face disappeared and he belched a painful scream that echoed so loudly that I had to cover my ears.

"Okay, okay!" The thief screamed, "I'll tell you. Don't burn me."

"Teega, I think you got what–" I started the thought, but she shut me down.

Another flick of her hand and the uninjured thief's right hand started burning. Teega's flaming aura lowered down to her shoulders so only her head was visible. Her face looked nothing like it had two minutes earlier. Her eyes and mouth were blue flames and her skin the color of red coals. When she spoke, her voice crackled like a campfire. "Speak."

The thief sat on his burning hand until the flame went out then looked directly at me. "The Marshes."

Annie stepped forward, her aura leading the way. "The Marshes aren't small. Gonna need a little more."

The thief hesitated, but Teega flicked her fingers and the other thief's hand was aflame.

"Southeast! West of the cliffs. You'll know it when you can smell the Sair Sea."

"Not possible. The winds carry away everything," I commented. "I've been south and I've been east to the cliffs."

"Then you missed it, moss'r," the thief spat.

Teega started to raise her hand, but I reached her mind. *That's enough, Teega. Come back.*

Her head spun to mine and the blue flame eyes darkened several shades. She stepped toward me and her aura flared a deeper red.

"Whoa, girl. Not going to let that happen." Annie put herself between Teega and me. Hundreds of dark green daggers hung in her aura and all were pointing at Teega.

I stayed Annie's anger with a thought and she turned her attention back to the thief. "Finish them. I got this."

Teega's aura enveloped her head again and she continued toward me. My heart raced, but not out of fear or danger; it raced out of excitement. Somehow I knew it would all work out even though I didn't know how. Teega's energy was an animalistic instinct almost like she wasn't in full control, but I'd help her to the light.

The closer Teega moved the more heat I could feel coming off of her. A bead of sweat fell from my forehead to my right hand. The instant the sweat hit, I felt an unfamiliar chill come over my body. The heat from Teega disappeared and the air was clear of the choking air that comes with a burning fire. My eyes remained focused on the blue flames of Teega's eyes.

"Um, Brim. What's going on?" Annie's voice stressed concern.

All my attention remained on Teega. I needed to get her back from wherever she went. "What are you talking about?"

"Look down."

I did. My skin was blue. Gone was the deep tan of my people and before me was a deep, icy blue. Never had my body reacted this way. Then again, never had a day like this happened before.

"Cool." I chuckled. "And cool."

Annie rolled her eyes. "You're an idiot. Just get her calm so we can get going please."

I looked up at Teega who had stopped walking toward me. About two feet in front of me there was a slight sizzling sound as the heat from her aura and the cold of mine met.

"We got what we need, Teega. You can come back now." I took a slight step forward which created another sizzle sound and a little haze from the different temperatures.

She responded to my words by throwing her hands up and releasing fireballs at me. I instinctively flinched, but the aura actually took care of the flames. They were immediately cooled into balls of ice that dropped to the floor and shattered.

I took another step forward. Clearly words weren't doing anything. Maybe I could use the memory she shared to bring her back home. I closed my eyes and brought forth in my mind's eye the memory of visiting her memory. Like I've done with Annie and transporting our consciousness to visit people across our land, I projected the memory onto Teega's consciousness. She was more powerful than before, but I didn't have to be gentle this time.

Jaired asked, *Help?*

No. I'd been feeling him watching everything happening in this room since I entered it, but he'd kept himself out of it.

He stood perched in the doorway between the rooms, but in his mostly harmless owl form. There is no doubt that he could have gone panther mode and he would have had both thieves sucking their thumbs like babies. However, that wasn't his style. Eternally the guru.

I broke through Teega's resistance and saw her sitting by her pillar.

"What is this?" She asked in definite confusion.

I waved my arm around, "This is my memory of your memory."

She gathered her energy and walked to her pillar. She reached out and touched it. "It's so real. As real as mine."

I chuckled. "Of course it is. It's my memory."

"Oh, right. That makes sense." She walked over to me and touched my arm as if she still didn't believe me. "I guess I didn't expect such accuracy."

"I'm well-practiced in this. Telepath and all that."

She nodded. "So why are we here?"

"Well, because you're being a flaming bitch right now to be exact." I know, I'm subtle.

"Excuse me?" Her eyes were wide with shock.

"Actually, you're not excused." I pointed to a spot on the gravel ground between the pillars and exerted my focus. To show a memory within a memory is something I'd been working on. It's...tricky and exhausting. However, it worked.

The gravel disappeared and an image of a flaming Teega could be seen through the haze of the confluence of auras. I shifted focus to earlier when she lit the thieves on fire.

"That's you. No warning. Just fire."

Teega shook her head and turned away from the images. "It can't be..."

"What can't be?"

She walked to the edge of the pillar platform and looked out into the fire orange abyss. "More stories. More tales of times long passed. More of something that should not exist."

I could feel that "respect my privacy of my people" feeling surging from her.

I spoke softly, "I want to pry, but we don't have time. Thieves are going to hit the borders of my people's homes and I cannot have that."

"Yet, I'm just me. There is no connection to what the bard sang and who I am." Teega was still lost in her own thoughts, trying to make sense of everything.

I walked to her and looked out into the abyss as well. In the calmest voice possible I said, "I understand what it's like not to know. It may not seem that way because I've lived so long and understand so much."

"I was about to say..."

"But imagine having all that time to know the world like the toes on your feet then have it all change. This news feels like ripples for your short life; it's like waves crashing for my life span."

Nodding, she replied, "I hadn't thought of that."

"So, we'll get to the bottom of these mysteries. I promise you. However, we need to stop these marauders."

"Okay. Okay. I can do this." She faced me and touched my wrist. "I don't know what's happening to me, but I know how to stop it. If the song is true."

I let out a breath of relief. "Good. How do we stop it?"

"Bow."

"Really?"

She shrugged. "Yup. I'll try to explain later."

"Okay. I'll see you in a bit."

I closed my eyes and wiped clean the memory from my focus. When my eyes opened I was back in the interrogation room in Our Place. Annie's curiosity nagged at me like an itch, but I ignored it. I took a deep breath, exhaled, and gave a deep bow at the flaming Teega. I didn't look up, but I saw the color in the room gain normality. The flames must have calmed dramatically.

Standing up, I noticed Teega's true self was slowly shedding the flaming aura. On a guess, I turned to Annie. "Bow. It'll bring her back. And no, I don't know why."

Asking Annie to bow to anyone is similar to asking the sun not to warm the land. Although, sometimes I felt it was more likely that the sun would listen to me.

Bow, little one, Jaired urged.

Grudgingly, Annie bowed.

We waited a few breaths then lifted our heads. Teega had returned to normal. Unburned, unscathed, and endearingly innocent as always.

She spoke in normal voice. "Hey guys. Sorry about that."

"It's okay. We got the information we needed."

"And one bad ass fire fiend!" Annie exclaimed. "Seriously, that was amazing."

Blushing, Teega looked away. "I didn't mean to. It just happened."

"If you could do that—"

"Annie. Drop it." I scolded. Sometimes I wondered if Annie was twenty years old instead of two hundred. "I asked you to take care of them."

She threw her hands in the air. "Fine. Boss."

Teega and I turned to watch her dispose of the thieves. I expected Annie to be quick, but she stood staring at them.

"Why aren't they on fire?" Annie asked in genuine confusion.

I looked to Teega for an answer. She had the glossy eyes of someone lost in a different thought. I reached out and gently shook her. "Why aren't they on fire?"

She shook her head and looked at me. "Sorry, I'm still trying to understand this. It's all coming back to me in bits and pieces."

"Any bits about how you were once a flame and now just you?" Annie queried.

"Best I can tell you is that it's part of a folk tale." She looked at Annie's confused face. "It's weird, I know. A song about a firewalker. It's something that has been passed on for ages and no one ever thought it to be real. Surely, you have similar songs among your people?"

I nodded. "Yes, we do."

"So this one I haven't heard since I was a child and I never told it to anyone because I don't have my own kin." She walked up to the thief who received the most flames and kicked his foot. He didn't move. She nodded as if verifying a theory.

Annie asked, "Dead?"

"No. Just passed out from the pain."

I stepped forward. "What do you mean pain? No flame, no pain."

"It's all in their head. And you should know more than anyone that what the mind feels can come true for the body."

"So you're telling me that they've passed out from pain of being on fire even though they were never on fire?" Annie's voice carried a hint of jealousy.

"Exactly. The song was often sung to keep children from lying to their parents because..."

"What you say can come true," I finished.

Teega just nodded.

We all stared at the thieves in awe of all that just happened. There were so many questions running around my head that we could have spent a week exploring the answers. A week I didn't have.

"I want to know one answer then we have to head south."

"I'll answer best I can," Teega assured.

"Why fire? If it's all in their head then why did you choose fire?"

Annie chimed in. "I want to know why we saw it if it's all in their head."

"I know Annie's, but I can only guess yours, Brim."

"Then guess."

Annie demanded, "Me first."

I laughed. "Okay, give the kid her toy."

Annie lightly punched my arm. "Don't be mad that you can't ask better questions."

"You mean simple questions." I retorted then promptly stepped out of reach from her next punch.

"You two are adorable," Teega commented. She almost sounded motherly. "Annie, what they saw you saw because you believed it as well."

"I didn't believe you were setting me on fire," Annie countered.

"No, but you believed they were terrified. That feeling was

enough for you two to see what they did."

"Like a shared dream," Annie paused. "Well, more like a shared nightmare."

"Exactly." Teega faced me. "Brim, my guess is the Yeryans are terrified of fire. They hunt at night. They are dark-skinned."

"I thought that, too. However, I also thought maybe it had to do with your people."

"My people? I don't follow."

"Your memory was filled with fire all around the cavern. For all the tiny fire pits and torches I saw, there was more glow caused by fires I couldn't see."

Teega sighed. "Maybe you're right, too. I hadn't thought about that."

"Tables have turned, huh?"

"What do you mean?"

"You laughed at me earlier for making assumptions about others because of my own life," I replied.

Teega started to object, but I stopped her.

"And rightfully so." I gave her a reassuring smile. "It would seem you made similar assumptions about us in regards to your people."

"Yes, I did."

"So it's settled. You're wrong, she's wrong, and I'm right," Annie summarized.

"Wait, why are you right?" I asked.

"Because I'm me." Annie pulled out one of her blades and walked to the first thief. She placed one foot on his forehead then swung the blade down and sliced through his neck. She repeated the same process on the other thief. With one surge of effort, her aura cleaned the blades of the Yeryan blood.

"Let's clean up this mess and leave," I stated. "We're wasting time."

CHAPTER 16

"Slow down, warden. Before we even bother with these soon to be corpses, I want answers from you," demanded Annie, hands on her hips. Her aura was still pulsing in that familiar frantic urgency. "You spent a lot of time with Teega and found out many things that I'm now in the dark about."

I stepped through her aura and put my face in hers. "Really? You want answers? What about earlier with your javelin ordeal in the forest?"

She tried to push back with her eyes, but she could not. Instead she looked down and mumbled, "That's different."

I reached out and actually poked my finger against her shoulder. She jerked up and looked at me in genuine shock. "You found a way to take my ice imbuement and magnify it. And did I freak out and make demands?"

"Jaired to—"

"No. You can't bring him in every time you need an out. You answer to me not him."

I spun on my heels and walked out of the room. I didn't have time to deal with her attitude and, honestly, I had no idea as to why I responded the way I did. Annie was too consumed with her own curiosity and frustration to pick up on mine. I've always been able to manipulate water to some degree, especially ice. However, I'd never been able to affect an aura around me the way Annie does. There were too many questions and not enough answers and it was causing my patience to wear very thin.

Too harsh. Jaired's thoughts greeted me once I entered the main room. His four eyes looked into mine from atop the perch.

I ignored him. *Let's get rid of these thieves so we can head to their den.*

Let the tree handle it.

"What do you mean, Master?" asked Annie.

I snorted at her formality, but she ignored me. Give it a couple hours and we'd want to talk to each other again. Sometimes being around the same people all the time can result in required quiet time between those same people.

Jaired's answer came in the form of several different mental images. The first involved the bugs soaking up the blood. The second involved small furry creatures eating and carrying away the meat of the thieves. The next involved birds carrying away the clothing for nests.

"Okay, okay. I get it. You can stop now," I said with an impatient wave. "Life will take care of it."

Anger surged from Jaired to me. *You should know this. Life takes care of all.*

Deep breath. Don't yell at a being that can kill you with talons and beak and fangs and claws. Since all I wanted to do was yell, I chose to not respond at all - mentally or verbally.

"Leave the bodies, Annie. We're leaving."

We left the anteroom and took the tunnels out of the main room up to the branches. As I stepped out onto the branch, I took a moment to take in the view. This specific branch had clearly been intentionally grown with the purpose of flight or just a place with a view. It was as wide as Jaired's wingspan when he was in flight form. Also, the branches around this one had been intentionally grown to accommodate the flight in and out as there was a gap in the otherwise impenetrable branches at a sharp angle away from the tree. The gap seemed to fit the wingspan of a mourar almost perfectly which always made me wonder if a mourar had in fact spoke to the tree and came to an agreement about the design.

Jaired never commented about the origins or convenience of Our Place, but he also flew down and up this branchless tunnel with the ease of me walking amongst the platforms at Varokkar where I grew up.

Once we reached the top, Jaired transformed into the silvery blue feathered flight form then took off out the tunnel. He only went to the edge of the tunnel then flew back and landed as quiet as always. His four large eyes bore down on me yet he set his left wing down for the other two to climb aboard.

"May I?" Teega asked with a bow.

"Ugh. Not you, too," I grumbled.

Jaired bowed his neck down to match Teega's and allowed her to climb up. On the flight here Annie had the good seat and it looked like the flight south Teega would be in that spot. And I'd be getting the bumpy ride near the back.

Sure enough, Annie jumped up in the air and let her aura slowly settle her down a little behind Teega.

"Hurry up, Brim. Jaired can't wait forever." Annie said with a wide I'm-very-pleased-with-myself smile. Teega joined in shortly after. Even Jaired flapped his wings in amusement - which I didn't think was possible until it'd happened.

"Come pick me up," I stated. Jaired lifted his wings high in that threatening manner that usually meant I was going to get knocked on my butt again. Quickly, I added. "I need to show you something from Teega's memory."

Jaired let his wing fall gently then jumped off the branch and took flight.

I watched him soar through the tunnel cut out of branches then bank south along the tree line. Since all these trees connected as if they were one, I could easily jump and swing my way to catch up with him. Granted, he had a grace that even surpassed mine and I had upset him a little bit today so I was going to have to step up my game.

I took a running start and leapt off the same branch that Jaired took flight from. Instead of flying, however, I somersaulted to my left and fell a good distance before grabbing a branch. With my falling momentum, I swung off the other branch and jetted myself almost out of the branchless tunnel. From there I jumped and swung my way south as beads of sweat started to form on my brow with each movement.

Jaired sent me an image of where he'd be after he dove to the ground. I sprinted along the branch, jumped to a connected one then did a forward, side flip away from this interconnected section of The Shims and into the open blue skies. As gentle as Jaired landing on the branch, my feet touched down on his feathers.

Teega exclaimed something in her native language and clapped with impressive joy. Even Annie had a look of awe that she quickly wiped away when I made eye contact.

"That's why he's the warden, huh?" Teega asked.

"No, that's why he's the best of our people," Annie remarked then turned herself forward again.

I shrugged and shimmied my way up Jaired's back to a few feet behind Annie.

I reached out to only Jaired. *Thank you. I needed that.*

A guide cannot sacrifice the student within.

I patted his side in agreement then I reached and nudged Teega's mind.

Yes, came her voice in my head.

I need to show Jaired the memory. May I?

A peaceful energy welcomed me before Teega's words did. *Of course. It is yours now.*

Thank you.

Teega's energy pulsed with concern. *Brim?*

Yes?

I'm sure Jaired knows this, but be...careful, Teega advised.

I know she meant to say respectful in concern to her people's privacy. *I will. And I won't surprise him like you did.*

She didn't respond, but I heard a faint laughter carrying on the wind.

———

After I finished sharing the memory, I asked Jaired, *Do you understand why I was taken aback, right?*

Yes.

I asked, *Any of it make sense to you?*

No.

How is that possible? I thought you were here since the beginning?

Jaired clarified, *Yes, the beginning of your people not mine.*

I took a moment to process the words. I looked ahead at the horizon. The clouds were thick and gray as if always waiting to storm. The Sair Sea was a distant and endless blue to my left and the trees of The Shims still stood tall and interconnected as they had been at Our Place. The trees grew up to the edge of the cliffs at the eastern edge of our continent.

Looking out upon my land always helped settle my thoughts and steady my body. A question finally formed and I asked Jaired. *Do you remember how you came to be? Being a youngling?*

No.

Earliest memory?

Foggy. Time is not the same.

Oh, right. We have gone rounds with this discussion before. I'm old, but he's really old. The closest I ever get to understanding is when he shows me parts of the forest when they were young. The only issue with those images is when he tells me that there were others before those saplings. Naturally, when I ask for how many seasons, he cannot tell me. One day, I'll find a way to come up with a common measurement.

I want to see your earliest memory, old one.

Jaired's connection with me didn't sever right then, however, it did lurch. As if we fell out of the sky and then lifted ourselves back up moments before hitting the ground. I tried to sense the reason for the lurch. It wasn't something I'd felt from him. It was anxiety with a hint of fear. And that scared me.

If this powerful being carried a hint of fear about anything then I should down right be shaking. Yet I couldn't deny the nagging pull of that memory and of the unknown. I had to find answers. There was too much between Annie and myself.

I was the only one of my people to ever bond this closely with a mourar. Our races may interact, but such a connection like the one between Jaired and me is extremely rare.

If anyone could help fill in the gaps then it would be him. I set aside my fear and reached out. *Jaired. I need answers. And so do you.*

The lurch faded away and the strength of his connection returned. The return was a welcoming warmth that spread across my body. I wasn't dependent upon him for my existence, but he had become a huge part of my life.

Agreed.

First the thieves, I said. *Do you know of this place the thieves mentioned?*

No.

I sighed. So much for the easy way out. *Okay, let's turn it on. Fly higher and fly faster. It's time to take these people out and get to the real answers.*

Jaired flapped his enormous wings a few times in agreement and we shot above the clouds.

CHAPTER 17

The clouds weren't as thick here as they were over The Sairs, but they were just as consistent. Thick and gray, the clouds around The Sairs could be seen from several locations throughout our land. All you had to do was find a clearing or climb halfway up a tree and you'd see them. They were beautiful because they were so expansive. Flying through them, however, not nearly as beautiful. Turns out staring at gray and only being able to see a few feet in front of you isn't very relaxing. Although it wasn't a huge concern because Jaired's multi-faceted vision could ensure we didn't wrap around a tree.

Thankfully, the wind wasn't strong up here. In fact, there was virtually no wind up here. It was a unique phenomenon with this area of our land. Cliffs separated the Sair Sea to the east and to The Shims. These cliffs hung out dramatically towards the sea which resulted in the winds, that normally come off the water, to hit the cliffs then curve off back toward the sea. They were like an upside down ramp that created the amazing phenomenon of no smells or winds from the sea.

A person could watch the beautiful blue waters, cresting white-tipped waves, and endless creatures diving from sky and jumping from the waters all without any winds to ruin the day. That meant no cold winds biting through clothes during the winter and no foul smelling winds that come from stale, hot mid-summer afternoons.

I know Jaired has spent a many of years flying up and down the eastern coast to hunt. No prey could smell him coming especially with the cover of the trees. So when he said he'd never heard or smelled the place that the thieves mentioned, it was a genuine shock to all. And I'm sure there was an element of pride for him since he always had an answer to any question.

Keep going above the clouds. I need to see, I requested of Jaired.

He obliged with two hearty flaps of wings and we were above the gray clouds. I looked to the sea and it was a calm as gentle waves lapped against the shore. Thanks to my vision, even from up here I could see some birds diving into the ocean then surfacing with a squirming fish in their beak. I wonder how often Jaired went over the cliffs and fished in the sea. I'd have to ask him later.

Anything? I asked Jaired. I hadn't felt anything from him except determination since we left Our Place.

He didn't respond in the slightest. I guess the determination came with some grumpiness, too.

I shared my thoughts with him. *I wonder if they found a way to hide from certain creatures. It seems almost impossible that you wouldn't be able to detect that after all this time.*

Hey, I can stroke an ego when I need to. And I need to because I needed to keep him sharp in mind and in body. As strong as Annie and I are, Jaired is a force to reckon with. He is a thunderstorm that only the oldest trees can ignore.

Possible, he grumbled.

Judging by his curt reply, I knew that thought was already going through his head. It was the only thing that made sense to me. Jaired was able to see more with his eyes than any other creature. His sense of smell was no different. However, there was clearly a gap in what nature had given him. One thing constant in nature is the fact that there is always a gap to ensure one thing doesn't rule them all. And I'd always given the control to Jaired whenever we were together. In fact, I'd become lazy in that regard. I always relied on him to give warning through sight and sound. That was a fault on his part as much as it was mine. As wise as he was, it is also the job of the student to not merely wait to be fed like a baby bird.

So I closed my eyes, closed my hearing, and opened up my sense of smell. I've only done this on a couple occasions with Annie. One time we were tracking an injured animal that had an amazing ability to hide its tracks in the dirt. Our people called it a ridger because it had ridges over most of its body that not only protected it from prey, but also helped with movement. The ridger could use it's five legs normally. However, if threatened then it would jump forward, tuck into a ball, and use the ridges to cushion the landing and propel it back upward at any angle to the next landing zone. Following feet are easy; following an unpredictable bouncing ball of spikes is not so easy. The sense of smell is the only thing that keeps a person from going dizzy trying to track it.

The best way to enhance your sense of smell is actually the opposite method of enhancing your sense of sound. With hearing, you tune everything out except for what you want to hear. With smell, you take in everything. The logic behind this is simple: identify all the ones you know then you can focus on the one that you don't.

Taking in all the smells from this height isn't as overwhelming as when I'm walking amongst the trees. Also, the smells are much purer so it's easier to identify. First, I could smell Jaired then Annie. She always smelled sweet as if she'd permanently walked amongst a field of flowers. My guess was the aura kept her that way. Teega threw me off because her clothes had smells from her homeland that I couldn't recognize. I kept them fresh in my mind in case some of those smells were part of the thieves. There were also couple other smells from Our Place that lingered on all of us. Once the proximity smells were cataloged then I really had to put my sense to the test.

Trees of The Shims had a different smell than the trees I grew up climbing in and around. My trees emitted smells that invigorated me. The older trees beneath Jaired's wings were not invigorating at all. They weren't stagnant either. Instead these smells were stable and constant. There were hundreds of trees, all interconnected through extending branches that stretched for most of the eastern coastline, yet each of them carried a smell slightly different than its brother.

What these trees did better than those in The Shaws was masking the scent of the lives in and beneath their branches. I caught hints of animal life - a few birds and a couple small, furry animals - and smelled occasional fish that leapt above the surface of an unforeseen stream. I know life existed beyond those few instances, but the trees provided cover beyond the physical.

"This is not going to be easy," I muttered to myself. I took a deep breath and exhaled the growing frustration as I prepared for a long day.

———

There! I pointed just over Jaired's head to the west. *I smell smoke.*

Four hours later... Annie words mumbled in my mind.

My reply was curt. *I didn't feel you helping.*

My apprentice's humor rippled through me. *I was moral support.*

Yeah, we were cheering you on, Teega added.

I just sighed. They came out of Teega's memory walk about an hour ago and had been restless since. It started with a question from Annie which only led to more questions from Teega. Then they both chimed in every other minute like two sisters teasing their little brother.

As happy as I was that they were now getting along, I was also growing impatient with them. My frustration reached the point where I started to contemplate ways I could kick them off Jaired and pick them up later. Thankfully, Jaired stepped in and calmed them down. Of course his way of calming was doing a sharp incline so they fell to the rear of his body then he stabilized again. Now I had the good seat and they were in the back getting all the bumps.

I reached out to Jaired's mind. *Jaired, do you smell it?*

I chose not to share my belief that someone had found a way to specifically exploit a flaw. Jaired's pride would surely get hurt if that happened. Moreover, the more people who knew of that flaw meant the more of a chance that others could find out.

No. No smoke.

Interesting. I guess that proves my theory. I'll store that knowledge away for another day. However, I wasn't going to let this opportunity to teach Annie to pass by. *Annie, do you smell smoke?*

She closed her eyes and took a few deep breaths. I watched as she moved her head in a couple different directions, hoping to catch something on one of the many breezes. I noticed that Teega looked at me in confusion.

Close your eyes, Teega. Take in all the smells and once you're used to them then try to identify the ones you don't know.

She smiled, opened her mouth to say something then shook her head instead. *I'll try.*

Annie opened her eyes. *I don't smell any smoke, boss.*

That's fine. It's more practice for later. I addressed Teega, *What were you going to say?*

The Dewarian opened her eyes. *I can't smell the smoke, but I can see the fire.*

Annie and I simultaneously expressed our shock. *Really?*

She shrugged like it was no big deal. When you asked Annie to smell the smoke, something in me shifted focus and I saw the fire. Actually, I saw more than one fire, but those don't matter.

My heart was racing with excitement. I could feel a tinge of jealousy from Annie because I knew she always wanted every cool gift she heard about. Whereas I didn't want that burden. However, I didn't mind if others in my life had them because I felt we complemented each other.

Yet again, I had so many questions, but I had to focus. *Slow down. You saw more than one fire? Why don't they all matter?*

Teega looked away in contemplation for a few moments. *That memory walk connected all of us together. Especially you and me. The smoke you're seeking is coming from the fire that I saw. It's the brightest in my mind. The other fires are from thieves, but not near their base. Not far away, but far enough that we don't have to worry.*

Annie asked, *Have you always been able to see these things?*

Nope.

Annie looked at me with great concern. *I don't know if we should trust our lives to this. No offense, Teega, but as risky as I am, I'm not that risky.*

Teega just shrugged innocently again. *I'm not saying what to do. I'm just telling you what I know.*

I was about to ask Jaired what he thought, but he'd already started to bank west and dove into the clouds. We had cover. We had a location.

Annie's aura stretched out to cover all of us. *I guess we're doing this.*

CHAPTER 18

I still wasn't used to looking at the world through Jaired's vision. There was so much to take in that it was beyond overwhelming. However, when you're flying through thick, gray clouds you don't have much of a choice.

The thermal vision showed about a dozen thieves gathered in a rough circle. I guessed it was their camp. There was no way it was the official camp since they had managed to elude us wardens for this long. I shifted my focus to another one of Jaired's eyes that could see through fog and clouds to ascertain exactly where they were. This vision didn't completely get rid of the gray that came with thick, moist air, but it was doable.

How many, Annie? As always, I could feel her next to me in my mind.

I count fourteen outside the cave. No idea how many inside. Her response was quick, concise. She was in the zone.

Cave entrance location?

Northeast of the cluster of five thieves. Look for the absence of life. Her response was immediate and clipped. She must have mastered the merging all of Jaired's vision simultaneously. He could see all life - animal and non-animal alike.

I shifted back to the thermal vision and saw the absence Annie mentioned. Jaired's vision couldn't penetrate the cave so only the gods knew how many were in there. Although Teega could see the fires. I asked, *Teega. Can you detect any fires within the cave?*

Like Annie, her response came quickly. *Yes. About five of them.*

Can you see anything else? Any thieves or creatures or anything?

No thieves or creatures. Although my ear hurts more than normal.

I don't like that. Jaired back up high, please. I could feel his hesitation. *Now.*

It was a gamble giving him orders, but I'd rather have him angry with me than the fear that was gripping my mind. It took him only a few deep thrusts of his wings and we were well above and beyond the thieves.

I reached out to Teega. *How's your ear now?*

Better. Back to the normal amount of pain.

Annie's frustrated energy ran right into me. *Why the sudden withdrawal, Brim? I was ready to hurt them.*

I know you were, Annie. However, I fear that her ear can communicate in some way to them. I'm not certain by any means, but I'd rather not risk it.

Surprisingly, Jaired concurred. *Hasty is not the way.*

Agreed. I gathered my thoughts. *Don't you find it interesting how there are so many gathered here and we didn't catch it? Not even Jaired.*

Annie surprised me and took a moment to reply. *That same thought occurred to me. Surely one of the wardens would have given us a heads up. As great as we are, we can't be everywhere.*

Did I just hear Annie being humble? Teega asked with a heavy sarcasm. *I must be imagining this.*

I tried to choke back my laugh, but the wind carried it directly to Annie. *She's right, though, Teega. Her and I have the greatest area to cover, but we should have heard something.*

Who covers this area? Annie asked.

Technically, Bilge is warden in this part of the land.

Teega asked, *Is someone sleeping on the job?*

I shook my head. *Not at all. Bilge is a bear of a man, stubborn* and moody, but steadfast in his loyalty.

And to you, Annie added.

Before Teega could ask why, I cut her off at the pass. *I saved his life.*

Teega's reply was surprisingly serious. *Seems to be a trend of yours. Building up favors for an army or something?*

Nothing of the sort. It's always happenstance.

I could feel Annie and Teega applying pressure against my mind to spill the story, but I ignored them. Annie knew I saved his life, but didn't know what happened. Not even Jaired knew what happened, but now was not the time.

Annie asked impatiently, *So where is Bilge? You wouldn't let any other warden slack with his duties.*

What she really meant was that I would never let her slack in her duties. Gods forbid she just say that or maybe grow up in that regard. *He's on a mission.*

Annie's aura started to expand in anger. *Okay, great. Pull him off that mission and tell him to get his ass back to his original oath.*

Not that simple, apprentice.

Annie persisted. *It's always that s–*

No, it's not.

Tell me what's going on, Annie demanded.

I took a long breath and let it out slowly. Anger was rising in me like a bubbling lava in a volcano. I tried to calm my thoughts, but I could not. *Annie, there are thieves in our land and their numbers are growing. They have infested our lands and we didn't notice. Do you know what that means?!*

I put energy in the last sentence that physically hit Annie and Teega in the chest and forced them to grab tighter onto Jaired. I continued, *It means that they are poisoning our land worse than I thought. Our home, Annie!*

Another force of energy hit them so hard that both of them lost their grip. Jaired had to come to almost a complete stop to keep them from falling to the earth below. I felt him touch my mind and immediately I thought he was going to scold me. Instead the touch was one of comfort, of sympathy.

This feeling I have been feeling. Jaired's words touched all of us in such a way that it put all questions to rest. Ants can hurry about and fight over this and that, but when a giant's foot falls and shakes the ground then all focus changes to the bigger issue.

Annie and Teega didn't glare, they didn't mumble biting words. They didn't even send any angry energy at me. They just sent energy of understanding.

The most acknowledgement they received was my lack of rejecting their energy. I shifted my focus to Jaired. *I need your eyes.*

Jaired acquiesced and pulled me into his consciousness. Immediately, I was bombarded with the different visions, but I closed my mind's eye and focused on what I wanted to see. I reopened my mind's eye and my vision was exactly what I wanted: looking at nature.

While I can feel what is happening to an animal or a tree or the tiniest blade of grass, I cannot see nature the way Jaired does. His thermal vision outlines living things in a vibrant red, the nature vision outlines life in different colors. The most vibrant and healthy in nature will appear as a transcendent and pure white while the other end of the spectrum will be a solid, evil black.

As I expected, the thieves' den was black as night. I'm sure they've gutted the area of as much nature as possible to keep themselves fed, clothed, and warm in excess. Thus, destroying all life around them. My heart began racing again in anger at their disrespect. Nature always provides what it needs if you protect and respect it - Tree Maker or not. I took a deep breath and let it out as I followed the black from their den and out into the rest of the land. What I saw struck me at such a core level it felt like my heart stopped beating.

Like veins in a leaf, the black spread out from the thieves' den in every direction. Despite a cliff being on the other side of the den, the evil fell down onto the beach and managed to slowly seep into the Sair Sea. The sickness also spread to the west, inland toward the confluence of The Snakes. Even The Tears were being infected as the southern part of the southern lake was tainted with some black. This kind of black didn't only mean evil, it meant death.

I shared the vision with Jaired and he immediately stopped flapping his wings and went into a hover. His concern shook through his body in the form of a low, but strong vibration.

Jaired declared, *I did not know it was this bad.*

Neither did I.

Something is giving them power.

Or someone.

Or someone, I repeated.

I let go of the vision and turned to Annie. *Jaired is going to share with you what I just saw. I need to reach out to Gregare.*

Annie opened her mouth to speak then closed it. I saw her chest rise and fall and her aura pull back to just protecting her as it does when she's calm. She finally spoke up, *I will do as you say.*

Teega queried, *Who's Gregare?*

Warden of The Marshes, Annie answered. *He's one interesting fella.*

I quickly added, *To say the least.*

I shut them out and focused my thoughts on my land, specifically on the wardens. My heart was still racing a bit so it took longer than usual. My view went from atop Jaired to the entire Shaws. With a few slow breaths I was able to see the tiny blue outlines of my wardens scattered across the land. All the wardens reached out with the standard "Everything okay?" feeling and I assured them thus. Gregare, however, I gave a specific and urgent feeling of concern.

He responded with feelings of concern and willingness to help. Gregare, for all his weirdness, always gave himself to the people. He was older and far wiser than me. Also, I will never forget his gesture of faith by helping me with the head warden appointment. I sent him images of Jaired flying to him with Teega and Annie in tow. He replied with visuals, his location, and where to safely land.

I disconnected and relayed the image to Jaired. *Make haste, my friend. I don't want to lose the opportunity.*

Jaired powered us forward and faster than I'd ever seen. A thrill of excitement, of the hunter in him, spread to all of us. Annie let out an encouraging yell while Teega laughed in joy. I tightly gripped his feathers and leaned forward to help with the speed.

CHAPTER 19

"You need a bath, Greg," I said with a smile as I stepped forward to hug the warden. "And that's coming from me."

A guttural sound that could be mistaken for a gurgling swamp came from the man. His voice was just a tad clearer than his laugh. "Must be bad."

I released and stepped back. It'd been almost a season since I'd last seen him without telepathy and he looked the same, down to the dirt smudges on his cheeks. Standing a head shorter than me with a ratty, twig-filled hat, he was thicker than most of our people, too.

In many ways, he looked like a Yeryan. Annie and I guessed his height was nature's way of best suiting him to the land. The trees in The Marshes were not towering like those to the north. These trees were two or three people tall, but the trunks were thicker and the branches, too. The leaves were also thicker and wider. Gregare had used them to make his hat since they repelled water and heat better than anything.

Gregare's clothes weren't raggy, they just looked that way from the wetness that came with protecting the marshland. We landed only a few minutes ago and my clothes were already soaked from the humidity as if I ran here from Our Place. Even though he was wearing more layers than I was, Gregare hadn't broken a sweat. He was even growing a thick beard and showed no signs of being hot.

"You have adapted well, old friend," I remarked. Gregare just gave me a wink.

Annie stepped forward and gingerly offered her hand only to swing it around her back and make an awkward bow. I stifled a laugh, Jaired laughed with a growl, but Gregare just nodded back in kind. Annie kept her eyes averted from his and walked back to stand next to a nervous Teega.

"My name is Gregare, Lady Dewarian," Gregare announced to a startled Teega.

She had been fidgeting nervously with her shirt while looking at him for a moment then quickly looked away. Once he said "Lady," however, she perked up as if he snapped a branch against her back.

Gregare stepped forward and Teega stepped back, her hands fidgeting even quicker. He stopped after one step and turned to me. "She didn't tell you?"

I shrugged. "I have no idea what you're talking about."

Annie seethed biting words at The Marshes warden. "We've been busy."

"Cease," I commanded and waved a right hand at her and energy knocked her in the shoulder. "You will learn respect."

No more complaints from you with my methods, Jaired said to me specifically.

I glared at him, but said nothing. "Greg, what are you talking about?"

"She's a thief." His tone was as matter-of-fact as the dull haze of The Marshes.

"Not completely," I said. "The transformation has not completed."

Shaking his head, he restated, "No, I mean she stole from me."

"It was to survive!" Teega interrupted with a burst of energy that caused a group of frogs to croak and jump away. She turned to notice nature's response then slouched her shoulders and shuffled closer to Annie in embarrassment.

I honestly didn't care about this right now. I needed to get to the thieves. I needed to stop them. As much as I wanted to yell that to everyone, I left that behavior to Annie. So I squatted down, put my elbows on my knees and rubbed my eyes with my palms. "Look, I'm really tired and really hungry. I don't want to deal with this right now."

"Tis something we can come back to, Brim." Gregare turned away from everyone and headed towards a clump of large leaf trees that had been growing out a mound of dark green and black moss common to the tiny hills of The Marshes. "I'll get the tea and food going."

"Thank you." I stood and looked to the others. "Jaired, stand guard please. Annie and Teega, don't piss off Greg."

Annie smiled her loving smile at me. "I'll wait until after your belly is full. You big baby."

The corner of my mouth twitched at the humor. I nodded in appreciation and followed Gregare into his hut. I heard Annie's feet, but I did not hear Teega.

"Teega, you'll be okay. He's not going to hurt you. Or kill you. Just feed you." Annie's voice was calm to the point of a lull.

I looked over my shoulder and my eyes met Teega's worried ones. *You are safe.*

I don't believe you. She looked at me, then at the hut, then out into the marsh. I could feel her confusion and a tinge of fear.

I forgot to prepare her for this part of our land. The Shaws has a specific distinction with trees being a certain way, clouds being a certain way, and most importantly, sunlight being a certain way. The Marshes has scattered clumps of trees that are a dark brown instead of dark green like The Shaws. Their leaves are almost black. There aren't any clouds and the sun is never visible except as you near the Traders Ocean to the south. Instead there is a permanent haze that alternates between a muddy brown color and a muddy yellow color. The haze prevented seeing into the distance with any great accuracy. It's definitely not a happy place compared to my home.

My stomach growled again as did my impatience. *Jaired, would you mind?*

Jaired had been in panther form since we landed. He jumped up, transformed into an owl and flew to Teega's shoulder. The moment he landed, the Dewarian noticeably calmed and started following the rest of us.

"But where is the hut? All I see is a mound of moss stuck between some trees."

It was Gregare who answered her question. "That is the hut, Lady. Always we must blend. Whether that's amongst the swamp or in our caverns."

I heard the subtle yet quick intake of air from Teega when she heard "caverns." It took a few moments, but eventually Teega's footsteps could be heard as we all made our way to Gregare's home.

I reached out to Annie. *What's with the Lady?*

Got me.

Did you ask her?

Tried. She's stone cold right now.

I shook my head. *Women.*

Yes, because you're such an open book.

I waved my hand at her again, but her aura was already at the ready and the energy I sent bounced off it and hit me in the shoulder.

I deserved that.

Her reply was a smile and sometimes that's all the words you need.

CHAPTER 20

The sun was setting in The Marshes as the only light that crept in the hut came through the smoke hole in the center. Jaired, however, kept covering the hole with his wings as he watched over us.

Gregare had to walk to the back of the hut and, with a heavy grunt, push a log out from the middle of the wall to allow some smoke to escape. Then he reached toward the campfire smoke with an open palm, closed his palm, then threw his fist at the open hole. The smoke followed the magical tunnel Gregare just made.

"That's a little better," Annie grumbled.

One day I will have to stop rolling my eyes at her. *Don't act like you're not impressed with his magic.*

Annie snorted. *Whatever.*

Fine. If she was going to be that way then a little reminder of the power of humility would do her some good. I cleared my throat. "Annie, are you still upset over what happened between you two? Wasn't that four or five seasons ago?"

Annie glared at me, which had to be the second time in the last two minutes, but said nothing. I smiled greedily and slapped my hands together in excitement.

"Looks like I'm telling the story to our new friend." I began, "So we were visiting The Marshes in search of a poison remedy."

"Those cold western marshes," Gregare mumbled. "You should

appoint a warden for that area."

"Too much for you, old man?" I asked with just the right amount of challenge.

Gregare looked up from the cooking pot above the fire and stopped serving. His face looked fierce in the light of the fire especially given the fire was the only substantial source of light. He pointed the tip of the ladle at me. "You will be served last."

"Still worth it," I retorted. Before he could worsen my punishment, I continued. "Annie was having a difficult time there. She'd never been in that cold and damp environment before."

Annie scooted closer to the fire as if the memory brought forth some of the cold. Even her aura pulled in close to her skin like a thick, green coat.

I looked to Teega. Her interest was definitely piqued, but she was keeping a noticeable distance from Gregare. She kept her body still with her hands behind her back. She wasn't fooling anyone, however, as the fidgeting of her hands was quite easy for a Tree Maker to hear. Maybe this story would put her at ease a little bit.

I continued the story. "We were trying to find Gregare because I had told him to hide as best he could so Annie could practice her tracking."

"And you had no idea where he was either," Annie whispered.

"Oh please. He has a tell. You just have to figure it out." I paused and winked at Gregare. He told me his tell just in case I needed to find him in the future. "We're walking along a bog shore and Annie was so focused on looking for the tiniest signs at her feet that she walked straight into a tree. Then she tried to stop from falling and put her hand on a thorn bush which caused her to jerk the opposite way and fall into the bog."

I sent an image of the mud-soaked Annie from my memory to everyone in the room.

The presence of Gregare kept Teega's laugh at bay, but the laughter in her belly couldn't be completely contained so it came out in a painful snort.

"I lost it. I laughed and laughed and refused to help Annie up as she was stuck in the mud."

"And her aura wouldn't do anything except attract more mud," added Gregare.

I laughed louder. "I forgot about that!"

The corners of Annie's mouth curved upward and I knew I had her.

"Annie, tell the rest," I ordered.

In the softest of voices, she continued the tale. "I eventually sat up and got to shore. Brim was too busy laughing to notice that someone was moving behind him with a spear in hand. I jumped over Brim to attack the enemy only to find the enemy had never been there and was covering up deep, peat hole.

I erupted in more laughter and a few tears started to fall down my cheek. "Greg, I owe you so much for that. She was dirty and stinky for months."

Gregare just shrugged, his face deadpan. "She needed to learn the lesson about feeling before she took action."

Annie finally looked up at Gregare, her aura starting to pulse in anger. "You could have warned me that there wasn't an enemy, it was just your magic."

"True," he replied without looking up.

"You could have helped get that stink off me."

"True," he repeated while stirring the pot.

I caught my breath and added. "You could have asked him for help."

He looked up from his stirring to meet Annie's eyes. "That is the most true."

In her pouting voice, she stated, "You wouldn't have helped if I did ask."

"Not true," Gregare and I said in unison.

Annie's aura transitioned from thick to translucent and pushed away from her skin.

"I believe you've been forgiven, Greg," I said smugly.

Before he could respond, Annie's aura turned to daggers and picked up some of the energy from the fire. They actually burned my skin.

"You," Gregare growled, "also need to learn when to let the bear sleep."

I rubbed my right forearm. "Yeah, probably."

Jaired finally joined the conversation. *You have no idea.*

"Something smells delicious," I said, excitedly hoping to change the subject. "I haven't eaten for two days."

I forgot to mention that part of being a Tree Maker is how we can go weeks without eating. The major side effect appears to be diminished powers and a little grumpiness. Supposedly there was a rare effect of sleeping for an entire season, but there were suspicious circumstances surrounding that situation. A while back, an elder fell into the season-long slumber after not eating for months. It ended up scaring a lot of the people.

I wasn't so easily fooled. I had my theory that Annie actually put something in his water, but I couldn't prove it. Honestly, I didn't want to prove it because I didn't particularly like that elder. Jaired didn't even bother acknowledging the request for help from the other elders. The elder eventually woke up with no idea why he was so tired although he mentioned his tea had an unusual emerald hue.

"Foolish boy. Food is too good to ignore." Gregare commented. He kept stirring the tiny pot above the fire. He reached into his left jacket pocket then his right before pulling out something and dropping it into the pot. There was a quick burst of yellow smoke and a loud pop then he resumed stirring.

"What was—" Annie started asking, but I stayed her question with a hand on her knee.

Shaking my head, I said, "No. You don't want to know. Jaired doesn't want to know. I definitely don't want to know."

She looked at me in confusion. "Why not? Think he's going to lie to us?"

I laughed at the same moment that Gregare snorted. "The problem is I know he won't lie to us. It tastes good and that's all I care about."

"You're the boss," Annie replied and reached out for a bowl that

Gregare had just filled up. Gregare walked right by her and out the hut. "But...what...where is he going?"

I just shook my head. "So easily you forget the rules."

"What rules?"

"The powerful eat first. Not the prettiest."

She seemed miffed at my answer, but also flattered so she let it go. With her elbow, she nudged me to look at Teega.

Teega had yet to sit down since we entered the hut. At first, she couldn't take her eyes off the hole in the center of the roof where Jaired was currently perched. I couldn't blame her since the first time I was here, I was blown away, too.

We were actually in the base of a massive, hollow tree. Gregare had been communicating with this living tree for as long as I've known him. He told me its top had been blown off during a rare storm and it was still recovering. However, with his help, the tree was healing quicker than normal. The gift to the warden for his help came in the form of a home.

The room we sat in could have almost accommodated Jaired in flight form if one side of his wings was folded in. Opposite the entrance at the back of the room was a wooden wall growing from the tree's roots. Gregare's bedroom and armory were back there. If memory serves, Gregare told me he was working with the tree on creating underground tunnels. He definitely had a preference to being inside or underground as opposed up in a tree like most Tree Makers.

Now Teega had moved onto the various collections of Gregare's. There weren't any skeletons since Tree Makers weren't those kind of hunters. Hunters of necessity used every bit of the animal for survival. Hunters of pride used every bit of the animal for boast. There were, however, various furs and skins that were molded, sewn or hammered into a functional object. In fact, I'm pretty sure he had made a fishing pole out of the thigh bone of an animal I'd never seen before. My guess is it was a bird, but there aren't many birds in these parts. One day, I'll have to ask him about it.

Gregare walked back in, grabbed a few more hand-carved bowls from a shelf and made his way back to the stew. He filled up one bowl and handed it to Annie. He did the same with a bowl for me although mine was bigger. Annie glared at me, but I shook my head ever so slightly. It wasn't polite to dictate how a host feeds the guests.

"Careful with that, dearie," Gregare whispered.

Annie stopped eating mid-bite and nodded her head in Teega's direction again. Gregare had approached her, with food in hand, and was whispering with Teega. His lack of response to seeing a different race intimated she wasn't the first of her kind that he'd seen. And he didn't make a fuss about keeping her out of his home so there wasn't any hostility despite whatever transgression had occurred. He wouldn't have done anything to her anyways with Jaired here.

Teega hesitantly took the bowl with her left hand, but had her right reaching toward a stick leaning against the wall.

I closed my eyes and tuned into the conversation.

Teega said, "I promise I wasn't stealing."

"I know that now, Lady," Gregare replied. I could feel the magic he was infusing in his words to calm her.

"And I didn't mean to touch your walking stick out of disrespect," she added then gave a slight bow. "I'm sorry, warden."

I opened my eyes and stood to watch the exchange. Annie followed my lead.

"No apology is necessary, Lady."

Even with only the flickering of the campfire light, I could see Teega's face was stretched tight from stress.

In a firm voice, she asked, "Why do you keep saying that?"

Gregare ignored her and grabbed the walking stick. The stick was same color as the leaves on Gregare's hat and had various carvings etched all over. The carvings seemed to be dancing in the light of the campfire. I wasn't sure if it was a trick of the eyes because of the smoke and hazy light or if it was magic. It definitely could have been the latter since Gregare knows magic in a way that no other ever could. He's not obvious about his magic; he's all about subtlety. It's the way in the The Marshes to avoid drawing attention to yourself. Although the dancing of the light also reminded me of Teega's garb from the memory walk.

"Help yourself, Lady." He held the walking stick out for her. "Just be careful; he's a bit ticklish."

She didn't grab the stick, but finally took a helping of the stew. The stress in her face almost immediately disappeared once she swallowed the food. "He? You name all your walking sticks?"

"Yes, she asks a lot of questions." I said between mouthfuls.

Gregare has never been a huge fan of questions. It's best you ask one or two that will get him talking for a long time. Too many questions and he'll just shrug you off and seek patience from the moonshine beneath his coat.

He looked at me. "Dewarians. Very into others. Not much into sharing about themselves."

It's a day of surprises, I thought. He did know about them.

"You've met others?" Annie asked.

Before Gregare could reply, I answered. "Really? You're going to ask that after what he just said?"

"Oh, go easy, Brim," Gregare scolded.

"What? You would have never let me slide with questions like that. You or Jaired."

She's nicer, Jaired's voice rumbled through us all.

I looked around the room at everyone looking at me and nodding in agreement. "To the hells with you. I'm just going to shut up and eat."

I walked over to the cooking pot, refilled my bowl then sat down next to Annie. They slowly walked back over as well. Gregare was the last to walk over, but carefully set the walking stick against one of the wooden poles holding up the cooking pot.

"That's the Brim we love," commented Annie.

"When did you last see one of my people?" Teega asked as she sat down across from Annie. She kept one eye on that stick. Something about it was obviously nagging at her.

"Long time ago. Too many seasons have gone by," he paused and looked up. Teega followed his eyes then looked back at her bowl. "Yes, about ten. Jaired's right."

Jaired and Gregare had a connection like Jaired and myself. It wasn't as strong, but there was a mutual respect. Honestly, I thought it was because they were both so similar. Not willing to volunteer information, not willing to deal with too many questions, and possessing that unwavering loyalty.

"Those markings look so familiar," Teega remarked as she motioned toward the walking stick.

"Ha! I would hope so. He's from your land, Lady."

Teega ignored that last part of being from her land. Her voice was now beginning to strain in fear. "Why do you keep saying 'he'?"

Part of my birth tattoo started to tingle. The tingle wasn't one of imminent threat, but it was one of caution. I set my bowl down and fixated on the stick to my right, just over Annie's shoulder. I also noticed the growing green of Annie's aura. She didn't notice the aura until it covered up her bowl. Immediately, she set her bowl down and looked to me.

I gestured at the stick and whispered, "Patience."

Gregare sat down next to Teega. He looked at her, took her hand, and said, "Do not fear. Do not be scared, Lady."

Before she could reply, he leaned forward and whispered something unintelligible toward the stick. The firelight swirled inside the carvings on the stick. Then it melted to the ground in one dark green mass before solidifying into in a curled, scaly mess.

I heard the slight hissing noise before I saw the head of the black snake stretch out toward Gregare. The snake's head was as big as both my fists yet its body was only as big as one as it stretched out a good eight feet. Flaming red eyes, strikingly similar to the fires I saw in Teega's memory, lit up the scales on his head and revealing the various carvings. They were also similar to the carvings on the pillars in Teega's memory.

Annie's aura solidified. Tiny, dark green daggers within her aura were pointing at the snake, tracking its every slither. I placed my hand on Annie's knee, suppressing her desire to act.

All eyes were on Teega. She was trying to push away from Gregare, but he held his grip tight. She tried to speak, but every time her mouth opened, she covered it with her free hand. The waves of fear coming from her were so strong, worse than the fear I felt in her memory.

Gregare gave me a reassuring nod and I heard a soothing coo from Jaired make its way down the vent and echo around us. The snake slithered until it was across from Gregare. Then it coiled up its tail and lifted its head until it was eye level with Teega.

Gregare nodded to the snake as if to give permission. The snake opened its mouth, revealing flaming fangs. It hissed for a moment then stopped almost immediately as words came to everyone's mind the same way Jaired's did. *Welcome, Lady Teega of House Hopki of the Hopki Caverns. I am Chawpki. The father of all Ceguurs. And your humble servant.*

The snake's telepathic voice was the most formal that I'd ever heard from any creature. And it was definitely nothing near to anything I'd expected.

Eyes wide in shock, Teega managed to gasp, "Oh. Hi."

Then she passed out.

CHAPTER 21

To my surprise, Jaired didn't bring the hut down. I honestly expected him to transform, fly up, and thunder down on the roof and bring everything to the ground. Instead, he flew down the hut's central vent and landed on the lid of the cooking pot. He perched there, while in owl form, and his eyes remained on Teega not on the snake.

I wish Annie's reaction was as calm, but it was not. She giggled like a little child and rubbing her hands together in joy.

I chided, "You're just like a kid, you know that?"

She just shrugged her shoulder at me, but kept her smiling face focused on the snake who had slithered back to the darkened corner of the hut.

Gregare was leaning over Teega, putting a wet cloth on her forehead. He had taken off his jacket, bundled it, and placed it under her head. He turned to me and asked, "Brim, is she strong?"

"Very. Do not worry." The words came out easy and with conviction. I stood and filled up my bowl. I noticed Teega was breathing steadily and, when I reached out to her consciousness, I felt her mind just as steady. With a tiny nudge of energy, I woke her mind.

Annie felt my efforts and immediately set her bowl down, stood, and walked to Teega's side. Jaired flew to Annie, resting on her shoulder. Her aura moved away from her and enveloped Teega.

"Are you doing that?" Gregare looked at Annie. "I haven't seen much of that magic."

"Not magic. Just instinct," Annie replied without taking her eyes off Teega. She grabbed Teega's hand and squeezed.

Gregare mumbled in an ancient language that Annie didn't know, but I did.

"Gregare," I boomed and my voice made him waver. "Do not complain. You can either educate or remain silent."

I can tolerate a lot, but if he's going to gripe about ignorant Tree Makers and not help then I draw the line.

He stayed squatting for a moment then stood to look down at me. He was pissed and I knew it. He always felt he was too wise to be scolded like that or that he didn't have to answer to anyone. He was wrong.

I turned my back on him and sat back down to eat. A simple gesture that I knew he'd understand. A back turned means the point isn't up for discussion.

The warden paced around the hut a few times then left outside for a few minutes.

Annie cleared her throat. "Is he mad at me?"

I finished my stew and set the bowl on the floor. "No. He just forgets how to be around people. He sees them often as they travel through this land, but he's always far away. I think the last time he talked to anyone was me and that was a long while ago."

Annie just nodded at me then turned her attention back to Teega. "She's waking up."

The snake let out a low hiss and started slithering toward her.

"Chawpki, remain still," I addressed the snake. "And please, do not speak."

The snake swiveled its head to me and nodded. I've seen a lot of things in my long life, but I've never seen a snake nod. That would take some getting used to.

I walked around the fire and knelt down. Reaching down and around her back, I lifted Teega up to a sitting position. "Come on,

Teega. You're safe."

Slowly, her chin lifted off her chest and her eyes opened. They immediately looked to the darkened corner of the hut where the snake slithered back and forth. So much for staying still.

"You're safe," I repeated. "He's not here to harm you."

"He is here to do exactly that. The Ceguur did exactly that to so many of my people." Teega's voice dripped with venom. She pushed me away and stood. "I should…"

"You should take a breath and go outside," I advised. I gently nudged her arm and we headed outside.

The Marshes is a moody land. There was a permanent dark yellow haze hanging around, tinting the color of everything the way Annie's aura did. A drizzle of rain had been soaking the world outside the hut. My feet immediately sunk into a couple inches of mud with each step. Thankfully, the winds in this area are almost non-existent.

Teega, I noticed, hadn't sunken in the mud as she stormed out the entrance and frantically walked around in a circle, mumbling angry words to herself. Occasionally, she'd look up, set her feet then ball her fists as if she was going to charge into the hut and tear it down. Then she'd take a breath, turn away, and go back to mumbling.

"What's going on?" Annie asked as she walked out of the hut.

Jaired flew off her shoulder and made his way over to a fallen, twisted tree trunk several feet to the right of Gregare's home. He transformed into the panther once he landed. I could see steam coming off his black fur and I knew he was repelling the rain with a subtle heat on his fur. Show off.

"You have eyes. Look around," I replied. "And Gregare is nowhere to be found."

I scanned the clearing again. There were no landmarks to the west and south. Endless marshland with the same scattering of moss and bushes. To the north, off in the distance, stood the trees of The Shaws. And to the east, I could make out the Shim Hills: tiny, bunny hills covered in the same colored moss as Gregare's hut. They looked like tiny green feet against the gray legs of the giant trees of The

Shims.

May I join everyone? Chawpki's words resonated in my head, a little loud for my comfort, but the audible slight hiss with each word was more distracting.

Teega spun on her heels and faced the hut. I turned with her.

The snake was even more black in this light. It moved almost like black lava across the light brown mud. His energy was powerful, deeply powerful, yet he was hesitant.

I could feel a different energy from her, the same energy as when she went all fire mode on those thieves. There was so much hurt and so much anger and it ran deep. So I closed my eyes and tried to recall the same feeling I had in response to her fire. Opening my eyes, I looked down at my hand to see a subtle, winter blue leaking from the tips of my fingers. I walked over to her and gently put my hand on hers.

"Now is not the time." I kept my voice gentle and squeezed my hand a little harder. The icy blue energy poured into her hand.

Teega took her glare off the hut and looked down at my hand. She squeezed her hand back and the icy blue retreated back to my hand. "Let go, Brim. He's mine."

My hand became hot and I had to pull back for risk of burning. Now I was getting angry and I am far worse than Annie on her worst day. Jaired reached out to calm me and I just shut him out.

Annie stepped closer to Teega and put a hand on her other arm. Her green aura tried to envelop Teega, but could not.

My fingertips were glowing blue and my voice turned just as chilly. I opened my mouth to release the thundering command that would have frozen her to the ground. My voice, however, was not heard.

"Enough!" Gregare shouted like thunder. The power of the voice picked all of us (except Jaired and Chawpki, of course) off the ground and slammed us on our backs. "This is my home! You are my guests!"

I coughed to catch my breath, but the air didn't come easily. Gregare had pulled all humidity and left this area dry, primed for lightning strikes. Tiny bursts of light swirled in my vision as I stared at the sky. Vaguely, I could hear Annie and Teega coughing to catch their breaths. I leaned up on my elbows and looked at the figure now standing just past the hut entrance. Somehow I'd forgotten how dangerous Gregare can be.

The shadow he was casting wasn't normal; it had grown at least twenty feet wide, covering the entire hut. His face was lit by the periodic flashing thanks to the crackles of lightning shooting up from palms. His eyes were completely black save for the tiny flicker in the center that danced at the same time as the lightning sparking from his hands.

"Please accept our apologies, Gregare." I said with all the respect I could muster while sitting in mud.

"Like hell, I'm sorry!" Annie stood, her aura solid green and in full-on murder mode. "I'm going to put him on his back and see how he–"

I closed my eyes just in time. Even through closed eyes, however, I saw the brightness of the lightning. Annie let out a cry of pain and I heard her thud to the ground next to me. I opened my eyes and saw her body smoking, but not burned. Reaching out, I put my hand on hers and could feel her awake, but barely.

"Stay down. Be quiet," I commanded.

I faced Gregare. His shadow had grown and the lightning crackled with greater intensity and greater frequency. "Release your skyfall and return, dear friend."

He ignored me and lifted his hands at Annie. "Younglings. Need to be taught."

I let out a sigh. This was going to get ugly.

Calmly, I stated, "Then teach. Do not punish."

He ignored me again and stepped forward. The hairs on my arms started to rise due to the energy from his hands. I hadn't seen him this angry in a long time. Clearly, he'd been pushing down something for too long.

"Greg. Do not take another step or you will be put down." I knew that I could take him, but I also knew that I wouldn't have to. He was one of my wardens and he was far older and, in many ways, stronger than me. The one area he wasn't stronger was with friends. Friends like Jaired.

Jaired was the ultimate predator. No one had heard, seen, or felt him stalk The Marshes warden from behind except for me. About ten feet behind Gregare, Jaired's silver claws were digging into the mud and his muscles were flexed in anticipation. His tail was steady and he was crouched, ready to spring at any moment. Even crouched his shoulders were at my eye level.

I tried reaching out to his thoughts, but I hit a wall. There was no hope reasoning with him so I had to reason with Gregare or watch my old friend be mauled by my new friend.

I lifted arms, palms up, to Gregare. A simple gesture of nonviolence and peace that I hoped the logical side of him would see. His eyes were no longer glaring at Teega and moved on to my own. I wasn't sure how I was going to disarm him and I certainly didn't have all day to talk to him. The thieves were growing in numbers and my gut told me they were massing for some grand gesture. Also, Jaired wouldn't tolerate this situation for long. Thankfully, the gods stepped in so I didn't have to.

A hiss came from Gregare's left. *Gregare, they did not do this to me.*

The Marshes warden jerked his head to the snake, an arc of lightning spiked straight up from his hands. "She threatened you. She's angry with you at levels you can't see."

As silent and quick as Jaired, the snake slithered between Gregare and myself. *I can see. I know what happened in the homeland. I know the depth of the hatred. What she doesn't know is the truth.*

"Getting yourself killed isn't going to get us to that truth," I added.

"Your brethren. I feel their loss. One after another." Gregare's voice was angry and so very sad. "All my creatures...all my friends..."

I swore under my breath. In the heat of this moment and a day of events I could not dream, I forgot my friend's affinity for animals. A love above his own people for all the creatures of all the lands.

I addressed my question to Chawpki. "How bad is it?"

He swiveled his head to me, his large slit eyes slowly changed from angry red to a soft yellow. They bore into my own and down to my soul. *Once millions. Now less than a dozen.*

The words were a punch to my heart. And if it was a punch to mine then I can't imagine what Gregare felt. I hung my head. So much loss, so much anger. This land is supposed to be one of flourishing acceptance for all creatures then the thieves came along.

"Is it the thieves?"

Chawpki let out an angry hiss. *Yes.*

Gregare bellowed and the clouds answered his call. I heard thunder boom. We all turned to the sound and witness clouds rolling in like dark purple bed rolls. The clouds were moving faster than nature could move them. I turned back to Gregare and his arms were high, his eyes the color of the clouds, and with each bellow the thunder answered in kind.

Danger was coming. In his anger, he could easily wipe Annie, Teega, and myself from this earth and possibly cause permanent damage to the others. I could not allow that and I had an idea that could possibly derail the coming storm.

I reached out to Jaired. *Show him the black that we saw. Make him feel the evil spreading.*

Jaired jumped over Gregare's head, twisted in mid-air, and landed with his ferocious snout barely touching Gregare's nose. There was a crack of lightning and a bright light lit up the area, but no strike actually hit near us. Jaired growled at the same level of as the thunder above. The growl snapped Gregare out of his trance. His eye color returned to normal and he looked down to fall into Jaired's gaze.

I turned to Annie, her aura still solid, and pushed energy at her to shake her from the murder focus on the other warden. Her aura responded with an audible pop at my psychic touch and Annie came back to reality. I didn't hear Teega until her foot stepped in a tiny puddle. She stopped just in front of me and a few feet from Chawpki. Her backside was covered with mud, but there were no signs of smoke or burning from any lightning strike. My guess was her ability to inherently see and produce fire kept even nature's ultimate fire out of her way.

"What is he doing?" Teega's voice was a whisper.

"Sharing the visions of the spreading evil caused by the thieves," I replied.

Annie let out her own low growl. She'd clearly been spending too much time with Jaired. "So what? He's not going to care. He's too full of anger."

"Annie, what is the opposite of anger?"

She shook her head at me. "Even now you want to teach a lesson?"

I nodded. "Especially now."

I took a few breaths as we watch Jaired and Gregare remain locked in the gaze. Chawpki had begun circling both of them.

"Is he getting longer?" Teega said, interrupting my thoughts.

"I was wondering that, too." I replied and looked at Chawpki. "Sure enough. Each time he encircles them he is lengthening himself."

Annie joined the commentary. "I can feel him. He is pulling away the pain."

"No, he's adding to the pain," Teega corrected. "I can feel it."

"Sympathy," Annie stated. "That's the opposite of anger."

I nodded again. "Exactly. And Chawpki is helping Jaired channel the evil and sadness caused by the thieves."

Eventually the Ceguur's body had lengthened to the point where the head nearly touched the tail. With his increasing length and width, the power behind his circling created a moat in the mud.

Jaired let loose another growl then stepped back. His front claws were still digging into the mud, but his energy had lessened in intensity and anger.

He knows, Jaired announced to all.

Suddenly, Chawpki increased his pace to the point where I couldn't even tell where his head was and where his tail was. I didn't understand why he was moving so fast - let alone how - until I saw the light blue aura that was rising up from his body and creating a dome over Gregare and Jaired. It took only a few breaths and it encased them. Once it had fully-formed, there was a bright, searing white light that burst in all directions from Gregare. I turned my eyes away, but not before part of the light had temporarily burned into my vision.

I slowly opened my eyes and made sure the light show was over. Turning back to Gregare, I noticed that Chawpki had slowed to a crawl and Gregare had fallen to his knees. The lightning disappeared from his hands. There was a rush of air as the humidity returned. I looked to the sky and noticed the clouds had transitioned from deep purple to a light purple.

Jaired laid down on all fours, resting his head on his paws. Chawpki was still slowing down, but the blue shield remained in place. I heard him hiss a sorrowful hiss that caused my entire body to shiver. In my peripheral, I saw Teega and Annie shiver as well.

There was another clap of thunder, but it was muted by comparison to earlier. Somewhere behind me lightning cracked and echoed across the land. Rain started to fall one tiny drop after another. Nature was calling out to me and my body started walking towards Gregare before I could tell it to.

I stepped over Chawpki and something in me knew that I could cross through the shield without harm. I knelt and put my left hand on Gregare's right shoulder. Annie, following close behind me, also knelt down next to me and put her right arm on the warden's left shoulder.

Gregare's eyes did not meet ours and they did not need to. The moment our hands touched his shoulders, we felt his sorrow. We felt the depth of his pain.

The rain started falling faster, but each drop that hit us didn't give us chills and did not soak our clothes. Instead each drop that found our bodies gave us a tiny bit of peace as nature mourned with us.

CHAPTER 22

"Um, Brim," Teega's voice was laced with concern. The others must have felt it because even Gregare looked up.

I turned around and Teega was standing just outside the circle, the gem in her necklace had begun to glow a vibrant red. I could see the beginning of another vortex. My heart beat faster at the idea of having another vision of that land.

Do not worry. That is a family heirloom, Chawpki announced to all.

The snake broke the circle and the light blue shield popped. He began slithering toward her and, to my surprise, Teega did not back away from him.

The color in Teega's face was draining. In a weakening voice, she said, "I can feel it pulling me away."

Chawpki reached Teega and lifted himself up to her height. His eyes began glowing red again and he opened his mouth, revealing those long fangs. Green began filling my vision, but I reached out to Annie's mind and pushed a patient energy to her. Slowly, the green faded from my sight.

"He would die before ever harming her," Gregare said in an emotionally-drained and cracked voice. The rain began to pull back its fall once his words hit the air. "His family has a blood oath to protect. It cannot be undone."

"Any oath can be undone," Annie snapped.

Gregare let out a sigh - oddly familiar to my own. "No, child. Not any."

"He's right, Annie. Nature can bind people so even if they try to betray the oath then it will take them out," I clarified. The green immediately faded from my vision.

Chawpki hissed something in the same language Teega had used to wake Annie back in Our Place. I watched as color returned to Teega's face and the red light from the gem swirled away from Teega and into Chawpki's open mouth. It took just a minute and everything was back to normal. Chawpki lowered himself and slithered back to Gregare's side.

"Thank you, Chawpki." Teega said as she tucked the necklace under her shirt.

Of course, Lady, the snake replied with a bow of his black-scaled head.

"Why did that happen?" Teega asked.

Jaired showed his fangs and let loose a growl that vibrated the ground. He strutted over to the fallen log, laid down then stretched out on the mossy earth. Everyone except Chawpki looked to me for an answer to the gesture.

I laughed awkwardly. "That's his way of saying it's not important right now."

"Who is he to decide..." Annie started questioning. She stopped immediately when Jaired growled again.

Teega seemed lost in a world that didn't include Jaired. I couldn't blame her, given everything that had passed today. She walked toward me and I saw the growing smirk at the corner of her mouth. "Are you going to sit in the mud all night? You weird outsider."

I smiled. "Eh, it's only mud."

As I stood, the wet mud fell off my clothes as if it were dust. I looked up to Teega and gave an arrogant shrug. "We're kind of a big deal."

"You know—"

"Yeah, I know. Arrogance or something like that, but you deserve it. You called me an outsider."

"Well, what is the true name of your people?"

"Oh, so now you don't mind asking such personal things." I looked at her and winked.

She smiled back. "You're right. That was personal."

"I honestly don't know." I replied. "I suppose I could ask the elders."

"Like they would tell you," Annie remarked bitterly. She rose to her feet, along with Gregare and they looked as I did: mud-free.

"True. They do like their secrets." I turned to The Marshes warden. "Greg, do you know?"

To my surprise, he shook his head. "It hasn't been spoken in so long. It might be back in my head somewhere. Although there isn't enough Rawin weed to smoke that would get down that deep."

A silence fell over us and our focus went back to the hut. A light smoke still drifted up from the fire, but during Gregare's outburst, part of the roof blew away. A log or two crackled and a few tiny sparks floated up.

I know it, Chawpki answered.

His words were hitting my mind, but he made an audible hissing when he spoke telepathically. It was still awkward because I was used to silence from Jaired - save his growls.

Teega looked at the snake. "How do you know? You're not from here."

Chawpki slithered forward a bit so he could fully see the Dewarian. *I know many things, my liege.*

Teega shook her head and smiled. "You're as bad as Jaired. So elusive."

Jaired whipped his tail out, transformed the sharp end into a soft fluff of fur, and playfully hit her in the hips. She toppled into the mud. Everyone laughed. Jaired growled again and the snake hissed in reply. I looked to Annie then to Gregare to check if they heard something. Both shrugged in wonder.

"What did you two say?" I asked.

The beast lord made disparaging remarks about how simple you mortals can be due to your inherent inability to think prior to speaking.

Annie smirked. "That's way too formal for Jaired."

The snake opened his mouth just a sliver which I'd learned was his way of smiling. *Yes, he is more precise. Consequently, more humorous as well.*

Chawpki hissed at Jaired and he replied with a couple growls that sounded eerily like laughter.

Teega stood and brushed the mud off her pants and wiped most of it off her face. She glared at Jaired, but the humor found her eyes.

Annie and Teega walked around Jaired, sat down, and leaned up against his other side. His only response was shifting his weight so they were more comfortable. I gave Gregare a reassuring squeeze with my hand. Then I walked over to sit across from Annie and Teega.

"As much as I want to hear it, I'm positive that everyone here wants to know something else." Teega looked around the camp, her smile falling on Annie next to her.

"Where do I start? Father of all Ceguur? Your 'liege'? You are royalty?" Annie fired off questions so quickly like she'd only been focusing on that since this all went down.

"Slow down, Annie. This part is for Teega," I said.

My apprentice furrowed her eyebrows. "Yes, but Teega is one of us now."

"Thank you, Annie." Teega's voice was warm and appreciative. "That means so much to me."

Annie returned the warmth with a deep nod.

It means a great deal because her family was killed, Chawpki stated to all.

Teega grimaced. A wave of sadness, anger and regret crashing all around her. Jaired whipped his tail a couple times as a warning then wrapped it around Teega's torso for comfort. She held onto Jaired's tail the way a child holds onto a parent's arm. Her voice, however, came out like the snake's hiss. "Yes. Killed by your people."

That is the story you were told. The snake slithered past Gregare and stopped between Teega and myself.

I tensed for a moment. Having a snake that size so close to me was something I still wasn't used to. We didn't have snakes in our land - as far as I knew - and we had very few creatures with the level of intellect and telepathy like Jaired. And it was a snake! Thanks to traders, our people had only seen their skins and tasted their meat. We had never seen any alive.

Teega's fury started to rise, flecks of golden fire starting to grow in her eyes. "That is not just the story I was told. That's—"

Chawpki shook his head. *Yes, that is what you saw, my liege. That is not the truth of what happened though.*

"My mother bled out as I was dragged from House Hopki! I saw the life drain from her eyes as my heart broke!"

The snake blinked and I saw something that no other creature - not even Jaired - had ever done: he cried faint fiery red tears. *Mysheran. She was a beautiful, caring person.*

"Do not speak of my mother," Teega seethed. The veins in her hands bulged as she gripped Jaired's tail tighter.

But I must, my liege. I was her adviser. I was her confidant. I kept her alive so the sickness could not take her.

"Lies!" Teega shouted. She tried to stand, but Jaired tightened his tail and rammed the tip into the ground, sealing her in place.

"I think I'll sit by Brim," Annie commented. She got up and made her way to my side. "Not really feeling like being in the middle of this."

Teega just ignored her. "My mother had no beast with her. She had me. She had my father."

I reached out to the snake's thoughts. *Tread lightly, Master Chawpki.*

Chawpki turned to me and nodded. He uncoiled himself a little more and lowered himself before Teega.

My liege, the loss of your mother will pain me long after the last breaths leave your old, refined body. That being said, I was her second. You just did not see me because you could not yet.

She crossed her arms and turned away like an upset child. "I would have seen a snake."

No, you could not because your mother veiled me. He paused until Teega turned back to him. *Brim knows of veils.*

"I know how to become invisible, but not to veil myself as something or someone else," I added.

The snake blinked at me in shock then turned to Jaired. The panther rumbled and the snake nodded. *You will in time.*

"What did she veil you as? A cup or a plate?" Teega threw it out in mockery.

Exactly, my liege. Chawpki coiled himself up. It looked like he was ready to strike, but great pride was swelling outward. *Every time someone placed a goblet in front of her, she would...*

"Tip the scepter to bless it," Teega finished. She looked across the endless marshes as if being pulled to that memory.

"She wasn't blessing it, was she?" I asked.

Chawpki turned his head to me. *That is the story she told everyone. I was tasting it for poison. And when she got sick, I used my people's gift to keep her alive.*

Teega shook her head, disbelieving. "She was never sick. She would have told me."

The snake let out a long hiss. *You are a proud people. You know she would not have told anyone especially the one she loved the most. She did not want you to worry.*

"Lies," she muttered under her breath, her gaze still far away.

Chawpki, words will not hold her. It will not hold any of us." I positioned my words carefully with the personal pride of the Dewarians. "Show her."

"No," Teega declared, fire in her eyes. "I will not be swayed with visions from that!"

I sprung myself off the ground, flipped backwards then landed with the sound force of a small quake. I directed telepathic words directly and solely for Teega to hear.

I'm saving your pride in front of all of us. I've saved your life. I own your life. I paused to voice the last line so everyone knew. "You owe me your fealty."

Teega wrapped her arms tight around Jaired's tail and scooted herself deeper into his black-furred body. The defiant child had disappeared and now she was just scared. The fire in her eyes were gone. Only the deep green of an innocent tree line could be seen; and her hands were shaking.

I looked down and could see why she was so frightened. It wasn't just because of my powerful (and somewhat dramatic) gesture. Teega's fright came from the ice that was freezing the ground and spreading directly for her. As a person that lives in the warmth of fire and underground away from all the elements, I'm sure it was terrifying to be encased in all that cold and ice.

Jaired lifted his head and bared his teeth at me. *Enough*, his voice boomed in my head.

Chawpki slithered between the growing ice and Teega. He opened his mouth and let out a deep hiss. Red mist started to slip out of his mouth and shroud the Ceguur, then expand to cover Teega and Jaired. The ice hit the red mist and instead of melting, it disappeared completely.

Whatever anger was in me disappeared quicker than that ice. I could not hide my excitement as I said, "Okay, that's amazing!"

"And I'm the kid," Annie mumbled under her breath.

I looked at her and shrugged. "Sometimes frustration gets the best of me, too. And this aura is entirely new to me."

I reached out to Jaired for answers with the aura, but he shrugged me off. Something to be answered later, I hope.

Gregare had walked over to the fire to scrape out the remaining stew. He walked back with a steaming bowl in hand and sat down next to us. "No, you don't. That's why you're the boss."

I turned away from Chawpki and the red mist and sat back down next to Annie. Jaired let out a soft growl and the snake closed his mouth. The mist dissipated into nothing. Teega was no longer shaking in fear, but there were more tears than before. The royal servant turned to Teega and bowed. He started to slither back to Gregare, but stopped once Teega started to speak.

"I remember now," Teega voice wavered and scratched. "She fell.

Someone shot her from a ship and she raised the staff. But she couldn't have raised the staff because she was on the ground. You raised up and sprayed the mist that burned all the arrows that tried to finish her off."

Turning back to her, Chawpki nodded. *Yes, my liege. Let me show you all.*

The Ceguur closed his eyes and started to glow a subtle blue, channeling some energy. I started to get an image of giant wooden ships, their sails on fire, but Teega's words canceled the memory.

"That arrow, it went through her. It should have killed her, my father told me. But the clerics healed her." Teega said in a sad voice. Apparently, Chawpki showing just a glimpse of an image was enough to uncover her buried memories. Tears still falling from her eyes, she asked, "It wasn't the clerics was it?"

No, my liege. Chawpki opened his eyes - the blue light fading - and stared at Teega. Slowly, it was getting easier for me to understand him and the hiss in my head was less. *I gave part of my life to save her that day.*

Chawpki moved to Teega and uncoiled himself completely. She leaned forward, one hand still tight on Jaired's tail, and reached out to the snake's tail tip. Her finger ran over a long gray scar.

I gave her my blood for many moons. Then I had to give more than blood. I gave too much. The snake words were sorrowful, but not regretful.

"What was there?" Annie asked. Annie even reached out, her green aura instinctively glowing around her fingertips as it protected her. The snake didn't recoil from her touch.

My people have two tails. We can get by with one, but...

I finished his thought. "I would not want to live with just one leg. My life could not be anywhere near the dream it is now."

Chawpki gave a low hiss.

Teega pulled her hand away and looked at her stomach. She pulled up her shirt to reveal a scar in her ribcage. Her finger ran over the scar. "I almost died by the same people."

Yes, my liege, the snake replied.

I knew Chawpki kept repeating those same words to build that respect and position of power beneath Teega. It was subtle, repetitive and wise. I doubt Teega noticed that she was being played, but at least it was in a good way.

"I'd pushed it away. My memory is only of my mother dying, my people dying. Your kind murdering them all." Teega sobbed for a moment. "So many Ceguur murdering so many of my people.

Your mother wanted you to think that. She needed others to believe we had turned so she could save us from them.

"Them? Who are they?" Annie asked.

Jaired bared his teeth at Annie and growled.

Chawpki hissed and whipped his head at Annie. *We do not speak their name.*

Annie put her palms up then bowed in submission to Jaired. "Okay, okay. Forget I asked."

I looked between Jaired and Chawpki and made a promise that I was going to find out what they were hiding.

"How did I survive?" Teega's voice still wavered.

Chawpki turned back to Teega. *My liege, that was my daughter. She also gave her other tail and so much more.*

Teega closed her eyes and wiped away the tears. "I do not remember her being there."

The snake opened his mouth in a laugh. *Your mother would not have it any other way. My daughter is like the beast lord. She could take shapes that I could only dream of. She was always by your side.*

Teega opened her eyes. "Did she die for me?"

No, child, she did not, the snake replied. *She was taken.*

Then Chawpki looked to me, his eyes burning bright red. *I believe she is the reason for all the destruction in your land. I believe she is giving the thieves their power.*

CHAPTER 23

We can all imprint ourselves onto people. These imprints allow us to feel when they are in danger, Chawpki stated. *Angwiki possesses a unique ability like no other Ceguur. She can imprint herself in such a way that she can see, feel, and hear everything the person is going through.*

I looked to Teega and caught her grimace. Any person wouldn't want their most intimate moments shared with others. I could only imagine how a member of such a private race would be terrified of anyone so easily prying into their life.

Chawpki caught her worry, too. He looked to Teega and gave another graceful nod. *They cannot share anything even under torture or threat of death.*

Teega let out a long, pent-up breath.

"Chawpki, you're bowing. I know it's out of respect, but there is something else there." I paused to pin down my guess. "A precognition, maybe?"

The Ceguur opened his mouth in a laugh. *Yes, indeed, warden. Most do not ascertain the second part.*

I gave him an endearing smile. "The likes of Jaired and yourself are rare. We're usually too caught up in the telepathic part to notice any other behavior."

Agreed. However, you are cognizant of the existence of others like Jaired and myself.

It was my turn to bow. "Picking up on my own thoughts, I see."

He hissed another laugh.

"But you always said to ask others before reading their thoughts. You repeat that every single time," Annie explained with an annoyance.

"And I will continue to repeat that," I reiterated.

Annie crossed her arms. "And he gets away with a simple bow?"

"His ability to read thoughts is instinctive, like your aura." I paused as another thought occurred to me. I turned to Chawpki and searched for permission. He gave me a bow of approval. I continued, "What I'm teaching you is not instinctive. Therefore, we have to show respect. He shows respect because he could flex his powers and share everything."

Annie glared at me, still disbelieving. "It's not fair. We are all equals."

"No, we are not, child," Gregare stated.

Lead her to it instead of stating the end results, I commanded to the stubborn warden. I'll make him ready for an apprentice one day.

Chawpki slithered over to him and transformed into the walking stick. Gregare grabbed the stick and leaned heavily on it as he pulled himself up. The warden's energy was still waning from the outburst earlier.

"Jaired can transform into more creatures than he shows us. Chawpki has more tricks than he lets on. I can do more than the lightning show you just saw," Gregare said. He looked to me. "And you, well, you have power that scares me."

"I do?" His comment shocked me. I mean, I know I'm powerful, but he's older and far more powerful. Or at least I assumed so.

Chawpki said, *He is correct. You are actually older than your memories reveal. Thus you are more powerful than you realize.*

I shook my head in disbelief. Yet the image from Teega's memory, my etching on the pillar, was older than anything I'd seen. I opened my mouth to ask a million questions, but shut it since it wasn't my time to be the student.

Gregare continued. "Annie, your aura could lay waste to our entire continent. We could end up like Dewaria."

I wondered if that's what happened to their surface. Now that is a loaded question, but definitely one for another time. As much as I enjoyed filling in the dark gaps of knowledge with light as bright as the summer sun, we had a mission to get to. Eventually.

"And me?" Teega asked softly.

"Fire so hot it could melt The Sairs," Gregare stomped his foot on the ground for effect. "Now tell me Annie, how is any of that fair?"

"Well, it's..." Annie flustered and re-crossed her arms.

"It's not. Existence isn't about fairness. It's not about right or wrong. It's about balance." The scraggy-bearded warden walked over to the fire and grabbed a log that was half on fire. Without warning, he threw the fiery log at me. Unlike my normal enemies, Gregare had serious power and speed behind his movements.

I had only the moment to see something coming at me, but no time to process it. Instinct took over. Instinct stopped the log midair, just inches before my face. Instinct filled me with anger so absolute about never wanting to face this challenge again. So I disassembled the log into all its components. The fire immediately disappeared and the smoke followed suit. Then the bark fell away to the ground. Finally, each ring of that log fell away as if I was reversing its growth. As the wood fell to the ground, it transformed into dirt. Where the log had started is where it ended.

Since everyone had been watching with awe, they didn't pay attention to the warden except me.

I saw Gregare grab a hollowed branch from under his cloak and blow a poison dart at Annie's face. Her aura immediately solidified and pushed out to disintegrate the dart. Then it did something I'd never seen: it formed a spike that shot out to the hollowed branch and disintegrated it. But Gregare had already dropped it on the ground and grabbed a campfire-sized boulder with his will and began swirling it around him. Soon it was a gray blur that he promptly willed toward Teega.

Teega's eyes widened in horror and she let go of Jaired's tail. Jaired didn't even move, as if he knew all of this was going to happen. Just as the boulder was arm's length away from the Dewarian, there was a flash of light that blinded my vision for a moment. When I opened my eyes, the boulder was gone. There was a pile of melted dark gray rock, peppered with scorch marks. Teega was still sitting on the ground, her hands were individual flames - not even her fingers could be seen.

Gregare reiterated with finality. "Balance. Rid yourself of the concept of fairness for that is a mentality of children. That is not who we are."

Annie was out of breath from the sudden test of ability. She gasped. "You should tell that to the elders."

"I knew you were a great guide, my friend." I smiled at Gregare. "One day, I'll get you that apprentice."

Gregare nodded a thanks for the compliment. He replied, "Yes, that would please the elders. You trying to upset them more?"

"I'll find one if it does!" Annie added excitedly.

"If we make it through this, we'll just throw Teega at him." I added with a hint of seriousness. Gregare looked to Chawpki and they both nodded to each other. Clearly that had been foreseen.

"Wait, you brought out all the instinctive gifts in us, what's so special about your true self?" Annie asked, "Do we need to threaten you without warning?"

Gregare gave a chuckle. "I knew my true self since I was young. The complete birthmark arrived before I could walk." He walked over to Annie and lifted his pant leg. His birthmark consisted of the outline of a man in the center and several individual shadows cast behind it to the left and to the right.

Annie crouched down to get a closer look. After scrutinizing it for a few moments, she stood. "What does that mean?"

Gregare didn't say anything so Annie looked to me for an answer.

I just shrugged. "This is the first I'm hearing about it."

"Over here." Gregare's voice came from behind us.

We turned around and saw him standing atop a tiny pile of fallen branches he'd stacked over the years.

"What the...?" I turned to the other Gregare still standing, pant leg lifted.

"Hey, over here," he said again.

I turned my head and he was standing by the cooking pot in the hut, a bowl in hand.

Annie turned to him, then the other him behind us, and finally the other other him standing next to us. She even reached out and lightly pushed Gregare and he did stumble. "Are you all real?"

"Yes," they all echoed. Then with a blink they all disappeared except the one standing with the help of Chawpki.

"Okay, that is definitely not fair," Annie said then smiled to herself as his point settled in. A look I'd definitely seen before, albeit, rarely.

She bowed to Gregare. "I concede to your point."

He nodded in approval. "Hope for you yet."

"You going to test Chawpki and Jaired so we can see them in action?" I asked.

"Ha! I'm no fool, Brim. Unlike you, I do not anger my betters."

Jaired growled and Chawpki hissed in assent.

"Very well. I'm sure we'll see something new by the end of this." I remarked. "But I need more food before we continue."

I walked back to the hut, the movement of the others told me they wanted more food, too. Except Gregare who just duplicated himself then merged with the one in the hut. I shook my head in amazement, walked to the hut then dished out another portion for myself.

Annie scooped herself another helping and stood next to me. She nodded politely to Chawpki then spoke. "Please continue telling us about your daughter."

The Ceguur melted from a stick back into a snake then slithered over next to the fire opposite Annie and myself. Teega sat down next to Chawpki while Jaired transformed back into an owl and hooked his claws on an open section of the roof.

Chawpki continued his recount of events. *After the attack and my queen died, a bedlam ensued. They killed and kidnapped Dewarians. Those who escaped went underground or to another port and sailed the ocean. Somewhere along the way, my daughter was one of those taken. Someone must have seen her protecting the princess.*

Teega asked, "What makes you think she's here? And she's helping the thieves?"

Your ear, my liege. I've seen that before just not at such an advanced state. Chawpki slithered over to Teega to get a better look.

To my surprise, Teega didn't recoil. In fact, she turned her body so the snake could get a better look. Despite all my confidence in my abilities and comfort with the animals of this world, having a massive snake with long fangs near my neck would have me on edge. Annie had the same thought as her aura instinctively spread away from her and began enveloping Teega.

Do not worry, Caryanne, I cannot hurt her, Chawpki commented without looking at Annie. *I can only protect.*

"Your words say that, but instincts may say otherwise." Annie said through gritted teeth. Chawpki hit the sore spot by using her real name.

No, child. I cannot hurt her. It is a law of nature. Chawpki paused and looked up to Jaired. *It's the same as for him. He cannot hurt Brim. He is bound.*

I reached out to Jaired and I could feel his humor. "Really? All your threatening words and close calls and I had nothing to fear?"

You should always fear me. The snake left out one part, Jaired replied.

Chawpki must have been unable to listen in on our exchange because he did not say anything.

"He says you left something out, Chawpki." I said aloud. "Apparently, he is threatening and I should fear him."

The snake turned away from Teega and looked at me quizzically. Well, as quizzical as a snake can look. *For us, hurt means seriously injure. To the point of near death. We can still cause you great amounts of pain.*

Jaired growled a laugh.

I nodded in understanding. He had lumped himself into the same group as Jaired on different occasions which meant he was as powerful as Jaired. I definitely didn't want to anger another powerful creature.

"So why does my ear hurt at different times?" Teega asked Chawpki. "When we flew over their cave, it really began hurting my head and my chest."

Chawpki moved back to Teega and coiled up next to her, far closer than before. His words reached our minds with such a deep sadness that we all wavered. *As common with your people, earrings are worn from birth. She bit you there at birth and that's her point of bonding. It didn't hurt before because you were not in proximity of my daughter. Now that you are, you can detect her pain which is great. She is reaching out for your help. She doesn't want to die.*

Teega reached out to the snake and ran her middle finger down from the back of its head to the start of the coil. The gesture was so controlled that I guessed it was an instinct she'd forgotten about. Chawpki responded with a low hiss and that subtle blue light which sent a wave of comfort throughout the hut.

The memories are coming back, my liege, Chawpki said. *Your mother used to do that when you were a child.*

Annie interrupted the rekindling. "Why is it discolored? Why do the thieves wear the infected ear like a badge of honor?"

The blue light emanating from the snake disappeared. *I do not know. However, I do have guesses.*

"And they are?" I asked. Finally, we were close to the truth and I wanted my land saved even if that meant interrupting the mending between Chawpki and Teega.

"Wait, before you get into that. I want to know what you call those people," Annie requested.

I jumped in on her behalf before Jaired brought his full force down on her. "She means the nickname for them."

Chawpki turned to Annie and addressed her. *I am the king of my kind. Jaired is the same for his kind. We call them–*

Jaired growled something fierce which is not a sound you ever expect out of a bird the size of normal man's torso. The growl interrupted Chawpki's words and his focus.

The Ceguur bowed deeply at Jaired. *Apologies, beast lord. I meant no disrespect.*

"What?" Annie, Gregare, and I all asked.

That information is Jaired's to share. I divulged it without knowing he had not.

Jaired kept quiet, but his four eyes had become completely black. I'd learned over the years that this coloration meant impatience. He was near predator mode where instincts took over. He jumped off the perch, flew down into the open roof hut and landed on the floor to look at us wardens.

To give a name to a people is to acknowledge they are worthy of acknowledgement as a people, Jaired said.

Annie looked at me in utter shock and I returned the look. Jaired never used full sentences like this. I felt like we were children sitting around the campfires at Our Tree listening to our parents tell stories of old.

Jaired flapped his wings to bring our attention back to him. *They are a thing. They are The Blackness.*

Teega failed at stifling a laugh. "Kind of dramatic don't you think?"

Jaired flapped his wings again, but the energy focused in an invisible, spherical cone that slapped into Teega's chest and pushed her a few feet across the ground, through the wall and out into the muddy clearing.

I leaned forward to check her final resting spot. She had stopped moving at the mud moat Chawpki made. She was unhurt, but also unclean. She'd spun around a couple times, fighting against the blow which only resulted her being covered in mud, front and back.

To my surprise, the blow did not affect Chawpki and he did not fight Jaired, physically or mentally. He just remained in place, shaking his head side-to-side in obvious disappointment.

Gregare mumbled and the snake hissed a reply. Gregare looked at Annie and me and said, "That would be one stubborn apprentice. Didn't I just finish saying something about not angering your betters?"

CHAPTER 24

Teega didn't say anything when she re-entered the hut. I noticed a smirk on Gregare's face, but I'm pretty sure she didn't notice it. Annie was trying to be busy by stuffing her mouth with stew. However, her aura pulsed excitedly and gave her away.

Chawpki greeted her, *My liege.*

Teega looked at him, but did not sit. Her eyes searched Jaired's for approval or forgiveness, I couldn't tell.

How do I apologize without offending him more? Teega asked, reaching to only my mind.

First off, drop the subject, I replied. *Continually poking a wound doesn't make it better.*

And the second thing?

Bow. Bowing shows another you acknowledge their power and wisdom. Bowing also shows respect. It worked on the pure flame side of you, remember?

Teega bowed to me and I smiled at the gesture. Then she turned to Jaired and gave a deep bow. Jaired didn't reply telepathically and he didn't bow back. Instead he flew back up to the roof and resumed his visual patrol.

I'd be happy with that response, I advised Teega.

Agreed. She replied then added a thought. *That mud got almost everywhere. I don't want him to finish the job.*

I let loose a laugh that filled the hut. The others just ignored us. Ahh, telepathy definitely has its privacy perks.

Chawpki slowly slithered in a circle and waited for Teega to sit down before he moved over next to her. He bent his head down low and Teega's hand instinctively stroked the scales just past his head.

I reached out to Annie. *I guess she's no longer afraid.*

Apparently, she replied. *Maybe we'll stop the talking and finally get to the killing.*

Another sigh from me and another tiny, playful smile from Annie. We both looked to Teega. Even though she was sitting in mud and she was covered in mud, she sat straight and with purpose. She sat like royalty.

"It is settled," she began. "We will find the person abusing your daughter. I will save her life as she once saved mine. Then I will end the thieves."

On those last words, tiny sparks flew out of the finger stroking Chawpki's neck. The snake's scales began to change color. The scales rippled in different colors of red, orange and yellow. The snake mirrored the fire within Teega.

Yes, my liege. We will end them. His words were louder in our heads as the hiss was louder to our ears.

"What can you tell us about them?" Gregare asked as he pulled weapons off the hut walls and stuffed them in a backpack.

Jaired growled and Chawpki hissed in reply. They did this for a few moments before Chawpki finally spoke to us. *We cannot interfere by providing all the answers.*

"Then why are you—" Annie complained, her voice starting to rise before Jaired's growl silenced her.

The snake resumed. *However, we can help once you find the source. It is one of the laws we are bound by. This is not our world to mold. That world...*

Jaired's growl rumbled throughout the tent. *No.*

Chawpki bowed. *Apologies again, beast lord. I am new to this deficiency approach when sharing information.*

"Why don't you want us to know more?" I asked.

The father of the Ceguur looked to Jaired again then looked out the hole where Jaired had pushed Teega. His voice came to our heads with resentment. *He believes the reason for Teega's loss and...other events...are due to my willingness to share too much information.*

Teega looked down at the snake. "Do you believe him?"

Chawpki kept his head level, but his eyes looked to Jaired. *No. However, I concede there might be validity in his assertion. Time will tell as he refrains from divulging information in order to test this theory.*

Annie stood and rubbed her hands together over the fire. "Great, we're just an experiment to the big guy."

He has faith in you. Faith is a power I sometimes forsake. Chawpki stopped sharing his thoughts, but left a feeling of regret in our hearts. He let out a low hiss then continued. *Faith might have saved those I was supposed to protect.*

No, snake lord. It would not have. What passed, passed for a reason, Jaired soothed.

Chawpki hissed in agreement then turned to me. *I am able to share one piece of information. One of The Blackness is here.*

That didn't make sense to me. I posed a question to Chawpki and I was relying on Jaired's energy to confirm or deny the answer. "Wait...the thieves aren't part of The Blackness?"

Jaired replied before Chawpki could. *Subjects, little brother.*

"Corruptible subjects. Easy to manipulate," I added.

Jaired confirmed, *Yes. Very.*

"If we end this one, this leader of the thieves, will the rest die?" Annie asked. She was reaching, hoping for an easy out. My stomach told me it was not that simple.

Jaired and Chawpki shared a few more growls and hisses to decide what to share. Gregare walked out of the hut with the bag of weapons before either could respond. Neither of them seemed to take notice or care.

We are unsure, Chawpki answered.

Jaired added, *We have killed infected thieves. More are infected.*

"Therefore," I turned to Annie, giving her a look of expectation.

She sighed, put her hand on her hip, and replied, "Therefore, logic says the head of the snake must be cut off and the rest will die."

Chawpki's hiss came with energy that knocked Annie back to the ground, her aura not catching the fall in time.

I stepped between the fallen and the snake. "It's an expression. One we will not use again."

Annie coughed as she caught her breath. "That is for sure."

———

We rested until the early morning when the night sky was slowly relenting to a new day. The rain, however, had started falling again. This rain, unlike what Gregare commanded, fell naturally in larger drops, easily soaking a person in a short time. It easily soaked me, anyway. Annie, on the other hand, was dry as can be; her aura ensured that. And I was dry like her thanks to that aura until I made a jab about Gregare putting her in her place. She thanked me for the reminder by retracting her aura to only shield her.

"You two are adorable," Teega remarked while fastening a hide pack that Gregare gave her.

"I don't see you dry either so there." My words clearly came before my thoughts.

Teega shook her head. "How you get to live so long and yet get to be so juvenile at times is beyond me."

Chawpki slithered over and opened his mouth to emit the red mist around Teega. Steam rose off her clothes and she smiled at me.

"Jaired, care to bail me out?" I turned to the black panther who chose to help ready himself for battle by stuffing his giant head in the pot and finishing off the stew.

He stood from his food, walked over to me then shook his wet coat fiercely. I managed to shield most of the spray from my face, but the rest of me felt like I had been swimming. Everyone laughed except me. I just smiled and went about gathering the rest of the potions and herbs Gregare had gathered to heal the poisons the thieves were notorious for using.

I figured I'd rather have everyone in a good mood before battle as opposed to being on edge. Some advocate serious times deserve serious attitudes, but I've learned such a recipe leads to mistakes. If situations are handled with same grace used during everyday life then there is no logic to change that approach to non-everyday situations.

Reaching out to Jaired, I asked him to switch forms. He was responsible for carrying us there so we didn't spend a day wading through muddy bogs. Then I reached out to Chawpki. I knew what I was going to say was not going to be taken lightly so I kept my intentions even and firm. *You are not going.*

The snake slithered away from Teega and headed my way. He uncoiled himself so he could look me in the eyes. Everyone stopped what they were doing and watched the confrontation. While our thoughts were not privy to them, the energy surrounding both of us was palpable.

You dare order me? That is my daughter. Your mentor has not punished you enough, Chawpki yelled in my head as an angry red light cascaded across his scales.

His emotions were nearly overbearing. They pushed against my mind like a glacier pushes on the ground beneath. However, dealing with Jaired during his frustrating moments allowed me to build up constitution to this pressure. I have also learned that giving any ground during moments like these with creatures like these will result in losing unrecoverable ground in all future disagreements.

That is exactly why. You will do anything for your daughter. My eyes were as unblinking as his. I willed my own power back against Chawpki's. *She will put herself in harm to protect you. The leader will see that as I see it now.*

Chawpki leaned closer to me. His fangs and eyes were all I could see. *I will destroy them.*

I leaned in and infused some ice in my words, literally. A blue mist followed my words. *No, you will not. This is not about you or your daughter. This is about eradication of the thieves.*

They are killing my daughter! Chawpki shouted in all our heads.

"They are killing my land!" My bellow echoed over the tiny hills and caused birds to fly out of distant trees. Tiny ice shards exploded from my hands as I repeated in a lower, more dangerous voice, "They are killing my land."

Teega walked over and stroked her finger down the snake's neck. "We will save her."

Chawpki's scales sparked with her touch and calmed him enough to move out of my face. I remained in place and held my gaze until he lowered himself and coiled down. Pride kept his head high as he slithered to Gregare.

I waited until the Ceguur turned his gaze from mine before I let a breath out and could feel warmth in my hands again. Annie and I walked over to Jaired, who had transformed as requested, and we threw a harness on his back. Gregare knew this day was coming and he kept the harness ready. It was a battle harness that provided pockets for our armament and protective hide undercarriage in case arrows or magic attacked from below.

"Give me a moment, Annie," I requested, but pushed my desire for privacy upon her.

She looked to Jaired and myself then shrugged her shoulders. "Whatever."

Once she walked away, Jaired reached out. *Handled that well.*

I fastened the straps around his right wing. *Thanks.*

My heart was already racing after the encounter with Chawpki and it began beating faster in worry of what I was about to say. With a gulp, I said, *You cannot stay either, my friend.*

Jaired craned his head back to me. Four eyes bore down on me and he sent an image of me flat on my back and his talons piercing into my chest. A foreshadowing.

As with Chawpki, I could not back down. I walked around the front of him so I could fasten the straps for the other wing. My gait was confident and I kept my head high, but my insides were shaking. I knew his beak could snap at my arm and rip it off before I could flinch away, but he did not. He let me by and I started to fasten the straps.

You will do the same for me as he would do for his daughter. I gulped as the sudden emotion caught me unaware. *And I'm afraid I would sacrifice myself to let you live.*

Jaired's wings instantly expanded then enveloped me to the point my world was dark. A moment that I thought would all be pain turned out to be a moment encompassed in love. It was unexpected. The tear that fell from my right eye was just as unexpected. No words were spoken. No thoughts were exchanged. Message received.

As quick as the moment came, it disappeared. He expanded his wings and allowed me to step out. I had to clear my throat a couple times before I could guarantee sound came with my words. "There is a tiny hill covered with thick trees that you should be able to land behind. It's just beyond the border of the Shim Hills and The Marshes. Then I need you back here to protect Gregare and the Ceguur."

"Protect from whom?" Annie asked. She walked up - no doubt sensing my sudden emotional imbalance - and put a hand on my shoulder.

"I don't know. There is something out there." I had been feeling a nagging pull toward the south, to the ocean. "Something is coming."

Jaired launched off the ground, flew in a tight spiral until he was nearly as high as the clouds. I watched him circle around a couple times before he came back down. *Nothing.*

"I sense it," I patted my stomach. "Gregare, do you feel it?"

"For a couple days now," the warden replied. "I have surprises in place, but I cannot be everywhere at once."

Annie let out a snicker. "Almost everywhere."

"There is a limit, Annie," Gregare corrected her. "I will need help."

"Chawpki will help you until Jaired returns," I added.

Annie and Teega looked at me in concern. I shook my head and ruffled Jaired's wing feathers as I walked by. Annie reached out and felt my sadness. Just as Teega opened her mouth to talk, Annie leaned over and whispered in her ear. I saw Teega nod in understanding.

"Load up, you two." I commanded. "Greg, run out and check

that hill to make sure we're clear for takeoff."

"Yes, sir." Gregare looked to the hill I pointed to and closed his eyes. Visibly, he did not change, but in a few seconds a duplicate of himself could be made out on the hill on the horizon. We all watched his duplicate walk the perimeter of the top then disappear. "You are clear."

"Keep them safe, old friend." I stated, my hand out for embrace.

He took it. "Same."

I gave a quick nod to Chawpki and he returned it. Then I made my way to Jaired. Annie and Teega were already mounted near his tail, leaving the commanding spot near his neck to me. I looked to the two, gave my best encouraging smile then jumped atop Jaired. "Let's cleanse this land."

Always with the perfect balance of ferocity and grace, Jaired flexed his wings and we soared off to the east.

CHAPTER 25

Jaired dropped us off behind a tiny hill just out of sight of the thieves' cave. There wasn't a long goodbye or a wishing of luck. He didn't even linger. He landed long enough for the three of us to dismount and gather our gear then he took off. Admittedly, my nerves were on edge as I watched him fly back to Gregare and Chawpki. I'd never gone into any serious fight without him at my side and this fight was going to be more intense than ever.

"I'm so happy that the normal light is back," Annie commented. "The Marshes are so moody."

I smiled at her. "I figured you'd be right at home."

Her aura filled with tiny white daggers in response to my jab. I just laughed.

"She's right; it's much happier here," Teega concurred. She walked in a small circle then bent down and ran her fingers through the grass. "And it feels good to be on grass again. All that mud..."

I nodded. "It takes a special person to find The Marshes appealing."

"Don't assign me there, please," Annie requested.

"Seconded," Teega voiced.

"Oh, you think you'll be a warden someday, huh?" I asked Teega with a raised eyebrow.

She stopped walking and looked into my eyes. There was that

flint of fire in them. It had yet to die out since she first ran her fingers down Chawpki's scales. "Yes, I do."

I entertained the idea for a moment. "I suppose stranger things have happened."

"But you're royalty. Don't you have to go rule or something?" Annie's voice carried a mixture of awe and disappointment.

Teega walked over to Annie, looked her straight in the face, and placed a right hand on her left shoulder. Annie mirrored the gesture. Then they touched foreheads. In a cracked voice, Teega replied, "I'm not leaving you."

Annie's eyes started to well up. "Deal."

"As for Brim...we might leave him," she added.

Annie smiled. "We'd have less headaches that's for sure."

"Hey now, I can still hear you."

"I know," both ladies said in unison.

I smiled, happy to see them calm before the storm. Moreover, I was pleased to see them bonding so quickly in just a matter of a few days. It's always been easy for us Tree Makers to bond with our kind. Bonding with other races, however, comes with great trepidation and often doesn't happen. Turns out that life-threatening situations and shared demonstration of unexpected powers can hasten the bonding process.

"All right, break it up." I ordered. As much as I wanted to enjoy the bonding between the species, I wanted them to focus on the coming minutes. They wouldn't get to enjoy the newfound friendship if they didn't make it through the day.

They separated, exchanged a bow, and Teega turned to me with a sudden look of concern. "I can sense them."

I took a breath as a hasty response can sometimes generate more concern. Then in a calm voice I replied, "That's not surprising considering what Chawpki said about the ear."

"I'm okay with advanced warning," Annie commented. "How many?"

Teega closed her eyes to focus. "I can feel seven of them outside the cave."

"And in the cave?" I asked.

"I can't tell. There is some barrier blocking my senses."

"Seven shouldn't be a problem," I commented then I looked to Annie. "Normally, I'd have you go crazy and oust them all, but I would like some sort of surprise here."

Annie nodded. "Agreed."

I didn't even wait for her to finish pronouncing the word. "Can you do that thing with the javelin like you did the other day?"

Annie kept nodding, picking up the excited energy. "I think so. I can't get them all. Not without Jaired."

"Three or four?" I asked.

"Definitely. Leave one. I'll stay."

"Hey!" Teega interrupted.

We both stopped talking and looked at her confused.

Teega continued. "You two are so used to completing sentences for the other person that you forget other people can't follow along. Keep me in the loop."

"Old habits, Teega. My apologies." I said.

Pulling my javelins out, I handed one to Annie and the other to Teega. "Teega, Annie will need complete focus so you'll have to protect her."

She looked disappointed at the dark wooden javelin in her palm. "With this little thing? It's barely longer than my hand."

Annie and I smiled at Teega's comment.

"Annie had similar thoughts when I first showed her the weapon," I said with a glance to Annie.

Annie grabbed Teega's javelin and flicked it outward. It made four clicking noises then extended several feet. It hummed with power and glowed green and blue, Annie's aura and my own.

"Ohh," Teega said. "Forget I ever said anything."

I noticed the energy coming from my imbuement carried more power than before.

Annie noticed it, too. "Do you think it's because of Teega?"

"I do," I replied.

Teega shook her head then pinched the bridge of her nose.

"You're doing it again..."

I chuckled. "Right, forgot. We both are picking up how my aura is stronger than it was before I talked you out of burning down Our Place."

"Okay, I'm with ya." Teega reached out for Annie's javelin then mimicked Annie's action. The javelin mirrored the other, auras and all.

"Teega, the thieves don't have any ranged weapons. And if you stay near Annie then her aura will protect you to an extent. The javelin is sharp and will instantly paralyze anyone that you hit with it."

"So he's saying that if they come then let them get close, but not too close, and jab them," Annie finished.

Teega took a few steps in the direction of the thieves, leaving Annie farthest from harm. "That I can do. Where will you be?"

On cue, Annie handed me her blades. "I'll go invisible and slit their throats once they are distracted by Annie."

"Simple enough," Teega replied. She started to pace back and forth in front of Annie with her eyes scanning in all directions.

As I watched her pace, I noticed how she likely never had to defend herself or even practice any defensive skills. I knew she was right-handed and the right hand carried the power when held away from the tip. Teega, however, was holding her right hand near the tip. Also, she was holding the javelin on the wrong side of her body which resulted in her torso always twisted. If I didn't intervene then she'd be next to useless protecting Annie.

I sheathed the blades under my tunic then ordered Annie to toss me the javelin. Annie, who had turned away to begin focusing her thoughts, flipped the javelin over her head.

"Teega, let me show you how to handle that," I said as I reached to my right and snagged the javelin out of the air.

"You're showing off," Teega said.

"No, I'm doing what's natural," I replied. She gave me the look of "I'm an arrogant outsider" so I clarified. "You will one day have the same abilities. It has nothing to do with how many years you can walk this land; it has to do with how much attention you pay to your surroundings."

"He's right, you know." Annie chimed in.

Her comment seemed to shut down whatever comeback Teega had in waiting. In a more willing-to-learn voice, Teega requested, "Show me, please."

"Hold the javelin with your strong hand near the back as to give you power to thrust. The other hand is mostly to guide the tip to the target." I positioned my hands and showed her. "I'm right-handed, like you, so I hold it like this."

"And, if your lead hand gets injured then you still have your strong hand to continue fighting," Annie pointed out.

Honestly, I didn't expect Annie to step up and help. Usually she would wander off to practice her abilities when I was instructing someone. She claimed it was because I'm a boring instructor, but I never believed her. Now, I realized why she really wandered off: she wanted to be the one instructing.

I handed the javelin back to Annie as I walked away. "You're right. And it's your time to guide her through this."

Her aura shifted to a soft glow from that battle-ready, thick green. "Thank you, Cassius."

Hearing my name caused a ripple of chills down my spine. Nature was telling me I was right, that this was part of her path. At the same moment the chills hit me, Annie reached down to scratch at her calf, right where her birth tattoo was. It was an absent-minded scratch, but I was certain that if she lifted her leg then she would have seen a change in that tattoo as she completed another part of her destiny.

I told myself to be patient. I would ask her to look at the tattoo once all of this was over. "I'm going to scan the area for any patrolling thieves. Annie, you have two minutes."

Annie gave me a curt nod then immediately began instructing Teega with tips on using the javelin. I watched for a few moments then headed north to scout the area.

———

A lot can be discovered in two minutes with increased speed and heightened senses. Also, a lot of training can happen in two minutes. By the time I returned, Teega was handling the javelin like a seasoned warrior. I walked up to Annie while keeping an eye on Teega. She was walking a perimeter around Annie, always stopping at random intervals to prevent patterns from being detected.

"She is ready," Annie boasted. "Do you know if her people are warriors?"

"I know as much as you do. They are traders. Their land was burned long ago and never recovered so they live underground."

She shrugged. "Maybe she's just a quick study then."

"I'm guessing that snake left out a great deal about Teega and her family."

"Why do you say that?"

I pursed my lips for a moment to align my thoughts. "First, royalty rarely comes to existence without a power struggle and power struggle means combat training. Second, her people survived."

"Ahh, yes. That's right," Annie said with a dawning expression. "Chawpki brought up how The Blackness killed her family, but never explained anything after that."

"Exactly. I refuse to believe that these people showed up just to murder the royal family then waved goodbye without damaging everything on their way in and out."

A silence settled over us as the shared idea settled in our thoughts. We both watched Teega walk the perimeter until she was closer to us. She noticed us watching her so I waved her over.

"There are two around the campfire and two in the tent just behind them."

"The other three?" Teega asked.

"Standing outside the other tent, closer to the cave entrance."

"Give me a minute, Annie, then let it rip." I shimmered invisible, my feet barely bending the grass blades beneath my feet. A little extra light-footedness while invisible never hurt, at least never hurt me.

Annie added, "Teega, resume patrol. Keep on your toes."

She literally started walking on her toes. I smiled at this change in walking as it gave a person the ability to react quicker compared to walking normally with weight shifting to the heels with each step.

Annie closed her eyes and gently lifted the javelin in the air. She removed her hand and the javelin hung there. Slowly it began vibrating. I could feel the energy pulsing from it and from her. The pulses increased with each of my breaths which served as a unique countdown to the attack.

I skirted the hill then made my way through the tall, dark yellow grass and the orange and yellow leaf trees. Ahead I could see the dull haze of campfire smoke climbing above the tree tops. Locating the thieves was a little trickier in my area of the forest than in The Marshes. Trees in The Marshes didn't have as thick of trunks and didn't grow so close together as they did here. The thieves' naturally dark skin and their dark clothes allowed them to blend easily into the surrounding nature. The backdrop of the light stone mountain, however, betrayed what would have been the ideal and complete cover.

Also, The Marshes had many smells - many of them pungent - and the thieves were a naturally smelly breed. Only the gods know why. Whereas in this area, unlike all the other areas along the coast, most smells came from the ocean. Even the sound of the ocean rushed up the cliffs and whistled through the cracks in the mountain and provided cover for my movements.

It took me a minute to reach the camp. Even though I was invisible, I chose to hide behind a recently cut tree stump. The thieves clearly underestimated the strength of the stump as they stopped cutting at a height of my chest. This area of The Shims was definitely younger and not as strong as those trees to the north. Although they weren't so weak that they fell like the trees in The Marshes. However, these trees burned hot and long so the thieves were smart enough to figure out they didn't need to gather as much wood.

Luck was also on their side as they cut enough trees to provide some vision from the camp out into the forest. They had cleared outward several yards from the cave entrance in a semi-circle. It was obvious from the trampled and patchy grass that the thieves' activity had increased significantly in recent weeks. While this clearing allowed them to easily see incoming enemies, it also allowed them to be easily spotted from within the forest.

I stopped at the edge of the flattened grass, next to a thick, knotted tree stump. The three were still standing outside the tent to my left. They were facing each other in a heated discussion. One person was waving his arms around - always a great way to prove a point - and the other two stood there with arms crossed. I smiled because their distractions were going to play in my favor.

A muddy path split between the two tents leading to the cave entrance. Opposite these three were the other thieves. Two thieves were sitting on logs with sticks just above the flames, roasting meat. They occasionally looked up at the three arguing, but shook their heads and returned their gaze back to the food. The tent entrance just behind them had a flap covering it. I closed my eyes to focus my hearing. Through the whistling wind, I could hear the three arguing, the sizzle of the meat above the fire, and the deep breathing of the other two in the tent.

The rapid pulse of energy from the javelin easily reached me from this distance as Annie and I were always connected. Quickly, I relayed the image of the scene to Annie so she could focus her target.

Other two are asleep, I told her.

She acknowledged my information with a brief feeling of gratitude then shut me out. Whatever spell she was about to cast clearly cost a lot of energy and even more focus. My hope was to help her with that focus once all this was done. If we all made it out alive and whole.

A roll of thunder boomed, followed by a sharp crack of lightning in the distance near Gregare's hut. Whatever had been coming from the south must have finally been revealed. The lightning lit the overcast sky and drew the attention of the two eating. With their attention away from me, I slunk away from the stump and toward the three arguing. Had those three been paying attention, they might have noticed the slight depressions in the mud from my feet. Thankfully, they did not.

Annie reached out to my mind and gave me a half of a breath's warning then released her spell. It took only two breaths and I looked to the thieves sitting by the fire. There was a streak of bright blue followed by vibrant green that pierced one in the back of the skull, exited through his right eye then struck the thief next to him in the left ear before exiting out his right ear. They fell without so much as a grunt. The javelin quickly zoomed into the other tent and I heard the distinct sounds of wood breaking bones.

Two of the three arguing thieves saw the streak of lights and the fall of their comrades. Both reached for their swords on the ground, but their hands never found the hilts. Instead, I leaped and landed right behind them. With the dagger in my right hand and the short sword in my left, I stabbed the thieves through their necks. The bloody tips easily stuck out their gurgling throats. The third thief was in shock, his eyes staring at the bloody dagger tips. I kept the blades in place, used the thieves to hold me up and quickly kicked my right foot at the thief's head. It snapped back with the crack nearly as loud as the lightning strike moments before. I pulled the blades out of the necks and all three thieves fell in unison before I could even finish a single breath. They may have numbers, but they don't have my people's art and skill in combat.

I remained invisible and closed my eyes to focus beyond the cave entrance. I couldn't sense anything. Something magical was blocking me out. I trusted since there was no sound coming out that it meant no one heard the commotion out here. I focused my hearing again and only the sound of the whistling wind could be heard. All seven thieves were dead.

I sent the all clear to Annie and Teega and informed them to skirt the clearing until they were up against the mountain. Just because these were dead doesn't mean brazenly walking through an open clearing was a good strategy.

A slight rain started to fall and I couldn't have been more grateful since the drops covered my footprints. I don't like risks and I gave a silent thanks to the gods for helping me out. Once back in the trees, I followed the clearing perimeter until I was up against the mountain. The whistling wind was much louder here and the pattering of the rain made catching any other noise nearly impossible. A slight green hue entered my vision which is when I noticed Annie and Teega approaching.

"That was," Annie paused to catch her breath, "challenging."

"She fell," added Teega. "I caught her before she hit the ground."

Annie was red in the face from exhaustion and no doubt a little embarrassment. I reached out and squeezed her right shoulder. "Proud of you."

She grabbed my opposing shoulder. "And you."

It was our ritual after any confrontation. Each touch allowed the other to take energy if needed. I wasn't even close to exhausted so I let her leech whatever energy necessary. After a few breaths, she pulled her hand back and nodded that she was good.

I asked the Dewarian, "Can you sense anything from here?"

She faced to the entrance. "Nope. Nothing."

"Then we go in blind," I stated. I put my right hand out and summoned the javelin. It took only a few moments and it flew back to me from the tent, shortened and ready for battle. I turned to Teega. "Do you need to keep it or could you possibly go firestorm on us?"

She shook her head. "That's not in control and I don't like not being in control. I'll stick with the javelin."

"That's fine," I assured her. "Annie, your blades."

The instant she took them her aura thrummed and covered all of us.

I gave them a stern nod. "Into the dark we go."

CHAPTER 26

I walked through the entrance with hesitant steps. A dull yellow light, coming from a torch at the end of a long dark tunnel, greeted my eyes. Tiny shadows danced out from the cage that held the torch and flickered off the surprisingly high ceiling. The Yeryans were barely over five feet tall, but these tunnels were at least twice that high.

"I wonder why these are so high," I remarked, but the only response was echoes of dripping water from sources unseen. At least that sound should cover the noises of our feet and, clearly, the sound of my voice.

"Teega? The ceiling height?" I pointedly asked the Dewarian, but she ignored me a second time. I turned around to the entrance and found out why. Teega was standing there with one arm out, fingertips touching the barrier of the cave entrance. She seemed to be in a trance.

"I recognize this magic," Teega said in a soft, mesmerized voice. "We use it in our homeland. It keeps the outside weather, well, outside."

Annie stood behind her. "Is it safe?"

"Yes." She looked around the entrance edges. "Although I don't know how to cast the spell."

"Cool," Annie remarked as she put her hand through the

entrance and retracted it. "Does that mean one of your people did this?"

Teega opened her mouth to reply, but I cut them off.

"Annie, let's focus." I turned to Teega. "Thief count?"

Teega closed her eyes and focused. "I can't tell. There are many, but I don't know where they are specifically."

Nodding, I scanned the cave tunnel. It was muggier in here than outside the cave, and it was definitely more wet.

"It's so grimy," Annie said. She ran her fingers along the rocky wall and water dripped off her finger when she pulled away in disgust. "Filthy."

Teega looked at Annie. "The water seems to be keeping the walls clean."

"Not that kind of dirty, Teega." I replied. "There is something evil here. I feel it, too."

"Because it's underground?" Teega asked, definitely affronted.

"Nothing of the sort. Part of our people live underground, Teega."

"I had no idea."

Annie interjected, "We don't talk to them often. The elders don't anyways. Brim is the only one in communication."

"Really?"

I nodded. "It's true. They are far north. Much colder up there and the underground keeps them warm, but it's not evil like this place."

"And not as dark, I hope," Annie remarked.

"The lighting is perfect," Teega squared her shoulders and took the lead.

Annie mumbled, "Perfect for you, maybe."

Teega ignored the jab. "Watch my back, there are several tunnels and several floors."

"How do you know?" I asked.

"You can hear it. Focus on the echoes and you learn to find your way without a map," Teega answered.

I didn't hear anything beyond the obvious, but I wasn't focused on anything else either. Once I closed my eyes and focused my gift then I caught the echoes she was referring to. "I hear it now. Although I'm definitely not used to it like you are."

"It comes with time," Teega commented as she continued down the tunnel.

Annie followed her and I took up the rear guard. The tunnel floor was a mixture of dirt and tiny rocks that gave a slight crackle when we walked. By "we" I don't mean Teega as I noticed her steps weren't making a sound.

"By the way, how are you walking so quietly?" I asked.

Teega looked down at her feet and shrugged. "I'm just walking."

"So you're loud as can be everywhere else, but here you're not even making a whisper," Annie said with an envious sarcasm.

"I'll teach you some day, but not today," Teega replied without rising to her tone. "Where is all this water going?"

"Dripping out over the cliffs is my guess," I said. "That might be why the smells and winds betray the cliffs here."

Teega suddenly let out a whimper of pain. She nearly fell, but Annie leaped ahead and caught her. Annie's aura immediately extended out to protect as she helped Teega slide down the wall onto the ground.

I pushed my senses out in hopes of finding the culprit, but all I could feel is the same evil fighting against nature. I hastened my pace and caught up with the two. Javelin extended in front of me and glowing blue, I asked, "What's wrong?"

The fire flint in Teega's eyes had turned from orange to red. Tears were trying to crest her eyes, but she was holding them back. With great strain, she said, "Ear."

I leaned closer, but nothing was out of the ordinary from when I first met her. The ear was sickly and black, but not nearly as bad as the thieves. I grabbed Teega's hand - which was hotter than normal to the touch - and told her to press it to her ear.

Her eyes widened at the idea of so much pain. "That's not going to happen. I'll pass out."

"No," Annie started saying. She squinted in concentration and her aura confined to encompass Teega's ear.

"Now that's a weird sensation. I can't feel my ear at all, but I can feel the..."

"Evil," Annie finished. "That's what Chawpki was talking about. My liege."

Teega gave a nervous laugh at the last part.

I asked, "Is the shock still running through your system?"

Teega nodded. "But with the pain gone, I can focus better."

I let go of her hand and gave her an encouraging nod. Teega inhaled deeply then lifted her hand and cupped her ear.

"Close your eyes, Cantiga," I ordered and added a pulse of energy when I spoke her name. Chills ran down my spine as I reached out and touched her elbow to watch the chills run up her arm and to her hand.

"Think of home," I added then I pulled my finger away from her elbow.

Teega's light green eyes closed and she released her breath. A rush of air ran through the tunnel. A bright orange light escaped between her fingers and lit up Annie's face as well as my own.

"Let go, Annie."

She looked to me and released her aura. The orange brightened to the point both Annie and I had to look away. I waited for the light to disappear and go back to the torch light then I looked back at Teega.

"It's gone," Teega stated. A relief washed over her and sent rejuvenating energy to Annie and myself. "I felt my calf burn for a moment then disappear."

Annie's eyes widened and glee filled her voice. "Oh, I want to see."

Teega's laugh this time was genuine and echoed down the hallway so loudly she clapped her hand over her mouth.

I grimaced and both females physically jerked back at the sight. Then they looked to my eyes and must have seen I wasn't too upset. "Annie, we'll look later. Teega, I will explain later."

"I'm a healer," Teega whispered in awe.

"Of at least one person," Annie clarified.

"Let's hope we don't have to find out if you can heal others," I added. I held my hand out, Teega grabbed it, and pulled herself up. "Annie will lead the charge, you will be in between her and myself."

"I can protect myself," Teega's defiance reflected in her hands as they began to change to flame colors.

"I know," I reassured her. I remembered my confrontation with Teega in Our Place and tapped into that energy then I reached my hand out and touched hers. While the color didn't change to blue, my touch was cold against hers and she pulled her hand back in response. I slowly retracted my hand.

"Remember, I am not here to make sure you feel good. I'm not here to placate your ego. I am here to protect. I am in charge." I kept my voice low, but as firm as the mountainside. "I will be invisible. And you will have to protect yourself because they can't see me."

Teega's eyes glared at me and I could see her twisting thoughts into words. I felt Annie reach out to her, but she kept the thoughts away from me. Teega forced an uncomfortable smile and forced an even more uncomfortable nod.

Thank you, I said to Annie.

She didn't respond with anything more than the same nod that Teega gave me.

Well, at least I have them back to being on edge, even if it is with me.

———

"They could have at least changed the height of the torches," Annie commented. "It's the same thing. Over. And over."

Teega chimed in. "I'm with her. I grew up in this world and I'm bored."

"The threat of death at every corner should keep you from being completely bored," I added. Both of them silenced immediately. Annie's aura glowed in response and I reached out to remind her to dull it to hide our presence.

The tunnels were crudely carved both in height and length. For every minute we walked there would be a lit torch crammed in a crevice. And it took about five minutes to traverse just one length of tunnel. There were a few steps down at the end of the tunnel that forked into two tunnels. Both were lit with similar torches as the entrance tunnels. Both were cut somewhat even and straight in their respective directions. Both seemed to stretch for miles with no indications of adjoining tunnels. Clearly there was some magic playing with our senses.

"More glossy moss and stinky humid air. Great." Annie let out a disappointing sigh. "At least let me snuff one of those thieves."

"I know you're bored, Annie, but stay focused."

Teega interrupted us. "Good thing they are lazy."

"How so?" I asked.

The Dewarian answered, "They stuck to building the basic underground dwelling."

"For those of us who enjoy fresh air and sunlight..." Annie said.

Teega turned to us. "You build in a swirl. For every turn, right or left, you split your tunnel, but you always choose the same direction to build down."

"But we didn't go down left or right." Annie clarified, "We went straight."

I shimmered back to visibility and asked, "And if both sides build down then how do we know which side they are and which side is full of traps or some bottomless pit?"

Teega turned around and walked back to the three steps we just took down into this tunnel. She waited for us to catch up then she pointed at the steps. "Notice how the steps aren't built equally."

I leaned down and took a closer look. She was right. It's amazing how something as simple as how steps are built go unnoticed. A downfall of always having eyes up, and on the prize. After a day like today, I should have known the prize wasn't going to be at the end of the horizon.

Annie knelt next to me and looked around. "I don't see it."

"Look at the other side of the step," Teega suggested.

Annie shuffled over a couple steps. "Ah! I see it. This side is wider. It also looks like they spent more time carving it."

"Except they tried to make it like they didn't spend time carving," I added. The step was carved distinctly wider, but they left the flat part of the step bumpier to compensate.

Teega nodded approvingly. "Both of you are correct. Look at how they carved the front of the wider step smoother than the narrow step. Also, the angle of the front of the step and the top of the step is a lot sharper than the narrow step.

Annie and I were completely intrigued. I even stopped thinking about the thieves for a moment to enjoy this lesson in underground structure. Her world was something almost entirely new to me especially considering my world rarely involved being enclosed. Our Place being the exception, but most of that had been formed long before I discovered it.

"What about the tops of the steps?" I asked Teega as I ran my hand along them. They were rough cut and dirty, but no water touched them.

"Intentionally carved that way," she answered. "They are preying upon the knowledge of people trusting what they feel."

Annie looked at Teega, confused. "What do you mean?"

"If both steps look the same to the eyes and feel the same under our feet then we tend not to think anything is different." Teega paused and ran her finger along the crease between the steps. "And they dug deeper here to keep the water away from the steps to prevent them from slipping."

I nodded. "We see that all the time with the animals and plants in our land. What we see as normal compared to everything else, we tend to not care about."

Annie brought us back to the task at hand. "It makes sense given what we know about the thieves."

Teega looked to Annie, confusion clear on her face. Annie lifted her chin, pointing to her neck.

The Dewarian said, "Ahh, yes, their white necks. What keeps them safe is what makes them weak."

Shimmering back to invisible, I said, "Their habits betray them."

Teega and Annie started down the right hallway, but I stopped them. "Now I know what to look for, I'm going to take the lead."

"I'll hang back," Annie said.

Teega asked, "Why am I the easy target? I mean I know you'll be hit first, but not be seen first."

"Because of that thing in your ear," I replied. "You may not like it, but you're more like one of them than not."

Teega cringed, but didn't rebuke the statement.

"How far do we have?" I asked.

Teega slightly tilted her head to one side to hear better. "Ten more tunnels at least. They went down more to the left to confuse, but they didn't count on me."

"I'm glad we can." I took the right tunnel and increased my pace.

CHAPTER 27

At least an hour passed before we encountered the first thief. He was sitting against the wall, completely passed out. He stunk of wine as did the leather wineskin he loosely held in his right hand. His left hand held a short, wide knife and smelled of cooked meat. It was small and dull enough that it posed no threat to us.

Annie stepped forward, lifted his chin and put a glowing green blade to the white patch of flesh on his neck. He didn't even stir.

Caryanne. Stop. I commanded with my mind. Then I remembered Teega's complaint about involving her with our back-and-forth so I used my spoken words. "We're not going to kill him."

"And why not?" Annie whipped her head around and her eyes burned into mine. "They're thieves, Brim."

"I know that, Annie. But I don't want someone to come across a dead one then raise whatever alarm they might have."

"I hate to agree with him, but I do," Teega concurred. "If one falls then the leader might notice or others might notice the string of bloody bodies."

Nodding, I added, "And if you look around, we don't have any place to hide him."

She pulled her blade away and turned right down the other tunnel. I searched the thief's pocket for any other weapons, but didn't find any.

"Must be a sentry that rarely leaves these tunnels," I remarked.

"What a life. I don't blame him for drinking himself into a stupor," Teega said.

"You two coming?" Annie's voice was irritated and growing distant.

"Let's go," I told Teega.

The Dewarian said, "Guess that means you're covering our backs again."

"She gets cranky sometimes."

"Maybe if you told her that you love–"

"Don't start," I grumbled.

She let out a light laugh and pointed her javelin ahead.

I took up rear guard and shook my head at the thoughts flooding forward. Gregare warned me about females. He croaked, "So pretty, so much fun, and require too much thinking for our little brains." Wise words. Of course, that wisdom didn't stop my feelings from developing for Annie. Nor did it stop me from confessing those feelings all those moons ago. My emotions started to get away from me and with them the energy escaped.

Teega picked up on the energy and let out another light laugh. Thankfully, Annie was too angry to sense anything and, judging by her angry aura, she presumed we were still laughing at her.

"Any luck sensing more of them?"

Teega shook her head. "For whatever reason, I cannot sense them individually. Only as a whole."

"Which is exactly what their leader wants," I guessed.

"He wants to know it all, but his followers only know of the masses."

"A clever one to be sure," I asserted.

Annie walked to the end of the tunnel then back to us. "Can you sense the leader?"

"Sort of. They all appear as darkness in my mind, but something is significantly darker."

"You think it's the leader?" I asked.

"Mmhmm," Teega affirmed. Her light green eyes had darkened

underground, almost to the same shade as Annie's. Also, the flint of fire in her iris had expanded outward and become more a red-orange almost like a streak of blood dripping over the sun.

Annie let out an impatient sigh. She flipped both blades up in the air, grabbed them by the handles as they fell and started walking to the next tunnel. "Let's go."

We made it through two more tunnels and almost turned to the next one when Teega stopped with a jerk. Annie's aura immediately appeared. I shifted to the side and leapt past them. I landed without a sound, pulling out my javelin and pointing it towards the end of the tunnel, expectant for someone to skewer.

Thankfully, whatever I held in my hand adopted the invisibility of my body so the javelin remained unseen. However, I noticed that my own blue aura was instinctively glowing and it wasn't retaining the invisibility like the javelin. Thankfully, the blue wasn't light like the sky. Instead, it held the dark blue of the Great Ice Shores. I had to trust to the shock of an aura hanging in the middle of a tunnel was enough to distract the thieves from putting things together.

With a careful step down and craning of my neck, I peeked around the corner. There were two thieves walking our direction. I pulled my head back and sent the image of the thieves to Annie and Teega. The next image I sent wasn't one of killing the thieves; it was one of knocking them out and dragging them around the corner.

Annie projected confusion and disagreement, but I saw her flip the blade in her right hand so she was holding sharp end. One day she would learn that she could manipulate whether the blade or the handle hits something without changing how she held it. Another lesson to add to the ever-growing list, I suppose.

I readied the javelin in my hand and stepped around the corner. Unlike Annie, I didn't possess the magic to propel the javelin through the air. What I did possess was the muscle and accuracy that accompanied centuries of training. I launched the javelin, a dark blue streak in its wake, at the thief on the left. Just a breath later, a green streak passed my vision as Annie's blade spun end-over-end at the thief on the right. Both projectiles found their targets in the middle of the dark-skinned foreheads and they crumpled to the ground.

"Remind me again why aren't we killing this scum?" Annie asked. Then she turned her head back to Teega and told her she was clear to come ahead.

Teega's head peeked around the corner then her body followed. Relief washed over her face.

"It's a guess. If Teega can see all the thieves as a darkened mass then it stands to reason that the leader can see when they disappear. My guess is if they are knocked out then they still show up in his vision, but they are out of our way."

I walked halfway down the tunnel to the collapsed thieves. I retrieved my javelin, reached over my shoulder and slid it through the loop on my tunic and my belt. Without so much as a backwards glance, I threw Annie's knife over my shoulder to her. Then I dragged the knocked out thieves back to the tunnel steps.

Annie sighed. "Whatever."

I grabbed one of the thieves by his collar and started dragging it back to the drunk thief. Teega followed suit and dragged the other.

Annie followed us down the tunnel. "Okay, but how do we make sure that they stay that way?"

"That's your job not mine," I said sharply. With two thuds, the thieves' heads hit the wine-soaked ground. I unsheathed my javelin and headed back the way I came. Without so much as a glance at Annie, I ordered, "So take care of them."

Teega looked to me then to Annie, "What are you going to do?"

"Come on, Teega. Time is wasting."

We walked passed Annie and I intentionally avoided her imploring eyes. She knew what she had to do, she had done it countless times during fights. Today's lesson was about being proactive. As we rounded the corner, I felt the pulse of building energy then a bright flash of green filled the entire tunnel. Teega stopped walking, but I did not.

"It's done," Annie announced to Teega.

She whispered, "What was that about? I've never seen him so impatient with you."

I smiled at Teega's whispering since she forgot how advanced my hearing is.

"It's as much my fault as his." Annie kept her voice quiet, but she knew I could hear. Teega had yet to figure that out.

"What is?"

"I don't want to let him down so I let him tell me exactly what I need to do most the time," Annie answered.

Teega asked, "And his fault?"

"He cares so much for me he doesn't want to see me get hurt in any way."

She let out a slow whistle. "You two need to get away."

Annie laughed. "Come on, let's get this over with."

I rounded the corner - hoping that conversation topic was over - and thankfully it was free of thieves. What Annie told her was true: it was just as much my fault as it was hers. I cared deeply for her and all of her failures fell on my shoulders. I possessed more knowledge. I had more experience under my belt. The gods gave me an immortal, near omniscient and omnipotent being for a friend. Of course, if I voiced these thoughts to Annie then she'd call me a fool. I'm sure anyone would agree with her, but that's just how I think.

"Annie, reach out to Jaired and tell him about the thieves. Those three might need some convincing to not dismember and eventually kill every single thief they see."

Teega agreed. "And Chawpki's wrath...I can only imagine."

"Good point," Annie replied.

"Teega, you should know that if you walk directly in front of her then she can follow without paying attention."

"What do you mean?"

"Normally, we close our eyes to communicate with our minds to those who are far away. However, I figured out a way to follow a person with my eyes open while not being here."

Teega gave an awkward laugh. "Okay, that's a little creepy."

"Yeah, I suppose it is, but it works in situations like these."

"You can keep that off my training list," Teega added. "What do I do?"

"Just make sure you're only a few steps away from her. Her body will mirror your steps and movements."

"You got it, boss," Teega said in her best impression of Annie.

I sighed. "Of all qualities to learn from Annie..."

CHAPTER 28

"Those two should be the last ones," Teega said between breaths.

Annie tried to laugh, but it came out as a gasp. "You said that about the last tunnel. And the one before that."

"It better be the last," I stated. I was still invisible so they couldn't see me panting. My hands were aching from dragging so many thieves.

For the last hour, we'd routinely encountered and knocked out two thieves per tunnel. We dragged the pairs back to the previous tunnel. As much as I wanted to drag them to the first tunnel with the three thieves, that was a lot of work and a lot of time. At one point, Annie pointed out that we would have to leave the way we came. I assured her that if they resisted then she could have free reign to kill all of them. We didn't have to be as friendly during the return trip.

Teega leaned against the wall, her hands on her knees and face to the ground. "I'm positive those were the last. When I see the darkness of the thieves, it's more spread out. Away from here."

"Gee, I wonder why," Annie said. She leaned against the wall opposite Teega, taking deep breaths. "Never thought I'd spend so much energy keeping those filthy things alive."

I remained invisible and controlled my breath when I spoke. I couldn't have them knowing their tireless leader was, well, tired. "Do you see Angwiki?"

Teega let out a long sigh. "No, Brim. I don't see Angwiki."

I'd asked this question after each pair of thieves we knocked out and each time I made sure to use the snake's name. By using the name, I hoped Teega's memories might be dislodged. While she didn't say anything to that affect, her mood and her voice definitely softened and saddened with each answer.

"You trying to bring her down or something?" Annie asked with great concern.

"Always on the defensive for anyone, but me, huh?" I retorted. Of course, she couldn't see me smiling, but she still could feel my intentions.

"Don't dodge the question, boss."

I shimmered to visibility and walked to Teega. I leaned against the wall next to her and gave her a friendly nudge with my elbow. "No, I'm not trying to do anything of the sort. I want all of us to remember that we're here to save someone important. We're not here to destroy lives."

Annie smiled. "That's just the side bonus. Like the fresh smells that come after a summer storm."

"Yes," I agreed. "Teega, if Chawpki is right - and I believe he is - then his daughter saved your life on more occasions than you're aware of. Something inside you knows this and is feeling the desire to free her."

Teega looked up at me, a slow stream of tears falling from her eyes. A hopeful smile broke through the sadness. "Let's save her."

I reached out and gripped her hand, assuring her. "We will."

She stood and wiped the tears from her eyes. Then she set her shoulders back and clenched her fists. Suddenly, her fists burst into flames. "I am coming for you."

Annie's eyes met mine and we nodded. We were done hiding. We were done being at peace with the world around us. Annie's green aura burst out like the flames on Teega's fists and lit up the hallway. I was tempted to do the same with mine, but not hiding from the world for me means being invisible. My power lies in being behind the scenes so I shimmered back to being invisible.

We walked down the recently cleared tunnel with Teega's flaming fists lighting the way. As we turned the corner to the next tunnel, I was surprised to find it wasn't a tunnel. Instead we were greeted by an open cave that was large enough to accommodate Jaired's largest flying form and then some.

The dripping water on the walls found a path through all those tunnels as it cut a steady stream about the width of my hand through the dozen or so steps leading down to the cave floor. The stream gathered in a calm pool in the center of the cave. Water from the pool gently flowed over into a stronger stream that ran across the cave and out of sight. A thick, but narrow stone bridge crossed over the mouth of the stream.

"I expected something...darker," Annie remarked. "Much darker."

"Me, too," Teega agreed.

They were right. This place had so much light to it - nearly as much as being outside. With the tunnels only being lit by the occasional flame, it made sense that the deeper we went then the darker the final stop would be. However, there weren't any flames lighting this stone lair. There were several, long slim cracks on the cliff side of the ceiling. These slits brought light in at so many different angles that they lit up the room like one solid beam of light.

"Those slits confirm this cave is at the edge of the cliffs," I commented.

"Which means that stream dumps down over the cliffs and onto the beach of the Sair Sea," Annie concluded.

"Exactly," I agreed.

Teega seemed uninterested in the location as her brow furrowed as she looked around. I reached out with my mind and nudged Annie to ask Teega what she was thinking. Like Gregare, I needed Annie to start thinking like a master with an apprentice.

Annie asked, "What's wrong, Teega?"

She shook her head and refocused on Annie. "Something is off. I can't put my finger on it. It's difficult because your land is different than mine."

I asked patiently, "What can you explain then?"

"There is a hidden entrance upstream," she pointed to the right of the pool. Her eyes were tightly shut and sweat was starting to gather on her forehead. "I think they know we're here."

Annie tensed and stepped ahead of both of us. Her aura solidified and both her blades were drawn. "Where?"

"I...can't tell. I just feel pressure on my chest. Like someone is pushing against me."

"Okay, let's take it slow so we don't get surprised," I said calmly. The plan formulated with each quick breath I took. "Annie, you are going to stay to the right of us at all times. Your eyes never wavering from upstream. That aura will keep us alive so long as you feel the threat coming from that way."

"Done." She took a couple steps down. "Nothing is getting past."

"Teega, your flames are still strong and you haven't lost control. Whatever you are doing to keep that focus then keep doing it."

She opened her eyes and they were bloodshot. She turned to me, her body slightly wavering side-to-side from the strain. She declared, "It's for Angwiki."

I shimmered back to visibility then put my hand on her right shoulder. "Put your right hand on mine. Take the energy you need."

The flame disappeared the moment her hand landed on my shoulder. "I don't know how."

"Close your eyes. I'll walk you through it." I took a deep breath and she mirrored me. We breathed in unison for a moment or two then I reached out to her mind.

Imagine that I am full of water and you are only half full. Then imagine water flowing upward from my body, out from my arm, and filling you up.

A strong pulse of energy - one of hesitance - surged from her. *I cannot. That energy is yours.*

I replied, *There is no more yours or mine. Only ours.*

What I didn't share with her was how our people always had extra energy. The energy allows us to go days without eating, allows us to heal others, and generally remain in a relaxed state. The more we give to protect then the more the world gives back what it would have spent on repairing the damage.

With extra focus, I pushed the image of the transfer of water onto her consciousness. She inhaled sharply at the shock, but I felt Annie reach out and calm her breathing. It took a few breaths, but I could feel Teega pulling energy from me.

How do I know when to stop?

When your breathing is as calm as mine is now.

Okay. Her breath was still slightly labored, but it was slowing. Another few breaths passed then she pulled away from me physically and telepathically.

I opened my eyes and saw Teega standing, unwavering, and looking rested. She nodded and I returned it.

"Very proud of you. You're becoming accustomed to our ways," Annie commented. "And those are looking much stronger."

Teega looked down at her hands and flexed them into fists. They were noticeably brighter and more diverse in color. "And they aren't draining my energy as much."

I turned my eyes from the brightness. "You're going to need that energy. You have to cover every other angle except upstream. I am going to check the perimeter for any traps or escape routes. Part of leading involves knowing you can survive. When you consider it's a leader of thieves then you know he has an escape."

"I'll do my best," Teega said.

"If you have to go all fiery volcano on everyone, just give me a warning." Annie added.

Teega laughed. "I'm sure the heat will let you know."

"Go ahead, Annie," I commanded.

Annie took each step carefully, her eyes never wavering from where the stream disappeared under the rock. Teega followed only a step behind. The flames in her hands licked upward a few inches when she inhaled and a foot or so when she exhaled. Yet they would dissipate whenever they touched Annie's aura.

I stayed at the top of the steps until both of them reached the bottom. Yes, they were bait, of sorts. I needed to take in the entire situation without being part of the situation. I wasn't worried about either of them. Only an idiot would think of attacking someone with flames in their hands.

No one jumped out of anywhere to attack the two. I closed my eyes and listened. All I heard was the trickling stream coming down through cracks in the cave and the larger, louder stream that escaped out of this cave. As far as my senses could tell, we were safe for now.

Instead of taking the steps, I leapt from the top step down to the floor. I reached out to Annie moments before I landed and she pushed out part of her aura to cushion my landing. I didn't make a sound. Unlike the tunnels, the floor was dry and smooth. Maybe this place was here first and the tunnels were made after as opposed to the reverse.

Anything? I asked.

They replied in unison, "No."

I'm going to check the perimeter then we'll find the entrance, I said. *Oh, and I'm going invisible.*

I shimmered and slowly made my way toward the cliff side of the cave. The light was much brighter as I approached that side of the cave. There were markings in random places along the wall. Most of the markings were in Yeryan yet they were marked at a height much taller than Yeryans and Tree Makers. A couple of them were definitely in Dewarian. The ones in Dewarian caught me off guard since Teega was the only one I'd seen in my land that had the thief's mark.

The rush of the stream grew louder with each step towards the edge of the cavern. I approached it carefully since I didn't know where and how fast it dropped out of sight. Annie may give me a hard time about being so cautious, but it saved my life on many occasions as it just did. I began to set my foot down on a stone by the stream, but the stone gave way. I watched the stream carry it away and out of sight. Judging by the sound and the light, the opening to the cliffs was probably a few feet after where the water fell out of sight.

This stream is more powerful than it appears. Do not step in it, I mentioned. *It feels evil. There is something or someone giving it power.*

"I feel it, too," Annie added.

It's opening to the cliffs could easily allow someone to pass through.

"Wouldn't they just fall to their death?" Teega questioned.

Yes. Unless that person is the one giving power to the water, I replied.

"So don't get in the water and don't let anyone in the water," Teega concluded.

Exactly.

I stepped away from the edge and moved upstream where the jump across was more narrow. I easily leapt over the stream and checked the other side of the cave. More markings in the same languages as the other side. Something nagged me to double-check the markings. I looked at the ones on this side, closed my eyes to reflect on the memory of the markings on the other side. That's when it hit me: they were mirrored.

The rushing stream was louder over here. *These markings are the same on both sides except they mirror one another.*

Teega asked, *What do you mean?*

I thought of an example that would be true for anyone on this planet. *Think of a quarter moon when you look at it in the sky then how it looks when reflected in a clear lake.*

I see, Teega answered.

What does it mean? Annie asked.

I didn't answer her because I didn't know. I knew it had something to do with all of this, but I couldn't pin it down. Hopefully, whatever it did mean would settle in a place of sense before it was too late.

Teega interrupted my thoughts. *There is one coming. From the tunnels.*

Burn him, I replied. Something was tugging at me like that vision I entered when I looked into Teega's necklace. I needed to keep investigating.

Hesitance surged off of Teega, but I didn't have time to encourage her. Annie had been the same way when we first encountered thieves a century back. They were sparse then and a lot more manageable. Likely because they did not have the blackened ear and were never moving in groups or with a sense of purpose like they have been over the past few months. Only by leaving Annie out to dry did she find her own footing instead of the one I molded through instruction. There was probably a better circumstance than this, but the gods don't let me in on their plans. Now will have to do.

I felt Annie push out energy that evened out Teega's erratic energy. An idea popped in my head and this moment was as good as any to implement.

I reached out to only Annie's mind. *She is your student now. Not mine.*

Excitement and reluctance greeted me first. *Really? Starting now?*

She's not a heathe, I scolded.

A heathe is a four-legged animal, with long white fur and long white claws, that stands nearly four feet when on all fours and more than double when standing on its rear legs. Extremely loyal, they possess some sentience, but only enough to bond themselves to those they know possess the same level of loyalty. Some of them have bonded with my people and they help patrol Varokkar. Heathes can grow four sharp and flaming horns from their head if threatened. Trespassers always change their mind when a giant, white beast with four flaming horns is barreling after them.

I know that. I'm just excited you trust me, Annie replied.

Even though her back was to me, I shook my head. *Annie, of course I trust you. And Teega is one of us. She likes you which is beyond unexpected.*

Okay, boss. That means stay out.

After I say this—

Oh boy...

I ignored her jab. *Learn from me. Let her fail. I never let you fail and that was a mistake.*

You are the best Brim. No one could be a better mentor. Not even Jaired. She'd laid so much appreciative energy behind her thoughts that I had to choke back tears. I didn't know how to respond. I will put it on the ever-growing list of things to discuss later. You know, because pushing emotions away is a great way to deal with them.

I returned my focus back to the perimeter. There was the same lack of remarkableness on this side of the stream. Just as I turned to Annie to finally address getting upstream, a glimmer of light from the last run of markings caught my left eye. When I faced the same markings straight on, the glimmer disappeared. I felt like a child, but I turned more to the left and the glimmer appeared in my right eye.

"Light them up!" Annie yelled to Teega and, in the process, completely derailed my thoughts.

Bright flame caught my attention and I watched in awe. Unlike in Our Place, Teega was not encompassed in flame. She kept the flames to her hands, but they were burning almost brighter than the sunlight bursting into the cave. The fireball she launched was traveling slower than I expected, but the thief hadn't appeared yet.

She controlling the speed of that? I asked Annie.

Oh yeah, Annie replied.

A thief rounded the corner, his knife in front of him ready for attack. As common of a Yeryan thief, his head was bowed low and completely unaware of the fireball. I watched him take a side glance at the open cave then jerk against the wall at the sight of the flaming death. He didn't even have time to cover his face before the fireball engulfed him.

To my surprise, there was no sound of screaming - not even the sound of the fireball hitting the thief's body. I looked to Teega and her right arm was outstretched, palm facing the thief. She clenched it in a fist and the flame immediately dissipated. I expect to see charred, smoking bodies crumbling to the ground, but nothing happened. The thief disappeared with the fire when Teega extinguished it.

That's new, Annie commented with a hint of humor.

Teega faced Annie and let out a long breath. The flames in her hands dwindled to a glow. *Brim, you are right. I thought of saving Angwiki and that just worked.*

I crossed the bridge and put my hand on Annie's shoulder. I gave her a squeeze of pride then walked to Teega. I reached out to grasp her shoulder so she knew I was there since my invisibility was still in full effect. Her eyes were intent and there was a focus that had been absent before.

In a whisper, I advised, *Rage will destroy everything including yourself. Power comes with focus.*

Annie exclaimed, "Hey, she's my student!"

I waved her off. "Teega, we are proud of you."

"Yes, we are," an unknown voice announced from an unknown location. It was low, creepy, and echoed off the walls like random thoughts in my head. "Very proud of you, Lady Cantiga of House Hopki."

CHAPTER 29

"Who are you?" Annie demanded. "Show yourself!"

Another laugh bounced throughout the chamber until it died away and only the sound of the sea wind remained.

"Speak your name if you are going to speak mine!" Teega yelled. The fire in her hands burned hotter, brighter with her demand. The red and orange flames tinted the otherwise bright, sunlit cavern.

This time the voice let out a low, evil chuckle that vibrated in my chest.

I remained still and frozen. I even slowed my breath and matched it to the softly whistling wind. Both of them gave up their place and their personality at the first sign of an adversary. While I'm sure the thief leader had heard me, he didn't know where I was. With time, Annie would learn to keep her cool better. My hope was Teega would be with us for a longer time and she could learn from both of us.

Annie turned to speak, but I willed such powerful energy at her mind that her body stumbled. Her wide eyes let me know she got the message.

"Teega, let's find a way in." Annie expanded her aura in short pulses to check for significant gaps in the rock wall. The aura bounced back with every pulse, failing to find any openings.

Teega walked over the stone bridge and began doing the same as

Annie except she used short bursts of flame. The flames would bounce off the wall and reflected sparks back at Teega. However, she didn't look away or even close her eyes as the sparks and the heat disappeared just a few inches before touching her body.

That would be nice, I thought, not having to worry about flames. I remained in place and watched them scour the walls, searching for a way in. The green flashes on the right and the bright yellow flashes on the left were quite a spectacle when combined with the natural light coming from behind me. Despite all their efforts, nothing gave way. The hidden passage stayed hidden.

"A little help, Brim?" Teega asked. The frustration in her voice augmented the flames in her hand.

I ignored her verbally and reached out to her mind. *Not everyone should reveal themselves in battle.*

Teega apologized with a hang of her head. It's the same gesture that Annie gave me in the beginning of her lessons. It doesn't matter how long someone has walked with ground beneath them, we all have something to learn.

I reached out to Annie and pulled her into the mental conversation. *Thank you for making noise, Annie.*

Why did you scold me, but applaud her? Teega's words carried genuine confusion.

I held back my reply since Annie was Teega's mentor now.

Annie took the hint from my pause. *Mainly because only one of the prey should draw the attention of the predator so the rest of the prey can escape or attack.*

I said, *And because she likes to make noise.*

I am quite good at it, too.

That you are. I looked to the runes on the walls. Those mirrored runes. *Teega, do you recognize any of them?*

Teega checked the runes on one side of the cave then crossed the stone bridge to check the other side. *A couple of them, but they aren't right.*

Annie asked, *What do you mean?*

We don't have several languages. What was spoken by our

ancestors is the same spoken to this day. Teega energy faded as something distracted her.

And… I prodded with a nudge of my will.

She continued, *What's marked here is almost correct. They didn't complete it though. It reads like someone cut them off in the middle of telling a story.*

For example… I encouraged.

This side here, she said, pointing to a group of markings on the wall farthest from the tunnels. *It translates, well, it should translate to 'water mountain' and the one on the other side should be 'air cave'.*

I pinched the bridge of my nose in an attempt to calm my thoughts. I didn't want to take a language lesson right now. And I definitely didn't want her to pick up on my frustration during a time like this. We aren't all immune to her fire, after all.

Should be? What did they leave out?

Teega sighed loudly. *I'm not going to explain. It would take too long.*

That's not good enough, Annie chided.

I know. Teega nodded respectfully to Annie and leaned down and picked up a rock. Her hands were still aflame and I was still in awe of how they had become an extension of her.

We watched her scrape for a couple moments, unsure of what she was doing.

She threw the rock in the stream and asked, *There, what do you see?*

Annie and I looked down at Teega's work. There were two overlapping, half circles etched in the stone floor.

Could be anything, Annie stated. *All depends on what angle you look at it, what you're talking about. That sort of thing.*

True. So if I told you it had to do with the sky, what do you see?

In unison, Annie and I answered, *Our moons.*

Exactly, Teega confirmed. *That's what is going on with the markings in my language. I know they are talking about the elements, but there is no context.*

Okay, we understand. So what does it mean? I felt a little better, but we were still without an answer.

A little frustration came with Teega's words. *I have no idea. That's why I asked you.*

Right, I replied. *The markings are mirrored and I believe the answer is in the mirroring. And if I'm as loose with my interpretations of the markings as you were with translating them then I believe you two need to act in unison.*

Unison how? Annie's confusion was as evident as Teega's.

Teega, you need to push forth fire on one side and Annie you need to push forth your aura on the other side at the same time.

Teega caught on to my logic. *And you think I should be on the side where water is marked because that's the opposite of fire?*

That's the guess, I answered.

Annie looked to me, still confused. *Where do we try this because nothing happened at the mouth of the stream?*

My guess is at the markings themselves.

Teega said, *Let's give it a try then, Annie.*

I watched Teega walk to the other side and stand in front of the water markings. Annie shuffled over to the markings on my side.

Now! I commanded with my mind. Instantly my vision went green from Annie's aura then clashed with the bright orange and red of Teega's flames.

Stop! I ordered and instantly the colors stopped.

Nothing happened, Teega said as she looked to the markings then to the mouth of the stream. *It's still blocked.*

I guess we try something else, Annie said with disappointment. *Sorry, boss.*

Patience, you two, I replied gently. And Jaired thought I was impatient. Yet they might be right. I stared at the markings on one side then the other for a few minutes and nothing happened. There was only the sound of the stream roaring through the cave and the sunlight flickering through the cave walls. It didn't make sense.

I thought for sure that the two of them would set it off and the entrance would be revealed. Yet it did not. Teega and Annie switched sides and tried again, but nothing happened as I expected. In frustration, Teega slammed the butt of my javelin into the ground. Shards of ice appeared upon contact and flew into the calm pond. They lasted a few moments then melted away.

"That's it!" I exclaimed out loud and revealed my presence. So much for the enemy being unaware of my presence. I still remained invisible because I'm not entirely stupid. They both looked to me for answers, but they were given commands instead. *Teega to the water side. Annie to the middle by that pond.*

Annie moved to where I pointed. *What are you going to do?*

Air to ice to be melted by fire to become water, I answered.

Teega asked, *Then what's Annie's purpose?*

She is nature. She is the mountain, the cave, then everything. Nature bends to her aura.

Annie nodded and closed her eyes. The aura burst forth from her like nothing I'd seen before. The entire cave filled up with such an intense green that even my skin changed color. Teega extended her hands and expelled flames onto the wall.

They are such show offs, I thought. I walked to the marking of air and closed my eyes. Focusing on the cold energy I infused in my javelin, I blew a breath of ice blue onto the marking. The cave immediately rumbled like we were a cloud and the gods rolled a boulder of thunder through it. I turned my attention to the mouth of the stream. A black entrance, similar to the one on the surface, appeared next to the stony bridge.

I think he heard us, Annie said dryly.

Teega laughed. *You think?*

While both of them withdrew their efforts and headed towards the entrance, I did nothing. I said nothing. My stomach was flipping end-over-end. Something was off and I didn't know what.

You coming? Annie asked as she stepped onto the stone bridge the same time Teega did. The moment their feet touched it, they were pulled in, Annie first then Teega, through the entrance by an invisible hand.

I reached out to find their minds, but there was nothing.

CHAPTER 30

The wind picked up from a whisper to a low howl. I still couldn't see anything through the entrance. Not even light could penetrate it. I walked over the bridge a couple times in case I missed something, but nothing caught my attention. My heart was beating out of control and my muscles were tense as if my life was on the line. Teega and Annie could be dead for all I knew and it took all my willpower to not bring this whole cave down. The truth was I didn't know what had happened to them.

I grabbed a tiny rock and threw it into the entrance. As I expected, nothing happened. Not even the sound of the rock hitting anything on the other side. I had no choice: I had to walk through and save them. I had to destroy the one who brought all this havoc onto my land. But I wasn't going to give him any more advantages than I had to.

I sheathed my javelin and remained invisible. Slowly and gently, I lifted my foot off the stone bridge, put it through the entrance, and set my foot down. A sudden sensation as if I was falling from unknown, but great heights washed over me. I was pulled through the entrance and my vision remained black for a few breaths or a few hundred, I could not tell.

"Welcome, moss'r," rasped the voice.

The darkness began to fade away as I opened my eyes. However,

I was not greeted with natural light like the previous cave. Instead, everything had a distinct, dark blue hue to it - the same hue that accompanied my own aura. Without any other source of light like the previous chamber, however, I could only make out vague shapes. Also, I couldn't move my hands, my feet, or my head. Nothing responded. What I did know is that I was suspended in the air because I didn't feel the ground beneath my feet.

"I suppose the invisibility is pointless," I remarked as casual as possible. I shimmered back to visibility and took a deep breath. The lack of control didn't slow my heart or relax my already tense muscles. However, I didn't want my captor to know this. An upper hand I intended to keep.

"Indeed it is." The raspy voice let loose another chuckle, but there wasn't an echo like before.

My eyes tried to find the source of the voice, but I could not. Since I couldn't twist my neck, my peripheral vision was limited. Annie and Teega were nowhere to be seen. I could make out the rushing stream which, to my surprise, did not originate in this cavern. It was pulling water from somewhere inland. Because it was enclosed, the cave was damp and probably naturally dark. However, a ripple in the stream reflected the light that must have been my suspended prison. Whatever held me was emitting a soft blue light.

I closed my eyes and took another long, deep breath to calm my heart then I focused on that soft blue light. When I opened my eyes, I was able to channel that blue light into my vision and the cave revealed itself. At least the part of the cave that I could see without moving my head.

The ceiling was covered in moss and vines that craned and crooked in, out, and around every crevice and hanging rock. There was so much of it that the room lacked the echo of the antechamber. I looked to the left and right, but my peripheral vision couldn't distinguish anything.

"Where are you?" I demanded.

I pulled my eyes off the ceiling and looked to the ground. My prison was suspended midair. Just to my right was some broken, burnt tree trunk. It was massive as it took up nearly half of the cave with its roots extending out of sight under the cave wall. The trunk only rose a few feet off the ground, however. My guess is that it once rose to the cave ceiling and beyond, but had been chopped down.

"I am here," the voice replied. "I am everywhere I need to be."

"Oh, how very mysterious." I had to stall him to better assess what was going on. "If you are everywhere then I am, too."

He let out another raspy chuckle. "Oh, I think not, Brim."

I felt a pressure against my head and I immediately shut my eyes. He was trying to get inside my head. Doubtless he thought he'd add another mind to bend to his own, but I'm not a simple-minded thief.

"Nope, you're not getting in here," I said. I actually tried to raise my arm and tap on my temple, but my arm didn't move.

"Not yet. But soon."

I imagined a wall of thorns standing in front of a wall of trees standing in front of a mountain. It was my routine for imagining physical barriers that my mind could use for mental ones. I opened my eyes and looked down. That's when I saw it.

The black and dark brown trunk moved. Except it wasn't the trunk; it was a being that looked to be an extension of the burnt trunk. As the shape became clearer, I learned it wasn't an it. It was a he. His limbs were knotty, long, and stretched thin with lean strands of moss-colored muscle. Only his joints had any semblance of skin as they were covered with a dark bark. His ears were sickly and blackened like the thieves, but in an advanced state. They actually pulsed an evil energy like separate heartbeats.

Loose clothing hung around his waist and an equally loose necklace dangled against his gaunt chest. With every other breath, however, the necklace circled, the large end circling up and around the thief leader's neck. Tiny jewels on the large end flickered between red and orange and that's when it hit me: the necklace was Angwiki! Just as I went to speak the name of Chawpki's kin, the being spoke.

"The more you search outward, the more others can search inward," the voice rasped yet again.

I understood the reason for the rasp: with every other turn

around his neck, the necklace pierced directly through his throat. Maybe he couldn't speak without Angwiki's help. I asked, "What shall I call you?"

The thief leader let out a little giggle like a child about to be tickled by a parent. He replied like he was singing a song, "Ohhh, Helios."

Then Helios looked upward at me and gray eyes glowed out of the darkness. Gone was the child as the evil thing gritted his wooden teeth at me. "Knowing my name for the remaining moments of your life will not change your fate."

If he expected an outburst of a plea then he was going to be strongly disappointed. So I changed the subject. Maybe I could keep him busy as I tried to find my way free. Yet no matter how diligent my focus, my body remained paralyzed. I asked, "Where are my friends?"

"There," he said and pointed a long branch-like finger to my left. He turned his other hand slowly and my prison turned with the gesture.

My eyes fell onto Teega first. She was suspended mid-air like me. Unlike me, however, she was encased in a tear-shaped prison of water. It swirled around her legs and arms in opposed directions and with enough current to immobilize her. The occasional spark tried to grow into a flame from her hands, but the water canceled it. Her eyes found mine and relaxed a little in the comfort of a familiar person.

I tried to reach out to her, but I could not. Something in here was blocking the mental connection.

Helios continued turning my prison until my eyes fell upon a giant rock prison suspended next to Teega. I could see Annie's emerald aura glowing between the hundreds of tiny rocks that encased her. I could make out an arm and part of her leg, but nothing else. Unlike Teega who was somehow free from the neck up, Annie was not. The rocks were slowly moving in closer, slowly cutting off all light.

Rage started to build up in me. It was the basic kind that is born into all creatures. Instinctive and powerful, it took all my will to temper it. Rage would not clear my mind and free us all.

"What do you want?" I asked. Everyone wanted something.

My prison rotated away from Annie and Teega. The thief leader stood to his full height then reached down with an open hand. He clenched the hand and vines crawled from underneath the burnt trunk and wrapped around his legs. They lifted him so we were eye to eye.

He was grotesque. My vision may have been tinted blue, but when I looked upon Helios, I saw true colors. And I wish it wasn't that way. It looked like his eyes were the only part of him alive. They were dark gray and lidless. The crude beard looked like the rotted roots of moss. There were holes in his cheeks like worms had once made home there. A sap-like substance oozed from the holes and dripped into his beard. He had no hair on his head. Instead the scalp looked burnt and ruined, as if it had been lit on fire, doused with water, dried, and lit on fire again.

I shifted my focus away from him in case he was trying to distract me visually so he could break me mentally. My vision remained true as I looked upon where he was sitting. It was an old, burnt trunk of a great tree that likely filled most this cave. However, I could see the chop and burn marks as part of it had been carved into a throne for Helios. He had carved this ancient life into being a throne for all his evil deeds. I could feel a little life coming from it, but Helios pulled me away from touching it.

"I have all I want," he stated. The vines slowly lowered him and he sat down, his knobby knees resting higher than his hips. "With you dead and those two dead then the thieves can thrive and I can do...other things."

"Other things, huh? Maybe get some rest. Eat some food. You're looking kinda off."

Helios held his hand up and looked at it as if it was for the first time. "Oh this, it's nothing. All part of the transformation."

There was a muffled scream to my left. It was Annie's. I tried to turn my head, but it would not budge.

"What are you doing to her!?" I bellowed. My voice boomed, but

I had no power behind my words.

He kept looking at his hand in absent fascination. It took him a few moments to register the question. His response came out casual like he was commenting on the weather. "Oh, she's being crushed to death."

Then he looked away from his hand and met my gaze. The gray eyes gave way to a white pupil that enlarged in excitement for a moment. "She's killed more of my underlings than anyone. She really must pay."

The threat steadied my heart and steadied my breath. My turn to take control. "Stop. Or you will be stopped."

He blew off the threat and turned his attention back to his hand. "He knows nothing," the thief mumbled under his breath. "He can cause no one harm. And neither can you."

I focused my intention on the encircling necklace. It looked like a string of leather, but I could make out tiny separations like scales. "Chawpki sent us. Chawpki sent your queen to save you."

The thief immediately stood and reached through the barrier of my prison. His rough, dry hand wrapped around my throat and squeezed. It felt like my throat was being squished between two massive trees made of the roughest bark. "Do not speak his name. He is the one who hurt my master. He set us back. So far back in all we need to do."

With his free hand, Helios pulled the necklace away from his body and threw it against the wall behind the throne. The necklace broke in two and fell atop the burnt trunk. The moment the pieces hit, the leather transformed into the snake it actually was. Angwiki let out a painful hiss that sent chills across my entire body.

The thief released his grip on me then turned to carefully scooped up both parts of the Ceguur. "My dear friend, what happened to you?"

I snapped, "You just threw her against the wall, remember?"

He didn't acknowledge me. Instead he cradled the snake in his right hand and whispered to it the way a mother whispers to a child.

I was dumbfounded by his behavior. "What is wrong with you?"

Helios ignored me again. His focus was on the Ceguur and her painful hissing as the body remained in two pieces. The thief leaned down and blew on the two pieces. An acrid, black smoke emitted from his mouth and hung in the air just inches from his mouth. With another breath, the smoke was whisked away toward the Ceguur. Light cascaded throughout the smoke like lightning in a cloud. Once it dissipated, Angwiki was whole again.

The thief excitedly clapped his hands in glee, pleased with the magic. Then they shifted to the dark gray of the mountain and he snapped his fingers. "Back, bastard!"

The snake hissed something close to a whimper then slithered up the thief's arm. She resumed circling his neck, however, she remained as a snake instead veiling as a leather necklace.

"Better. Better." He said then began stroking the snake with his left hand. The thief stood and walked to Annie. With an unseen command, my prison rotated to see what he saw. He stopped in front of Annie's prison. Only a few green rays were creeping out of the rock-built tomb.

"Let her go," I ordered. Thoughts of her gone from my life started to shake my confidence. There were so many things that I wanted to say, but never told her.

Helios waved one hand and the rocks parted near the top of the prison so Annie's face could be seen. I could see the early stages of bruising on her face and neck from the crushing rocks. My heart lurched in excruciating pain.

Her eyes met mine and she gave me a smile. She knew what was coming and she knew it was inevitable. She playfully bit her lip, raised an eyebrow at me because she knew it always twisted me up inside like a little boy in love.

Helios watched the exchange with interest. He turned to me. "You have nothing to offer me and neither does she."

He clenched his fist and the rocks immediately closed all the gaps and started to collapse in on themselves.

My heart knew it was the last time I'd see her beautiful face.

CHAPTER 31

I tried to scream, but I could not. I began to shake in pain and my chest physically hurt as I watched Annie's prison of rocks close in tighter and tighter. In just a few breaths, I saw a drop of blood slowly trickle down the lowest rock then fall into the roaring stream.

I broke. I'm not ashamed to admit it. I cried.

The moment the tear fell something happened: the blue hue in my vision started to fade away so I could see the cave for what it was. Another tear fell and my vision became nearly clear. More tears and I would wiggle my fingers and my elbows. Most importantly, the tears gave me access to the world around me.

I could feel the power in the water as it coursed through the earth, giving nutrients to those who needed it and washing away waste to allow for growth. I could feel the vines clinging to the life all around the cave as they ran away from the poison caused by Helios. The burnt trunk wasn't dead as I thought, but it was in such pain that I had to turn my attention away or else it might break me. Losing Annie hurt, but the pain of one of the oldest parts of my land suffering was the deepest pain.

"You, young lady. You are a great treasure and I wish to keep you alive," Helios spoke to Teega. He didn't notice that I was regaining what he had stripped and I wasn't going to let him. "But my master wants you gone and I would be nothing without him."

He reached out with his hand and started to swirl it in a circle. The water began to swirl much faster than before and Teega strained to keep her limbs from ripping off at the joint.

Let me say goodbye, the snake hissed. Like her father, I could hear the hiss with my ears, but the telepathic words were formal and hiss-free. *Please, my master.*

Helios stopped moving his hand and the water in the prison slowed. Then he looked down at his other hand that hung at his side. He squinted as something caught his attention. He reached down and he started twirling a loose string on the piece of clothing around his finger.

I watched him smile as he twirled his finger then the string would come loose. The smile immediately disappeared and he'd grimace in frustration. He started twirling the longer string - a growing smile on his face - and the string would loosen again. Frustration wiped away his pleasure as quickly as a hand can block sunlight from my eyes. Something definitely wasn't right in his head as he went from sinister to child-like and back again without hesitation.

Angwiki slithered off his neck and wound her way up Helios's arm to the tip of his hand. The Ceguur bowed her head at the Dewarian. *Lady Cantiga, my child. Please forgive me.*

The water had risen almost to her nose, but Teega could still see the snake. She gave a nod of acknowledgment. The necklace that she'd kept under her shirt was now swirling around her head, glowing bright white.

I saw Angwiki's eyes widen when she recognized the necklace. Angwiki let out a soft hiss of a whisper. *Your father. Remember him.*

The moment Angwiki mentioned Teega's father, the necklace stopped swirling and the gem held still against the current in front of Teega's face. I saw an image of a face appear in the white light.

The image was of a man with dark hair and sea green eyes like Teega's. His hair was pulled back and held in a ponytail by a thick, golden ring. His face had a masculine, defined jaw with a short-cropped goatee. I could only see the side of his face from my position, but he looked like a cleaned up and clean-shaven version of…

No, it couldn't be him, I thought.

Teega's eyes widened in recognition of the face. She struggled with her right arm to grab the swirling necklace, but her arm snapped at the shoulder joint and flopped uselessly in the water.

I grimaced at her pain. While I couldn't physically help her, Helios must not have figured out I could help her out telepathically. *Take my energy. Take it all.*

I opened myself up and found Teega in the depths of the darkness of whatever magic Helios bound us to. Teega looked like the tiniest star on the darkest night, but she was there. I gave all the hope and energy I could to stabilize her other arm. I felt her pulling the energy at such a pace that my head began a dizzying spin.

Teega kept her eyes closed and I could feel her newfound focus. She reached up with her left arm to grasp the glowing white jewel on her necklace. Once she did, the swirling began to slow and the water began to lower.

The thief leader must have sensed the shift in energy because he jerked his head up. He reached out to snag the snake before it wrapped around Teega, but Angwiki flung herself into the aquatic prison.

"No!" He screamed, "Get back here, now!"

Helios reached out to command her back to him, but Angwiki remained atop Teega's head. Chawpki's daughter curled around Teega's head and protectively opened her fanged mouth toward Helios.

Angwiki released a long, angry hiss. *You cannot touch me here. You are not my master anymore. My true master is back.*

The water was almost still now and Teega's presence was almost fully detectable now.

"No, my old friend, I am not your master. We are friends." Teega's voice was full of a familial love.

The snake slithered off Teega's head and moved down to her hand that held the jewel. Bright rays of white light escaped between Teega's firm grasp. Angwiki nudged the clenched hand with her head and Teega relaxed her hand. The snake slithered forward a little farther, opened her mouth and swallowed the jewel. The glowing light of the gem rippled throughout the snake as it traveled down to the middle of its body.

"Stop! Stop! Stop!" Helios screamed like a child who had his toy stolen.

He stepped away from Teega and Angwiki and headed towards me. He pulled a long knife from behind his back. The knife shone bright red like it was ready for cooling after being shaped at a forge yet no heat radiated from it. While I didn't recognize the metal, I did recognize the ancient tree that the white handle was made out of.

There is a tree in the old forest that can be seen almost as easily as The Sairs if you are far enough south. It stands in the middle of The Sairs. Long ago my people named it something boring, just like they did with the original name of The Snakes, but the official name never stuck. After generations coming and going, nicknames came and went. I just call it The First and that works for me.

Likely the first tree that made the rest of these, The First is as hard as the mountains, but can be persuaded to give part of itself for a cause. I should know as I'm the only one who has traveled to it and the only one who managed to bring back part of the tree with me. A story the elders begged to hear, but it's a story I told no one. And there is no way on this planet that The First gave into this abomination of a being so it could wield a blade that devastated so many living things in our lands.

The rage came back to my chest like a forest fire and I channeled it into a fierce fury. Even as Helios raised the blade to my throat, I did not care. The robbers and rapists of our land, of my land, would not be allowed to exist any longer. I reached out to the white handle and felt its sadness. I felt its story of being torn from a limb with a burning axe and a twist of evil magic. I knew how it had been twisted and shaped so it could hold a metal that was stolen from another land. I knew that very blade had murdered so many innocents. I felt everything that had been happening and I snapped.

My prison of ice exploded outward, knocking Helios back

against the burnt tree trunk that he claimed as his throne despite the tree never granting such passage. His head hit the back of it and his dazed, gray eyes rolled back in his head. His eyes closed for a moment then slowly opened as he focused on my suspended body.

"Foolish little thing," I growled. My voice was poison and my words carried power that even shocked me. Each word spoken made the thief jerk his head left and right as if he was being punched. "You came to my land. You threatened those I loved."

Teega's prison followed suit and burst outward. Teega gently floated to the ground. The water from the prison went in all directions and had no effect on anyone except the thief leader. The moment it hit his bark-like skin, it sizzled like acid eating through skin.

I smiled condescendingly. "You can forcefully manipulate nature, but it still betrays you, I see."

Helios flinched at the initial pain, but did not complain directly about it. He tried to play casual by brushing off his leg like it was nothing. With a grimace and a tense, raspy voice, he said, "Tree Maker, you know nothing–"

"We are not makers. We are not gods." I waved my hand and an invisible force slapped his head back again. Nature was lending its power to me, keeping me suspended and adding its dangerous energy with every word I spoke.

The thief leader tried to move against my willpower, but the water had eaten through his legs so he was unable to do more than twist his torso.

"We are bound to nature as much as nature is bound to us," I declared. I reached out to all the living things in the cave. The weight of uncertainty within me began to transform into power of certainty.

Nature needed to exact balance on those who had sickened its world. The strongest are the trees since they reach to the skies to provide homes for those who fly above. I did not forget that the trees provide life and protection to those in the ground. Their pain had been pouring into my being. That pain punctuated when my eyes fell upon warped, black, burnt limbs of the usurper's throne. Nature witnessed the abomination through my eyes and granted me its power. A power beyond anything I knew.

"You could never understand," I growled again. My voice shook the cave and caused crumbles of dirt and tiny rocks to fall from the ceiling. "Never."

He rose to speak, lifting his paralyzed lower body up by his arms. The arrogance in his eyes told me that he had prepared some message of how I'm a pawn in some game or how he is more powerful than anything ever could be. Possibly he would have weaved some great long tale about how he'd mastered the elements in ways I could never understand. I'll never know because I reached out to the wounded and deeply saddened, defeated stump that had supported this evil thing for too long. Then I poured in all my hope and power and commanded it to take back its life. So it did.

The sole branch that had been twisted and burned so it could provide back support for Helios suddenly straightened. Then it curved down towards the thief's head and skewered it quicker than the blink of an eye. The leader's eyes went wide and his mouth remained open as I saw the burnt branch pierce his tongue.

"Finish it," I willed.

CHAPTER 32

"No!" Teega yelled and interrupted the focus of my willpower.

"What are you doing?!" I yelled back. I looked down at Teega. Angwiki twisted up and down from wrist to forearm completely whole in her true form.

Anger replaced my tears. My voice shook the walls again. "Annie's dying and he's holding her there."

Teega's face softened and she had a steady stream of tears falling, but her eyes displayed a strong conviction. "I know, Brim, I know. But we must find out who his master is."

The cave shook again as nature shook inside my chest. "My land does not care about the rest! Only what this thing has done to it!"

I turned back to Helios and lifted my hand upward. The burnt branch resumed skewering his throat and tongue. The thief showed no pain. He gargled with the strangling of his throat, but his dark gray eyes stayed locked to my own. A green ooze started forming at his mouth and the corners of his eyes. I could feel nature turning his abusive magic against him.

"Kill me," Helios stated with a gulp. "Do it."

His eyes smiled and his mouth tried to follow, but the growing, spreading branch prevented it.

Teega reached my mind. *Brim. Stop.*

The way she touched my mind changed. Her power was deeper.

It could have been because of her rekindled bond with Angwiki. I didn't know exactly why. What I did know is she felt familiar to me the way Annie does. And to my great surprise, nature listened to her.

The branch stopped spreading and the life within Helios remained in place. Teega walked to the sitting thief. Helios disregarded Teega and kept his gaze upon Angwiki.

"Come back to me, little one. I will forgive you," Helios said in an attempt to sooth the snake.

He reached out with his right arm, but Teega shut him down by lighting his arm on fire with just a flick of her fingers. A second flick of the fingers and the fire disappeared along with his arm.

"Angwiki, I need answers," Teega said. "You gave him the power by biting those ears. Let's use that against him."

With pleasure, Angwiki spoke to our minds followed by a long, satisfying hiss. Angwiki slid off Teega's wrist, extended her body a few inches and floated to Helios's shoulder.

"No! No! No, you won't!" The thief shrieked. He frantically slammed the side of his head against his shoulder to block the snake from getting to his ear. When Angwiki made her way to the other ear, the thief slammed his head to the other side to block that one.

Each second that passed could have been Annie's last on this planet. And Teega wasn't going to let me finish it before she has her answers from Helios. So I reached out to the burnt throne and another branch sprouted, rose, and wrapped around his neck to hold his head in place.

Angwiki gave me a nod then turned back to the thief and struck his ear, white fangs gleaming against the darkness of the thief.

He yelled out, but Angwiki didn't release her bite.

I extended my focus to Angwiki to ask what she was doing, but she was blocking me out.

Teega filled in the blanks for me. *She's draining his power and, with it, his knowledge.*

I nodded and tried to control my rapid breathing. I looked to Annie and saw the green glow was completely gone and all that remained was rock. Also the dripping blood was falling faster.

That's enough, I commanded.

I extended my right hand in front of me, my knuckles white from holding a painful fist. Then I reached inside myself for the power granted by nature. It coursed through my body and I could feel the burnt tree pleading even more for balance. It wanted a reckoning and I was the one to grant its wish.

I didn't have time and I didn't care to warn Angwiki. The Ceguur must have felt the surge of danger because she released her fangs and floated back to Teega's outstretched hand.

I hope you got what you needed, I said. Then I flattened my fist and power rushed out. The branch inside Helios's body suddenly sprouted dozens of limbs in all directions. Then those limbs sprouted more limbs. Each growth pushed away flesh and bone from his body. He didn't scream because limbs tore through his entire neck. He could only suffer as the tree regrew itself. The final limbs pushed out of his head then the head exploded. Bits of brains and bones scattered through the cave, falling everywhere except on us.

I heard the thuds of all the rocks falling away from Annie's prison. Then I watched her mangled body hang in the air for a moment before falling to the ground with a loud, echoing thud.

The power surging in me left as soon as my eyes fell upon Annie. I dropped to the ground and ran across the cavern to her side. Blood was soaking through the clothes at her stomach, back, thighs and feet. Her face was as pale as the winter moons. The single curl of hair that normally danced freely in front of her forehead was soaked in blood and stuck to her face. She was not breathing.

I knelt down and scooped her up so her bloodied shoulders could rest on my legs. I gently held her head as my chest tried uncoiling and crying through the pain. Except I had no more tears and the tears wouldn't help in this moment. I squeezed my eyes shut. Hope flooded me as I tried to give her all my energy as I had done hundreds of times over the long years we'd spent walking amongst The Shaws. Nothing happened.

Teega fell to her knees next to me and threw her body across Annie's. Her voice cracked into a sob. "Angwiki. Help. Please show me the way."

The snake slithered off of her wrist, landed on the floor then extended her body to the length of my arm. She swiveled her head to me and she asked, *Who is she to you?*

"She is everything," I whispered.

Angwiki reached out to my mind, pushing against it with that eternal power of her father. *Show me.*

I opened my mind to the memories of Annie. All her good and all her bad and all of her time spent defending this land. I felt Angwiki pulling emotion from my memories which broke my walls that kept me strong. I pulled in the deepest breath that I could as to avoid breaking down again.

Angwiki pulled away from my memories and my mind. She looked to Teega, but spoke to both of us. *My child, sit up. She is not dead.*

Teega didn't move. Chills spread across my body as I was moved by how she protected Annie. "No, I will give her my life."

Angwiki coiled up and raised herself up to eye level with me. She opened her mouth and let out a mist. Instead of the mist of protection like Chawpki's, hers was the emerald green of Annie's. The mist flowed towards Teega and enveloped her head.

The mist must have been doing something more than just clouding Teega's vision since she immediately sat up. "What are you doing?"

Healing you so you can heal her, my child. Angwiki's response was calm. She uncoiled and shrank back down to the size of the necklace. Then she slithered up Teega's body to her neck and began circling it.

"Teega, your ear," I said as I pointed to it.

Her ear was slowly losing the color of death. I could feel whatever within it was dying. Tears began to fall again from my eyes as my hopes began to feel like they were becoming reality.

Teega closed her eyes and put her hand to her ear. I heard her mumble in her native language. Angwiki repeated each word spoken the very moment after Teega spoke them. Energy thrummed from them and I could feel death giving way to life. Together they sounded as beautiful as the morning singing of blue neddills that lived in Varokkar.

Teega opened her eyes and pulled her hand away from the ear. The ear was the same as the other now except for the two piercings. The piercings I knew were actually bonding bites from Angwiki. Teega's eyes were not the same as before though. They were dancing in colors of the fires I saw in her memory walk. Then something bright caught the corner of my eye. Teega's pant leg had bunched up when she knelt and revealed the birth tattoo. It was burning bright again and I watched new lines carving along her calf.

Teega flinched, but Angwiki slid off her neck, and onto the floor. She dispelled another tiny bubble of green mist that fell upon the calf. Teega let out a sigh of relief and we all watched the tattoo become complete. If the healing of the ear didn't convince me then the tattoo did.

The gods chose to mark her as a healer standing on the ground in the middle of an archway. The left side of the archway had swirls indicating the rising air that fueled the flames directly above Teega's outline. The flames fell down the right side and turned into waves of water that eventually fell into the earth. She could give one to cancel the other. A healer with the antidote to every poison.

My voice cracked, "Annie..."

Teega turned away from her calf to Annie. When she spoke, her voice was no longer wavering. She was in complete control. "My friend is correct. She is not dead, Brim."

Teega closed her eyes and I could feel her pulling in the energy from every corner of the room. Her left hand burst into bright white flame. She reached out with the other hand and a jet of water leapt from the roaring stream directly to encompass her right hand. Then she brought the flaming hand up to her mouth - the fire still doing nothing to her - and brought the other hand with the swirling eddy of water to her mouth. There was an immediate hissing of heat and water as steam rose.

Teega took a deep breath then leaned down to Annie's bloody, broken face and let the breath out. Somehow, her breath tunneled between the confluence of fire and water then came out blue on the other side. The blue misty breath fell on Annie's face and hung there for a long moment.

I gripped Annie's hand tighter in my own, urging her to come back. I urged the gods to help whatever magic was happening. Slowly, the blue mist began to dissipate as it fell into Annie's nostrils. One shallow breath led to another then another then she jerked straight up.

"Cassius!" Annie exclaimed, "It's a trap! Don't come in!"

I wrapped my arms tight around her. "I got you, Annie. It's over."

Annie leaned back into me and took my hands in hers and wrapped my arms tighter around her. I felt my arms become wet from Annie's tears.

Well done, my child, Angwiki said. *My pride for you grows.*

Teega's voice cracked again as she turned to her childhood friend. "Angwiki...so much time lost..."

We shall make it up, my child, Angwiki replied. *You are grown now. We can have fun.* We heard the "fun" in our head normally, but the accompanied hiss was longer than normal.

Annie let out a laugh through her pain. She pulled away from me and turned to Angwiki. "I'm so happy you have a sense of humor. Your dad is boring."

Angwiki opened her mouth and I instinctively put myself between the snake and Annie. Then the Ceguur let out a series of low hisses that pulsed with such humor that I even laughed. *Yes, he is.*

Annie leaned forward and slightly tilted her head. *I'm Annie.*

Angwiki, unfamiliar with the gesture, looked to Teega. She made the motion like Annie and Angwiki nodded. The snake stretched forward and put her head against Annie's. *Angwiki.*

"Thank you, Teega." My eyes met hers and I knew we were bonded for all of life. "A debt I can never repay."

She smiled. "Well, actually that would make us even."

I had to be firm on this point. "Even would be if you saved my life. You saved hers. She is far more important to me than my own life."

Annie looked up at me, tears falling down her beautiful face and she kissed me.

My instincts didn't pull me away as that kiss let me truly know she was alive.

"You should have never come in here," she whispered after the kiss. "You could have died."

"Not an option, Annie. Never an option with you."

"Ugh, you two are so sappy," remarked Teega. "Come, my lord, let's go before I puke."

Angwiki corrected, You are the queen now. You are "my lord."

"I don't like the sound of that. And since I'm the queen, you cannot tell me what I call you."

The snake hissed another laugh then slithered up her outstretched arm and found her way around Teega's neck.

I let go of Annie and stood. My attention turned back to the burnt trunk and where Helios used to be. I could feel the trunk starting to heal inside even if the outside still looked sickly. I walked over to it and knelt at the base of the trunk. The remnants of the thief's body were nowhere to be found as even in this cave as nature had cleaned it away. Gently, I put my hand out and rested it upon the flat area.

I had to search my thoughts for the right words. *I am sorry you were so sick for so long. Ancient one, thank you for helping me.*

A massive wave of energy bombarded my thoughts and I grabbed onto the trunk to prevent from falling down. I felt blood starting to drip from my nose. The entire land was trying to talk to me all at once and it was too much.

Pictures, I struggled to form the word in my head. My brain was hurting from the pressure of its power. (And I thought Jaired was strong.) I repeated the message. *Pictures.*

It understood and the pressure stopped. It flashed images of healthy growing trees in the clearing on the surface just outside the main cave entrance. It sent an image of this cavern that was no longer dark green and sagging sickly, but was vibrant green and full of plant and animal life. Then it showed me burnt forests and hills that I recognized from Teega's memories as her home.

I felt something sliding onto my hand and I opened my eyes. One of the new branches had reached towards me.

Annie asked, "What's it doing?"

The branch sprouted tiny new limbs that circled around a few times to form a round base then it broke itself off. In my palm was a tiny sapling with a couple green limbs and a couple tiny green leafs. And I knew just what to do.

"This is its thanks." I said then turned to show Teega the future in my hand. "This sapling will regrow your land."

CHAPTER 33

The trek back to the surface went much quicker than the trek down. The thieves we piled against the tunnel turns were now awake, but they were disoriented without their leader. Annie and I laughed as they pushed each other down upon laying eyes on Teega's flaming hands. I suppose seeing a snake fall from her neck then grow to be as tall as Teega and as thick as her torso also added to their fear.

At first, Angwiki wanted to kill them all as her anger ran deep after years of being under their control. To my surprise, however, Teega was the one who passed on my lesson about rage. Angwiki resisted at first, but a quick whisper in her native tongue and the snake ceased her pursuit. She transformed to a bracelet-size snake and found her master's wrist.

To everyone's surprise, the clearing outside the cave was already losing ground against the growing trees and bushes. Ground creatures had already taken away the dead bodies while the air creatures tore off parts of the tents to use for nesting. Even sunlight had cleared a way through the rain clouds to foster the rehabilitation.

We made our way to the hill where Jaired had dropped us off to find him waiting for us. He was in panther form and was finishing up, rather grotesquely, one of the thieves that tried to run away.

I saw his left ear twitch at the sound of Teega snapping a branch that snagged on her shoulder. I looked to Annie and gave her a look of disappointment. She had so much to teach the youngling.

Jaired gulped down the remainder of the thief's thigh meat then bounded toward me at full speed. Angwiki had never seen such a creature and immediately transformed into a massive snake and put all of us between Jaired and her.

"Whoa, Angwiki," I stated. "He's with us."

Jaired didn't care. He leapt in the air, transformed into a tiny bird that flew over Angwiki's coiled body then transformed back to the panther and landed at my feet. His four eyes bore into mine and I felt him probe my mind first for injury then for the transpired events. Satisfied I was safe, he closed his eyes and bent his furry head towards me. I met it with my forehead and rubbed behind one of his ears.

"We are safe, old friend." I assured. "How are the others? Gregare? Chawpki?"

Fine. Cleaning up the rest.

"Anyone hurt?"

He reared back his head and let loose a few short growls. Laughter amongst animals is something you never really get used to. *They were no challenge. Became bored so I left.*

Angwiki, head still has high as mine, slithered over and knocked her body into Jaired's. He snarled and whipped his tail back at the snake who barely dodged it.

The snake hissed, *You left my father? Alone?*

If I did, little one? Jaired bared his teeth then released a long growl that shook the ground.

Angwiki started to grow larger and her rage went along for the trip. I could feel her pulling energy from the world around her. Teega walked over to her servant and reached out her hand, no doubt to run a finger along her back in an effort to calm the situation. Before she could take two steps to intervene, however, a sudden hiss, louder than a river waterfall, filled the area.

Chawpki's voice immediately entered our minds. *That is no way to treat our brother!*

Everyone turned to watch a massive, dark purple tornado form in the clouds and immediately funnel down to the edge of the clearing. Teega, Annie and myself raised our arms to block debris from hitting our face as the funnel swirled dangerously close to us. Then there was a sudden, blinding burst of light.

When I opened my eyes, the tornado had disappeared to reveal Gregare atop Chawpki. Except Chawpki was no longer the size of a walking staff or an eight-foot snake. He had transformed into something so large you couldn't even call it a snake. Unless snakes were thirty feet long and six feet thick. If he coiled up, he would look like a not-so-small, charred hill.

We owe them our lives. Our existence is tied to theirs, Chawpki continued. Despite his size, he moved with the quiet grace of Jaired toward us. His body didn't even dig into the ground.

Angwiki held her height, *But father—*

He hissed so loud I had to cover my ears. Angwiki uncoiled and laid on the ground, only her head was raised, but she avoided eye contact with her father.

Jaired, please excuse my child. You may enact whatever lesson you deem worthy. Chawpki added, *I will not intervene.*

Normally, such a statement would have made me laugh because I'd seen how awesomely powerful Jaired could be in every form. However, Chawpki was huge from twenty feet away and was only growing larger as he moved closer.

"Um, I'm going to step over here," Annie stated. Her aura pulsed out and protected her as she walked away. "Really far away from whatever is going to happen."

I wasn't worried about my safety. The matters of the omniscient and omnipotent are not for me to ponder. So I turned my attention to my fellow warden. "You all good, my friend?"

Gregare slid off Chawpki and landed gracefully on his feet. He was without a hat and the lightning had made his hair disheveled. Tiny sparks bounced from his hands. "Ohhh yes. We had so much fun."

I laughed. "Of course you did."

Gregare ran his hands through his long hair, flattening it against his head. Then he stroked his black beard to calm the wayward tufts.

He turned his head to the side and looked in the distance for a moment.

The way he looked, in that profile, was too familiar. I reached out to his mind and started to relay images of the man that formed in Teega's prison once Angwiki mentioned Teega's father.

Before I could ask the question, Gregare shut me out. He glared at me, his white pupils flashing like lightning strikes inside the black irises.

"That century you went missing…" I whispered.

Gregare shook his head left to right and his hair was disheveled again. He stepped toward me and the air suddenly became dry as if readying for another lightning strike from above. Thunder rolled from the purple clouds in the distance.

"Not today, Cassius." His voice came out just as loud as that distant thunder.

I acquiesced his request, but I held my ground. "Another time."

I looked away and no one noticed our exchange - not even Annie. A deadly Ceguur the size of a small mountain can have an effect on a person.

Gregare was more than willing to change the subject as he turned away from me and toward Jaired. The air was no longer dry and the angry energy coming from the warden had shifted to a playful one.

Gregare reached out to Jaired, but included all of us in his taunt. *I suppose if you're going to be a coward then they are all for me.*

Jaired let loose a fierce growl that shook the branches in the trees around us. Angwiki cowered and Teega jumped back as Jaired leapt toward Gregare, his claws out reaching. I thought for sure my friend was in trouble then I remembered his gift.

Jaired's claws found nothing as Gregare's duplicate disappeared. The mourar's tail whipped left and right in frustration.

I looked to the cave entrance and saw Gregare standing with his staff in hand.

The Marshes warden smiled wide. *You're getting slow, mourar. Maybe you're best fit to be a pack animal.*

More roars of laughter from Jaired filled the area. He turned to

Chawpki then to Angwiki and spoke. *Youngling. Do not challenge me again. Or you will look like that man flesh.*

We all looked at the decimated and bloody body of the thief that lay just a few feet from Angwiki.

Angwiki looked to her father and opened her mouth to speak, but Chawpki silenced her by baring his fangs. Angwiki rose to meet Jaired's eyes. *Yes, mourar, Father of All. I am in your debt.*

The air was tense. And I needed everyone not to be tense because what we had coming was something far more challenging than this could ever be. I reached out to Jaired and impressed upon him what was waiting in the Burnt Lands. *Take her with. Let her fight with you.*

Jaired whipped his tail in frustration again. No one heard our thoughts, but they felt our tension. *No, Brim. She needs to learn.*

There is something you need to learn from me, I retorted. I felt anger rising from Jaired. A Tree Maker telling a mourar what should be? That wasn't going to go well, but I continued. *Humility forges bonds.*

I have no need. He replied then snapped his tail upward before striking the tip into the ground.

We all will need it in the coming days, I said. I pulled the sapling from my pouch and held it out for him.

Jaired's eyes went wide upon close inspection of the sapling. *From The First?*

I nodded then opened my thoughts for all to hear. Given to me from our land. This will restore the forests of Dewaria.

Chawpki and Angwiki let out a hiss at the same time. Jaired gave a bow to me as he knew it was great when the land reached out to one of my people with such a gift. He spoke directly to me. *Very well.*

Then he stalked to Angwiki and the snake did not move. Jaired stopped just a hair's length from Angwiki's fiery eyes, baring his fangs. To my surprise, Chawpki didn't even blink his giant eyes at Jaired being so close to his kin. *You want your debt cleared?*

Yes, Angwiki hissed softly.

Then kill more thieves than me, Jaired replied. He let out another roar and bounded toward Gregare and the cave entrance.

Chawpki shimmered and shrunk himself to Jaired's size and made his way to the thieves' cave. *No, Jaired. She must out do us both!*

Angwiki narrowed her eyes and looked to Teega. They had a connection I could not compete with and it was one I barely understood. It was as if the years apart had only been a few days. Teega turned to the cave entrance and lifted the javelin, pulling her arm back ready to launch. Angwiki didn't miss a beat and slithered so fast that she was a blur. Teega threw the javelin and Angwiki leapt upon it just as it left her fingers. The javelin blurred through the air and stuck in a rock crevice just above the entrance.

Gregare gave an approving nod to Angwiki as she slipped gracefully off the javelin. Then she mockingly stuck her tongue out at Jaired and Chawpki then slithered out of sight into the cave.

Annie and Teega laughed then I joined them.

"And they call us children," Annie remarked.

"Let them have their fun," I said. My eyes turned south to The Marshes and to Traders Ocean beyond. Then I looked down at the sapling in my hand and a vision started to surface in my mind. My heart started racing and my hands started to shake so I had to push the vision away. "It will be a while before we can laugh again."

ABOUT THE AUTHOR

Buddy teaches life lessons – and computer support – to high school students by day while playing video games and writing by night. For more information, visit www.buddyheywood.com.

51693912R00144

Made in the USA
Middletown, DE
13 November 2017